On
Santa's
Naughty List

ON SANTA'S NAUGHTY LIST

Shelby Reed

Lacey Alexander

Melani Blazer

POCKET BOOKS

New York London Toronto Sydney

Pocket Books
A Division of Simon & Schuster, Inc.
1230 Avenue of the Americas
New York, NY 10020

First Pocket Books trade paperback edition November 2008

POCKET and colophon are registered trademarks of Simon & Schuster, Inc.

For information about special discounts for bulk purchases,
please contact Simon & Schuster Special Sales at 1-800-456-6798
or business@simonandschuster.com

Manufactured in the United States of America

10   9   8   7   6   5   4   3   2   1

Library of Congress Cataloging-in-Publication Data
On Santa's naughty list / Shelby Reed, Lacey Alexander, Melani Blazer.—1st
Pocket Books trade pbk. ed.
     p. cm.—(Ellora's Cave anthologies)
1. Erotic stories, American. 2. Christmas stories, American. I. Reed, Shelby.
Holiday Inn. II. Alexander, Lacey. Unwrapped. III. Blazer, Melani. When I
close my eyes.
PS648.E7O54 2008
813'.60803538—dc22
                                                                    2008002778
ISBN-13: 978–1–4165–7764–5
ISBN-10:   1–4165–7764–5

ONTENTS

Holiday Inn

Shelby Reed

Prologue

*J*esse Proffitt stretched out on his son's bed, Daniel's thread-bare stuffed whale clutched to his chest, and stared at the glow-in-the-dark stars glued to the ceiling.

They'd buried Daniel this morning, under a light drizzle that had commenced three days earlier when a drunk driver struck and killed him on the street in front of their house. A hit-and-run. Daniel was chasing a neighbor's dog. The dog made it to the other curb.

Daniel didn't.

Jesse tried to swallow, found his throat too thickened with unshed weeping. Outside, the rain intensified and drove itself against the earth, like his roiling grief. Even nature seemed to know that a six-year-old so full of life and spirit wasn't supposed to die like this.

He was Jesse's greatest joy. His life. His world. Jesse couldn't think past the pain. It filled his ears, his nose, his eyes, his mouth, choking him. It bubbled and seared like molten lava in the center of his chest, eating his insides, his soul, everything except his heart, which had gone brittle and shattered into a thousand, free-floating shards.

And still the world was spinning in its callous, insolent way, when it should have gone still in reverence. Still Toni Braxton sang from the small stereo in the kitchen, begging someone to un-break her heart. She had a deep, rich, soulful voice that Jesse would recognize anywhere. Funny that amid all the pain, he could muse over Toni Braxton and her lush vocals. He wondered if she'd ever lost someone she loved to the black void of death.

Silence would have been more appropriate now that all the mourners had gone home, but Sheila couldn't stand the quiet. She never had liked stillness, so Jesse and Daniel had given her that damned mini-stereo last month for Mother's Day, and it never went silent. She was moving around the kitchen to its constant yammer even now, on the day she'd watched their son's coffin lowered into the ground.

The refrigerator door opened and closed. She was putting away the casseroles brought by well-meaning neighbors. She hadn't eaten a bite of anything since Jesse called her from a bystander's cell phone three days ago.

Sheila, come home . . . Daniel's gone. He's gone from us, he died in my arms . . . our boy is dead, and I couldn't even tell him goodbye.

Not that her inability to feed herself had much to do with grief, necessarily. She'd been too thin when Jesse married her a decade ago, and he'd long since grown sick of admonishing her to eat. It was a *thing* with her. Emaciation meant power. It also meant a bony, unyielding body curled away from him every night in bed. But the slow dissolution of their marriage hadn't really bothered him so much over the past few years, because Sheila had given Jesse a terrific son, the best friend a man could want, and Jesse could stand anything.

Anything but this.

On the kitchen radio, Toni Braxton sang about un-crying her tears.

He hadn't, yet. Hadn't cried. Couldn't. He'd stood at the foot of his boy's grave and held Sheila up, and her ninety-nine pounds felt like a thousand, crushing him. She'd wailed and Jesse had been her wailing wall.

Now he lay on top of their son's quilted cartoon bedspread and closed his burning eyes, breathing in the fast-fading scent of Daniel, the echo of his laughter, his husky voice shouting for Jesse to come kiss him before he could go to sleep. And Sheila moved like an automaton around the kitchen, straightening, cleaning, anything to avoid the bleak reality that remained, which included her husband.

The phone rang down the hall and Jesse's body gave a startled jerk. Soon the sympathy calls would quit coming, and people would move on with their lives, while Daniel Proffitt's parents sank in the quicksand of loss. No one could save them, not even themselves.

Sheila's voice, tear-choked, murmured over Toni Braxton. Inaudible words. A pause, followed by the click of her black high heels on the wooden floor, leaving the kitchen. Coming nearer.

"Jesse? Where are you?"

He didn't answer. She didn't need an answer. Her narrow shadow fed the falling darkness in the hall, and then she appeared, her face a ghostly white mask in dusk's gloom.

"Jess?"

"Yeah?"

"That was the sheriff's office." Her words quavered as Jesse sat up to look at her. "They arrested him."

"Who?" he responded automatically, even though he already knew. Even though Jesse's blackened mind had already decimated the man a thousand times in the last three days.

"The driver who killed Daniel."

He sat up to look at her, then said flatly, "All right."

When he looked up, the doorway was empty.

One

"So where are you, Anna?" Maggie Shea spoke around a mouthful of something crunchy, unashamed to munch in her older sister's ear over an already-scratchy cell phone connection. "Made it down through Rocky Mount yet?"

Anna glanced in her rearview mirror and maneuvered her Toyota sedan into the passing lane. "Not even close. Traffic's crawling. Drivers are road-raging. There's a reason why I hate traveling over the holidays, you know."

"But this is my first Christmas in my first house . . . Mom and Dad are going to be here any minute, and I can't handle them alone. You know how important it is that you be here." Maggie's voice rose in a plaintive fashion that sent Anna scurrying away from the argument.

"I know how important it is to you," she affirmed quickly, "which is why I'm taking my life in my hands and inching two states through this godforsaken parking lot they call I-95. I wouldn't miss your party for the world."

"Or Christmas with your best sister."

"Or Christmas with my *only* sister."

"At least you have good weather," Maggie pointed out. "No snow, and you were so worried."

"So the weatherman says." Anna eyed the early afternoon sky through the windshield. One small cloud drifted close to the horizon in a sea of blue. "I just have a funny feeling about this."

"You do?" Alarm sapped the humor from Maggie's voice. "Is it a run-of-the-mill anxiety feeling, which would mean nothing, or a pit-of-the-stomach bad feeling, which would mean psychic intuition?"

"Strictly run-of-the-mill," Anna reassured, giving herself a mental kick. Maggie was so superstitious. "So I'll see you in about three hours."

"Call me every half hour so I know you're safe."

"You're a pain in the ass."

Maggie chuckled and hung up without saying goodbye—she'd always believed uttering those magic words would bring bad luck. Such idiosyncrasies had long ago ceased to unnerve Anna. Her younger sister's quirks made her lovable, if a little impossible. Her whole family was that way. Maybe that craziness was what had driven Anna to become a genealogist. She craved explanations for why the leaves of her family tree were so . . . colorful.

The party didn't start until dinnertime, and two hours into the drive, weariness strung tight bands across the back of her neck. She needed something to fortify her, pep her up, give her a jolt of temporary social enthusiasm, since all she really wanted to do was turn around and go back to Alexandria, Virginia, where her empty apartment and too-small artificial Christmas tree sat waiting.

Coffee would have to do, and a break from the stress of creeping along I-95 with all the other fools too entangled with their families to say, *No, thanks, I just want to stay home this year.*

It took another mile before a harried driver took mercy upon her and let her into the right lane, and with a sigh of relief, Anna swung off the next exit ramp and into a crowded gas station.

No parking spaces remained, so she pulled into an illegal spot on the grass, beside a dusty maroon Harley, and climbed out.

Despite the vibrant glow of the sun, the cold snatched the breath from her lungs. Icicles hung like crystalline fingers from the eaves of the convenience store, and customers pumping gas into their vehicles huddled against the wind's assault. The frigid currents shoved Anna along, whipping at the thin silk wrap she wore over her velvet minidress and loosening the pins that held her brown hair in its carefully crafted chignon.

Damn, but it was chilly. Whoever had the guts to ride the motorcycle she'd parked beside had a hide of steel.

Stepping into the warmth of the convenience store, she glanced around for the coffee machine and spotted it in the back. A tall man in full leathers and boots stood at the counter beside it, his dark head bowed as he doctored a cup of steaming coffee.

The motorcyclist, no doubt. Everyone else in the store was either elderly or weighted down with kids and junk food, moms and dads dressed in goofy Christmas sweaters and college football jackets.

Anna couldn't have explained why she hesitated in the entryway instead of heading straight for the coffee. The cheery store was crowded, Christmas music trilling under the steady hum of voices. There was nothing particularly scary about the man at the coffee bar, other than the fact that he was the proverbial biker—bearded, broad-shouldered and powerfully built. He probably wouldn't bite her if she walked up beside him and reached for the coffeepot.

When the glass doors behind her swung open and a blast of cold air stabbed through her clothing, she jolted from her rumination and forced herself to walk. The biker didn't look at her when she stopped at the counter beside him, but he did move aside to make room for her. Painfully aware of his dark presence, she poured herself a cup of coffee, and glanced around for the sugar.

He was blocking it.

She cleared her throat. "Excuse me. May I . . . ?"

He backed up a step and met her gaze.

Wild blue yonder. It was all she could think. His eyes were the iridescent color of the Caribbean Sea, made all the more electric by his dark beard and mustache, and the stern features they half hid.

An unexpected surge of sexual awareness washed through her as she reached in front of him and grabbed a couple of sugar packets. The scent of piney winter and worn leather emanated from him, and she quickly stepped aside again, surprised at her reaction. She liked clean-cut, polished, cerebral men who were familiar and utterly unthreatening. Grizzled bikers weren't her type. Unpredictability held no appeal for her, and this stranger's somber, fiercely blue eyes radiated it.

Maybe the lack of sex—a year's worth since her last breakup—had addled her brain. Or maybe it was just the idea of spending yet another Christmas as a single girl.

Somehow her relationships always met a tragic end just short of the holidays. It was a running joke in her family. Even Anna never bought her boyfriends Christmas presents anymore, because inevitably they would hit the high road by December 25th. And this year was the worst, because this year, for the first time, she really felt alone in the world.

So she gave her steaming coffee a slow stir and let herself indulge in the wayward pleasure of standing beside a man she didn't know. A mere five inches separated them; they stood too close, really, but he didn't seem to notice, and just the sheer thrill of breaching his personal force field pumped her pulse into a high, erratic dance.

A quick sideways glance told her his profile was more handsome than she'd thought, even with all that facial hair. She'd never kissed a guy with a mustache or beard. It might be prickly on her lips, too distracting. More likely it would be silky soft, delightful. It would glide a shivery path across the sensitive column of her throat along with his lips as he kissed his way down her naked body. Maybe when those lips found the curve of her breast . . . and then closed hot and hungry over her nipple, drawing on it, tonguing it, and that beard and mustache tantalized every inch of her aroused flesh . . . she would never want to go back to a clean-shaven lover. And *oh*, to feel the brush and tickle of that bearded chin on the tender flesh of her thighs, between her legs, and then the probe of a soft, wet tongue sliding down her cleft, savoring her, while his strong hands cradled her ass and lifted her like a loving cup . . . *oh my God.*

Pre-orgasmic shivers fluttered through her muscles, and she felt herself go wet beneath the velvet dress. How insane to get so excited simply by standing next to a complete stranger. Maybe she was having some kind of holiday mental breakdown.

Face burning, she stirred her cooling coffee one last time, then glanced around for a top.

The biker was, of course, standing directly in front of the stacked lids, and she wasn't about to reach past him again. Shouldering her purse, she started to turn away when he said, "Need a cap on that?"

His voice was low, quiet.

"Oh." She swung back and looked everywhere but at his face. "A medium one, please."

He retrieved the plastic top and handed it to her.

"Thanks." Delight quivered in her stomach as she stared at the front of his leather jacket, and out of sheer nervousness, she continued, "I can just see myself sloshing coffee all over this velvet dress."

"Going somewhere special?"

She glanced up at his gaze and away again, seared. Yep, those eyes were still blue. "A Christmas party."

"Have fun," he said without smiling.

"You too."

Jesus. He didn't look like he was headed anywhere fun. There was a starkness to his features that belied holiday cheer of any kind.

"Merry Christmas," she added uselessly as he walked past her. He might not even celebrate Christmas. It didn't matter. He was a stranger, a passerby in her day, no one she'd ever see again, although she would remember those gorgeous baby blues for a while. A woman didn't forget eyes like that. And if she ever had the guts to replay the intense sexual fantasy she'd conjured about that beard . . . it would definitely have to be somewhere private. Like in her lonely apartment, with her lonely vibrator, which probably needed dusting off by now, for all the action it saw. The morose thought stole the vague excitement lingering inside her.

She sipped her hard-won coffee without tasting it and watched through the store window as the biker climbed on the Harley parked beside her white sedan, slipped on his full-face helmet and rolled out of the parking lot. It was a sexy sight, a man straddling his motorcycle, sheer roaring power between his strong thighs, his face a mystery beneath the black-shielded fiberglass mask.

Only when the rumble of his motorcycle faded did Anna recognize the hollow sensation in her chest.

She felt as though she'd been left behind.

_ගෙන_

It took her a while to notice the dense clump of clouds that had dulled the glaring afternoon sun. She set her coffee cup in its holder and directed her sedan onto the interstate, where traffic had miraculously resumed moving at a pre-holidays pace. Spirits lightened by this heavenly phenomenon, she dialed Maggie for her thirty-minute check-in, dutifully reported her location and after hanging up, adjusted the radio to a festive slew of Christmas tunes.

That was when the first snowflake hit her windshield.

Glancing up in horror, she studied the fast-growing cloudbank and groaned as flakes drifted across the hood of her Toyota. How could this be happening when the weatherman had proclaimed Christmas weekend to be blue-skied and crystalline all the way down the Eastern seaboard? How, in this day and age of radar, computers and high-tech gadgetry, was it possible *to miss the gigantic storm* now brewing over North Carolina?

Within minutes the highway surface was wet and dusted

with fine talc, and the heavens had turned to steel. Anna slowed her car to a crawl, noting with increasing anxiety that the traffic around her had thinned dramatically. People were actually pulling over on the shoulder of the road, hazards flashing their sense of alarm, unwilling to forge through what was fast-becoming the impossible.

A whiteout.

"No freakin' way," she muttered, and picked up the cell phone to dial Maggie.

An automated voice on the other end announced there was no available signal.

Ahead, red lights flashed as the pickup driver in front of her unexpectedly hit his brakes. Instead of slowing, the truck skated sideways and made a helpless, graceful slide into the grassy median.

Anna clutched the steering wheel with both hands, hunched forward to see the road, her heart hammering. The highway ahead was almost deserted. It seemed she'd moved into a foreign, cold, frightening land, where the only sign of humanity was the gentle tinkle of Christmas music beneath the roar of her heater.

Soon her entire world shrank to the two feet barely discernible in front of the car. No exits appeared. Nothing but hard-whipped snow, which clumped in the windshield wipers as fast as they could clear the glass. If this kept up, the blades would freeze and she wouldn't be able to see anything.

Anna swallowed the lump in her throat and tried again to call her sister, but it was no use. The storm must have knocked out a tower. Either that, or she truly had entered *The Twilight Zone*. Praying she wasn't overshooting the highway altogether, she eased into the right lane and took her foot off the accelerator in preparation to pull over.

Suddenly a pale red dot appeared through the miasma ahead, a ghostly neon orb that swayed and then shot hard into her path. She gasped and hit her brakes, slid a little and finally maneuvered the Toyota to a stop. In the dim glow of her headlights, a black-garbed figure lay in a tangled heap on the abandoned powder-coated highway, his motorcycle's rear tire still spinning.

Anna threw her transmission into park and leaped out into the storm. She couldn't tell if the rider was a man or woman; the black-shielded helmet hid his face. "Are you okay?" she called, slip-sliding with little aplomb to his side.

For a second the motorcyclist didn't move, and then he slowly pulled his legs free of the bike and sat up in the snow.

A man.

Hunkering down beside him, Anna brushed the white powder off his back and helped him pull off his gloves. "Oh God, did I mow you down?"

"No," his low voice was muffled. "I cut across your lane. I didn't see you." He unfastened his helmet and pulled it off, leaving his dark hair ruffled, but suddenly all Anna could see was a familiar pair of piercing blue eyes.

"Funny meeting you here," he drawled with no humor whatsoever.

She scrambled back, slid, and hit the snow on her bottom. "You're the guy . . . the . . . coffee . . ."

"Right." He raked a hand through his hair, straightened his

spine, winced a little as he rubbed the thigh on which he'd landed. "We must be the last two fools left on the interstate."

"I was looking for an exit," she said foggily, her heart pounding.

"Me too. There aren't any."

"I noticed." Drawing a deep gulp of frozen air, she let her
worried appraisal move down his long legs. "Are you okay?"

"Yeah." He got painfully to his feet, his breath puffing out
in rapid clouds beneath the whirling snow, and offered her his
hand. "Are you?"

"Oh. Yes." She grasped his fingers and allowed him to help
her up, then quickly withdrew from his warm touch and backed
up against the hood of her car.

The snow seeped into her velvet pumps as she watched
him set his motorcycle upright. He was incredibly strong to
handle the machine with such ease. Young, too, more than
she'd thought the first time she saw him. And those amazing
eyes . . .

The shiver that quaked her frame didn't have everything to
do with the frigid air snaking beneath her thigh-length skirt.

He didn't appear to harbor the same romantic notions. After giving the motorcycle a once-over, he swiped his helmet
from the ground and flashed her a solemn glance. "You should
get back into your car where it's warm."

"I'll wait to make sure you get safely on the road."

With a shrug that said *suit yourself*, he pulled on his helmet, flipped down the face shield and straddled the bike. "Take
care," his voice came muffled at last.

"You too." She picked her way around to the Toyota's driver's side, shaking hard from the cold and excitement. Any second and the roar of his bike would fill the air, he'd ride off and she'd never know why their paths had crossed.

Hell, who needed a reason? She sounded like Maggie, searching for keys to the universe. Maybe the insanity was genetic after all.

Inside the car, Anna pulled on her seat belt and cranked her heater, all the while taking guilty pleasure in the sight of the biker's strong form straddling the motorcycle as he tried to start it.

And tried. And tried.

Her pulse jumped in her veins, a wayward thrill tickling her nerves. Frustration wrote itself in every lean line of his body as he attempted again and again to start the Harley, and failed.

His bike was dead. She couldn't leave him stranded out here in the middle of a blizzard.

She couldn't take him into her car, a dark, unpredictable stranger.

The motorcycle fired finally . . . and sputtered out. His head dropped forward in abject frustration. And all the while, Anna's heart performed impressive acrobatics, because it had already made the decision for her.

He dismounted, kicked down the stand and stood with his hands on his hips, studying the Harley. After a minute, he gave its exhaust pipe a scolding nudge with the toe of his boot, then gathered his backpack and trudged over to her car door.

Butterflies swooped and soared in her stomach as she lowered the window expectantly.

"I hate to ask you to do this," he said, leaning low to meet her eyes through the full-face helmet, "but—"

"Of course."

"Just to the nearest exit."

"No problem."

And hitting the unlock button, she invited him in, a dark, bearded stranger with the bluest eyes she'd ever seen.

Two

Anna drove at a snail's pace through the storm, her fingers clenched and sweaty on the steering wheel, every muscle in her body tight with awareness of her silent passenger.

When she stole a glance at him, he was staring out the window, one elbow resting on his helmet, his forefinger stroking his mustache. He seemed to be somewhere else, and not one bit interested in making her acquaintance, which should have been a relief.

It wasn't. The scent of leather, male exertion and melted snow filled the car's interior, stole her common sense, plucked at a female place deep inside her that made her want to lean across the console and bury her nose in his short, tousled hair. He was all male, impenetrable, a rock. Under those smooth-fitting black leathers no doubt dwelled all kinds of lean, hard delight. But beyond the physical allure, he radiated a strange melancholy and a raw sensuality that was as frightening as it was appealing.

He wasn't her type. She was nuts to want him, yet she did. So much that she could barely sit still beside him. Her mind played tricks on her, flashing images before her eyes that were carnal,

outlandish and wholly reckless considering her focus needed to
be on the icy road.

*Lost in the sheets of some generic fantasy bed, she would let him toy with
her, tease her with slow, circling thrusts, let him rub against her until she shuddered and came, and came again. Then, when enough was enough, she would
clutch his damp back, roll him over with wild strength granted by lust and sit
astride him, her hair loose and tangled as it thrashed her breasts in time to her
movements.*

*"Faster," he'd order, his hips pushing hard beneath her so that she rose high,
impaled on his steely cock. Instead of obliging him, Anna would pin his broad
wrists to the mattress and slow the enticing rotation of her pelvis. He could
only touch her when she allowed, even though every grinding slide of her sex
against his hard shaft threatened to dissolve her power and render her mindless
and vulnerable.*

*But it was her fantasy, and she was a siren, capable of wringing helpless
cries from even this dark, dangerous man. After an agonizing forever, after perspiration dampened their bodies and his legs slid against the mattress in restless
agony, after his harsh exhalations had turned to low groans and his hands
twisted in the sheets . . . she would reach behind her, let her fingers find the sensitive sac beneath his cock and fondle him, and the tender flesh would tighten like
magic beneath her skilled caress, a harbinger of the impending explosion.*

*"Fuck me," he'd growl, his dark head thrashing on the pillow. "Fuck me
hard, Anna—do it now!"*

*And with her own orgasm simmering like hot oil in her belly, she would
free him, ride him fierce and fast, revel in the hard slap of flesh meeting flesh,
the rising commingled scent of their desire, the rising song of their ecstasy, until
every muscle in his strong, sweat-slicked body tightened and bunched, and he
churned out pulsing jets of fire within her. While he was still quaking, still
calling her name, she would soar to the sky, crest and fall into a hundred tiny*

deaths of sanity. The aftershocks of her orgasm would milk him until he sank into the mattress and she fluttered like a fragile leaf atop his strong body. Then he'd stroke her damp hair with all the tender gratitude of a sated lover, kiss her temple, and say—

"How about now?"

She visibly jerked and embarrassment scalded her cheeks. "I'm sorry?"

"There's an exit coming right up." He turned his head to study her.

Anna swallowed and stared at the road. "I didn't see the sign."

"There were two of them," he offered, and when her gaze darted back to him, he was regarding her with grave intensity. God only knew how much of her thoughts were written on her burning face.

"Well, thank God." She maneuvered the car carefully onto the exit ramp and crept to a stop sign half buried beneath ice and snow. "Do you have any idea where we are?"

"Nope. There's a gas station." He gestured to a faded blue and red billboard, but when they rolled by the station, its windows were boarded up and tall brown weeds poked through the abandoned snow-coated lot.

Anna's unease tightened into trepidation. Where *was* everyone? They couldn't be the only two people out in this freak storm. Where had the rest of the world gone?

In the distance, a row of golden lights sparkled through the blowing collage of white. "A motel!"

"That'll do," he said.

Minutes later the Toyota pulled in front of "Holiday Inn," only this motel didn't belong to any giant hospitality corporation. It was a one-floor motor lodge, circa 1960, with a green and red retro façade and snow-frosted gables. Anna was comforted to see the variety of vehicles parked in front of the rooms. She and the biker weren't the last surviving life-forms in the universe, after all.

A rotund, bearded man dressed in Christmas red—complete with plaid suspenders—waddled down the walkway with towels under his arm, and gave them a cheery wave as he passed.

"Merry Christmas! Come in out of the storm!" he called, before disappearing inside a room.

Anna smiled and turned to her passenger. "Maybe you can call someone to pick you up here, or . . . or . . . ?"

"Yes." He didn't say who that someone would be . . . a wife? Girlfriend? Before Anna could cross the line into nosiness and ask, he reached across the console and touched her elbow. Just a brush of fingertips, but she felt it down to her marrow. "Thank you for the ride."

"You're welcome," she replied breathlessly as he climbed out into the waning storm. It seemed so abrupt, their parting. So sudden, like something had been left unresolved.

Oh, well. That was it. The adventure was over, the stranger gone, her foray into reckless behavior ended. A snowplow rolled by the motel on the two-lane highway, headed for the interstate. She could get back on the road now, and spend the next one hundred miles mooning over what could have been with that sexy, forbidden stranger if she'd had even *one ounce* of raw courage . . .

Her sister had won the guts lottery in the family, however. And Maggie was going to love this story of the one-night stand that never was.

Anna made it to the interstate ramp and braked to dial her

sister's number. Still no signal. If the storm continued to abate, she would only be a little late for the party. The Toyota revved a high squeal when she accelerated.

"Oh, no, you don't," she muttered, shifting gears. In reply, the car jerked and sputtered, made an ungodly sound she could never describe to any mechanic . . . and shut off.

"No, no, no! Shit, shit, *shit!*"

No amount of coaxing could get the engine to turn over. Tears lodged in her throat, she hit the hazard button, climbed out and stood in the middle of the deserted ramp beside her lifeless sedan. What the hell was she going to do now? Not a soul was in sight, not even the snowplow, which was just as well, since her dead Toyota was sitting smack in the center of the road.

It was a long, cold walk back to Holiday Inn, and by the time she reached the office, her feet were screaming in their soaked velvet pumps and her nose was so cold, she wasn't sure it hadn't fallen off her face. Every muscle was rigid from shivering, and when she stepped into the golden warmth of the tiny, wood-paneled lobby, she got as far as the nearest plaid sofa before collapsing.

"It's a nasty one out there, eh?" The jovial voice from behind the counter startled her into an upright position. She hadn't seen the clerk when she walked in, but suddenly there he was behind his wood-paneled station, white beard, bald shining head, dressed in a red-and-white-striped shirt and those crazy plaid suspenders.

Santa Claus, Anna thought dazedly as she got to her feet. How *apropos*.

"What brings you out in such a storm, my dear?" he asked, much too merrily for her current mood.

"My car has stalled on the interstate ramp," she told him in a carefully restrained voice. "Do you know of any nearby service stations that could help me?"

He rubbed his whiskered chin. "Not this late on Christmas Eve."

She closed her eyes, drew a deep breath for strength. "How about a room, then?"

"'Fraid we're all full up for the night. Lots of travelers thrown by this freak storm." He nodded at the large picture window. "It's coming down again, harder than before."

He didn't have to be so cheerful about it. Anna wasn't one for weeping, but the urge to do so, and do it loudly, surged in her chest and suffocated her response, which would have been, *You've got to be shitting me.*

"We're 'bout to close up here, go home to our families," the happy little man continued, as though they were sharing a congenial fireside chat. "How about you? Are your loved ones close by?"

She shook her head, self-pity choking her ability to speak.

"That's too bad. I'd like to let you stay here in the lobby, but I'm off the clock now, and I've got orders to lock up for the night. Cash register and all, you know. You can use the phone here to call the highway patrol though. Maybe they can help."

Hell of a Santa Claus he'd turned out to be. Resisting the urge to tell him exactly what she was thinking, she dialed the number on the old-fashioned rotary phone with stiff fingers, and when the highway patrol dispatcher told her it might be morning before a patrol car could reach her, *". . . what with the storm slowin' things down and lots of accidents ever' where . . ."* Anna knew there'd be no Santa this year.

"Thank you," she called to the little man, who had disappeared into a back room. *Not that he deserved it.*

He poked his bald head around the doorway, his blue eyes twinkling. "May your Christmas be filled with magic, dear."

"Same to you," she gritted, tears stinging her eyes. Frankly it was the thought of hiking the half mile back to her car that grieved her, even more than spending a frigid, blustery night—Christmas Eve!—in a car with no heat.

In thirty years, she'd never felt more alone.

Three

Jesse ran warm water in the sink and let it pour over his fingers, soaking in its comforting heat, letting his weary mind drift, if only for a moment, away from reality. He hadn't felt anything but sadness in so long, and the acid of grief had eaten holes in his brain, through which his thoughts seeped, disjointed and agonized.

But there had been a single breath of clarity, of normalcy, today of all days. The pretty brunette in her tin-box Toyota, all wrapped up in silk and velvet like the sweetest Christmas gift. The tenderness about her, the endearing clumsiness, the kindness in her big brown eyes, the sexy way her swan neck flowed into her graceful shoulders. The curve of her breasts beneath that wacky, useless shawl she wore, as the relentless wind whipped her chestnut curls free from her fancy hairdo.

He'd wanted her. The realization struck him now, brought a rueful smile to his lips as he stared down at the steaming water trickling over his fingers. *I guess you're not as dead as you thought you were.* In another lifetime, he might have had the balls to ask for a parting kiss from such a beautiful woman. A brief taste of her full, sensitive mouth would have lifted him up and out of the bleak movie his life had become. And it wouldn't have been so out of place to ask for a kiss. For a while, they'd shared an adventure. Two strangers whose paths had intersected not once, but twice— and while Jesse didn't believe much in fate, the scenario certainly offered some interesting possibilities to his writer's imagination.

But he hadn't asked to kiss her. Hadn't even thought of it until now. One more missed opportunity, and normally he didn't care. Tonight, though, it mattered. He regretted the way they'd passed through each other's lives. Even now he could picture her moving among the guests at her party tonight, sipping champagne, smooching cheeks, shaking her sweet backside beneath that short velvet dress to some sultry beat on the dance floor.

That tugged his mouth up into a smile, but when he caught his reflection in the mirror, the pleasure faded from his bearded features. He hardly recognized himself anymore. How had he come to this? People lost children every day and moved on. Why couldn't he? Why had he lost everything when he lost Daniel? His entire life—his writing career, his marriage, his home, his identity—slipping away like the water gliding through his fingers.

He'd let it all go without a fight, except for Daniel's ghost. It was killing him, day by day, pulling him out of this world and into another where nothingness reigned. He was drowning, letting himself drift further and further from recovery. He had become a ghost himself.

The water in the sink abruptly went cold and he straightened, shutting off the spigot. A coffeemaker sat on the counter to his left, but he didn't want coffee. He needed something stiffer. Whiskey. A tiny flask was tucked inside his backpack for occasions such as this, when the nights got too long and his isolation too profound. He'd never been much of a drinker, but at this moment it promised a welcome escape.

He loosened the flask's lid, then hesitated. The bitter medicine might go down easier with a little cola, and maybe he'd sleep for a while, his only break from the pain that drove him. He'd passed a soda machine near the motel office, although there was no guarantee it would work. Everything about the tiny motor lodge seemed lost in time. Just like he was.

Retrieving a handful of coins from his jacket, he opened the door and stepped out into the covered walkway, just in time to see a slender, familiar figure limping away from the motel and into the wind-whipped parking lot.

"What the hell . . . ?" Hunching against the blowing snow, he jogged after her. "Hey!" *Christ, he hadn't even asked her name.* "Miss!"

The heavy precipitation swallowed his call. Only when she paused to adjust her thin, soaked shawl did his voice reach her, and her head shot around, her fawn eyes wide and liquid with tears, wet strands of chestnut hair frosted with ice.

She was shivering. Crying. An unnamed sensation fisted around his heart as he reached her. Without thinking, he folded her into his arms to protect her from the swirling storm, and she didn't resist.

He meant to ask her what she was doing—was she *crazy?*—but she melted into him just right, as though she belonged in his arms, and only when the wetness of her garments soaked through his shirt did he pull back to meet her brimming eyes. "What the hell are you doing out here?"

"Hugging a stranger?" She laughed, but it sounded choked.

"After I dropped you off, I thought I could get back on the highway. The storm was letting up. I mean, it appeared to be. I'm not crazy enough to get back on the road in a blizzard. But—you saw that the storm had let up, right?"

"Sure," Jesse said, his embrace absorbing the hard shudders of her body. She might be a little nuts, but she smelled like a rose in winter, soft and rich.

"I barely made it to the on-ramp and my car died," she was saying. "No warning. There's nothing wrong with that car, I'm telling you. I take such good care of the cheap piece of junk! And it flat-out died!"

"The nerve of it," he murmured, knowing she wasn't listening as she clung to him, her words coming in warm exhalations against the bare skin where his collar fell open.

"And then the snow just poured on my head like someone had dumped a bucket of ice on me, and—and I walked back here, but there are n-no vacancies."

"I took the last room." He cursed under his breath and tightened his embrace, his chin finding the top of her head. It felt too damn good to hold this woman, standing like a crazy man with her out in the storm.

She was sobbing now, her shoulders heaving, whether from the cold or the tears he didn't know. "It's not your fault. Ugh, look at me. Normally I don't do this. It's just that . . . it's C-Christmas—"

"Come on." He started to lead her toward his room, but she stiffened and withdrew from his guiding arm.

"What are you doing?"

"Taking you somewhere warm."

"Your room?"

"The office looks locked up and closed," he said. "Do you have a better place in mind?"

She bit her lip. "I don't know you."

"No, you don't," he replied, shivering himself now. "But I'm not about to hang out here and freeze to death just to let you get better acquainted. You want to come in or not?"

She lifted her chin and studied his eyes, her teeth chattering. "Fine. I'll accept your offer as a return favor for helping you on the highway. Only until the snow lets up and I can call a tow truck. And no funny stuff."

"Speak for yourself," he pointed out, poker-faced.

Her head tilted in consideration. "Well, true. I could be a serial killer for all you know."

"Maybe you'll have mercy on me and take a break from all that violence. After all, it's Christmas Eve." And when at last a smile twitched on her delectable mouth, he led the way into his room and shut the door behind them.

Despite her bravado, unease swirled around Anna as unrelenting as the blizzard's wind. Here she stood inside a stranger's room, staring at him, and he at her, his bright blue eyes giving nothing away. And outside the world had disappeared in a miasma of white fury.

If this man wanted to hurt her, he could easily have his way. He was, as she'd earlier suspected, strong-limbed and lean. He'd shucked off his leather jacket. His plaid flannel shirt stretched taut across his broad back as he finally moved, leaned to pick up the ruined shawl that had slipped from her shoulders and hung it in the tiny closet to dry.

"I was going to make myself a drink," he said, his voice quiet in the room's hush. "Would you like one? I can grab you a soda from the machine."

"That would be great." Still quaking from the cold, she eased down onto a worn wingback chair and squeezed her chilled hands between her nylon-covered knees to warm them.

He disappeared outside again, and she sat in utter stillness, shell-shocked by the unbelievable reality of this day. She no longer felt like crying. This was all too interesting to give into despair just yet.

After a moment she retrieved the phone from her wet purse and dialed Maggie's number. This time the call went through, and for a moment hope swelled in her heart. But there was no answer; not even the machine picked up. She dialed again, to no avail.

The entire day was beginning to feel like one fat cosmic joke.

The biker reentered the room, two soda cans hugged against his chest. Snow dusted his dark hair, and he shook it off like a big dog and shut the door with his foot.

"It's bad out there," he said, and leaned behind Anna's chair to crank the heating unit, close enough for her to study the smooth seat of his leather pants.

He had a nice ass, she managed to note through her misery. Muscular, but not the bulky bubble-butt of a weight lifter. His physique was obviously compliments of Mother Nature. So was the easy way he moved, with enough liquid ease to indicate innate sensuality—half the reason for Anna's discomfort. She might not trust him, but she trusted herself even less. Desperation did funny things to a woman's code of ethics. Right now she could hardly remember what her mother had taught her about strangers and motel rooms with only one bed.

Outside, the wind wailed a mournful elegy, but warmth had begun to return to Anna's limbs, and since the biker had retreated to the bed and seemed to be keeping his distance, she relaxed a little.

"Before you even think it, I don't plan on getting wasted." He retrieved a small flask of whiskey from his knapsack and splashed a finger into a glass on the bedside table. "I just want to warm up, and I'd suggest you do the same."

"Plain soda, please," she said stiffly. "I'd like to keep my wits about me."

If he was insulted by her obvious doubt of him, he didn't show it. After he'd handed her a glass of cola, he finished making his drink. Then he sat down on the edge of the queen-sized bed with the glass cradled in his big hands and wordlessly met her gaze.

Anna swallowed a mouthful of cola and glanced away. His eyes were so clear, so piercing, like the azure marbles she'd collected as a kid. She wanted a longer look at them, but they stung her. "What's your name?" she asked finally.

"Jesse." His lashes lowered as he studied her mouth. "You?"

"Anna."

He lifted his glass in her direction. "To being stranded in the middle of nowhere on Christmas, Anna."

"Cheers," she echoed, and took a long gulp. Silence blanketed the space between them, and underneath, an unnamed tension roiled and flowed. After a beat, she said, "You know, Jesse, I think I will have a little whiskey with my soda."

He obliged her, then returned to his post on the edge of the bed, and they finished their drinks without speaking. Outside, the storm raged, and soon the lateness of the afternoon swallowed what remained of the frail, frozen daylight. Jesse reached over and turned on a bedside lamp, filling the room with a soft golden glow.

Thawed at last by the whiskey, Anna kicked off her ruined pumps, curled her feet beneath her and sank deeper into the chair's winged embrace. Despite the strangeness of the situation, it was damned good to be off the highway. Weariness weighted her eyelids, and she forced them open again, not quite secure enough to sleep in this man's presence.

Without a word, he rose and withdrew a blanket from the closet, tossed it to her. Keeping his distance, even though less than an hour ago he'd wrapped her in his arms and she'd come more than willingly.

"Thank you," she murmured, and the words held a deeper import.

He gave a short nod. "I'm going to sleep for a while."

She tensed again, her gaze following him as he pulled back the covers and threw one pillow to the foot of the bed. He didn't offer to give her the bed and he didn't offer to share it. He pulled off his boots, tugged his shirt free from the waistband of his pants and stretched out on the mattress.

"Wake me if you need anything," he said, and just like that, he fell asleep, leaving her in peace, wholly surprised, and inexplicably disappointed.

~ ⌒⌒ ~

While he slept, Anna crept into the bathroom, locked the door and ran herself a hot shower. She hung her soaked clothing up to dry and stepped beneath the steaming spray, where she lingered until the water went tepid. When she was done, she wrapped herself in a towel and sat on the toilet lid, unsure of what to do next. It wasn't appropriate—or smart—to flounce around the room in nothing but a towel while her clothing dried, even if the biker wasn't awake to witness it. On the other hand, she couldn't sit in the tiny, steam-filled cubicle all night. Gritting her teeth, she put her clothing back on, which no longer was drenched, but merely damp and icy to her tender skin. It was hell, but at least she was clean and somewhat thawed.

Shivering, she eased the bathroom door open and tiptoed into the room. The biker had changed positions on the bed; he lay on his side away from her, silent, the steady rise and fall of his back indicating he truly was asleep.

He looked cold.

Moving stealthily, Anna drew the side of the bedspread over his huddled form, then backed away to watch him, half frightened, a quarter miserable, and the rest . . . well, titillated. Knowing that nothing would happen between them gave her love-hungry mind free rein to entertain a million erotic scenarios. *Two strangers, both solitary, stranded in a storm, sharing a motel room with one bed out of sheer desperation. And sheer desperation would ultimately drive them together.*

Sounded like a movie . . . a juicy one.

She groped for the chair behind her, curled up on it, and covered herself with the blanket he'd offered her earlier. After a while her thoughts slid into a sleepy collage of fragmented fantasies, and finally, dreams.

─◌◌─

Anna didn't realize she'd dozed off until the sound of water rushing through creaking pipes roused her back to life.

The bed was empty, the covers rumpled. From the bathroom came the sound of a shower running, the thud of soap hitting the tub floor. After a minute the water shut off, followed by the clack of shower curtain rings sliding on a metal rod.

He was in the shower. Naked. With one thin wall between them.

Afloat in that languid place between sleep and wakefulness, she let her eyelids slide closed again while a naughty picture of his body slid through her mind. *Jesse.* The name suited him. Tough yet tender. He'd welcomed her into his room. He'd put his arms around her in the parking lot, protected her from the storm.

Such a man would be an incredible lover. Anna couldn't say how she knew this. But she'd felt it, a galvanized shiver of awareness, while she stood in the sheltering circle of his arms with the snow blowing all around them. Awareness of his strength, and of the vague vulnerability that contradicted it. She'd been wrong to think him an impervious rock. Now that she knew his features, she read the unnamed history in the lines around his crystalline eyes—laughter. And the shadows beneath those eyes—grief. He'd been happy once. What had stolen that from him and brought him to this solitary place on Christmas Eve?

Unexpected desire surged low in her belly, burning her everywhere, pulsing heat between her thighs, making her painfully aware yet again of how long it had been since she'd known the touch, taste, scent of a man.

This one, with his paradox of darkness and light, mesmerized her. And being just a little afraid of him seemed to feed that fascination. She wanted to unlock his armor, see what dwelled beneath.

What if, for once, she took the road less traveled and followed the whisper of recklessness in her mind, the one that echoed the hot fantasies she'd entertained since first seeing him in the convenience store? What would he do if she threw all caution to the wind and met him at the bathroom door?

Merry Christmas, she'd say. May I unwrap you?

Before the scenario could play to fruition in her overheated mind, the door squeaked open and steam billowed out of the bathroom, followed by the delicious scent of soap and shampoo. Jesse appeared, his lean hips enfolded in a towel, his naked back turned to her as he retrieved the knapsack he'd placed by the sink.

She sat as still as a deer and watched the liquid play of sinew under his golden skin, her throat dry, her pulse pounding. Rivulets of water trickled over the ridges and dips of his musculature, rushing to meet at the low dip of his back.

When he lifted his head, she froze.

The clean-shaven, sharply chiseled face reflected in the mirror belonged to someone new. But those eyes . . . deep, bright, exquisitely blue . . . they were the same. Filled with buried sadness, but under that, something more. Man's awareness of Woman. He knew she appraised him, measured him, contemplated the possibilities, and she didn't deny it by looking away.

They stared at each other in the mirror for much too long before Anna finally found her voice. "You shaved off your beard and mustache."

His mouth quirked and he rubbed a hand across his chin. "It's been a while. I feel kind of naked."

"You look different."

"You don't like the change?"

Her cheeks warmed as she tucked away the memory of her earlier fantasy. "Believe me, a part of me definitely liked the beard. But you're quite handsome this way. I like your face."

"Thank you," he said, his eyes finding hers again. Searching for his own answers.

Holy cow, she wanted him. And what, truly, did she have to lose, alone on Christmas night for the thirtieth time in her singular life?

One . . . two . . . three . . . jump. "So what are you thinking, Jesse, when you look at me like that?"

"Wondering what you're thinking when you're looking at *me* like that," he volleyed.

She had to smile, even though her heart threatened to hammer its way through her rib cage. "That's funny."

"Maybe a little."

Try, try again. "Well? Do you like what you see when you look at me?"

"Yes," he said, without preamble. Not that she gave him any choice.

Her brows lowered. "You're nice to say that, but I kind of put you on the spot just now."

"Maybe a little," he repeated.

Anna bit her lip. "Well. I like *you*, Jesse."

His strong throat moved when he swallowed. "That's good, seeing as how we're stuck here together."

An arid comment, but not a rejection.

She eased forward on the chair, her heart pounding. "I want to know you." The truth quavered just a little. Playtime was over.

He let the shaving lotion slide back into his knapsack, the muscles of his back flexing as he straightened. "Why?"

"I don't know. I'm drawn to you. Not just physically." When he didn't respond right away, she snapped out of her pleasurable haze and closed her eyes, humiliation chilling away the desire that had turned her insides to warm, sweet liquid. "Jeez . . . what am I doing?"

"I'm not sure." He braced his hands on the counter, all clean and sexy, watching her in the mirror with those blue, blue eyes. "Keep talking and maybe we'll figure it out together."

Not a rejection at all.

Just like that, the fire returned, rushed through her, simmering low in her belly. She licked her lips and straightened on the chair, the blanket sliding from her lap onto the floor. "I felt like this when I first saw you at the gas station, you know."

"Like how?" he prompted, his voice gone husky.

"Like . . . all squirrelly and . . . and hot." Her fingers dug into her thighs through the short velvet dress, braced for his rebuff, prepared for something far more frightening—his reciprocation. "You scare me to death. I haven't been with a man in a year, and even before that, I've only had a couple of boyfriends. I'm a long-termer when it comes to relationships. This isn't like me. I don't pick up strangers. You're a stranger."

"That's right." He turned at last to face her, but instead of approaching, he leaned his backside against the counter and let his sultry gaze slide down to her feet and back. "You want to change that?"

She tried to clear her throat, but all that came out was a squeak. Her body was aching and inflamed as though he'd touched her inside and out with his strong hands, yet all he'd done was make a few noncommittal comments, look at her with those watchful bedroom eyes, standing there unabashed in all his half-naked beauty . . .

Anything could happen next.

"Anna," he straightened away from the counter, the word playing on his lips as though he'd sampled it and liked what he tasted. "That's your name?"

"That's right," she said hoarsely.

"Anna," he said. "Come here."

Four

When she didn't move right away, Jesse held out his hand, his heart lunging in his chest. Jesus, she looked vulnerable. She was small, so fragile in the face of an incredibly gutsy move.

Her proposition had sideswiped him. He couldn't have guessed she wanted him . . . didn't know why she did, when he had so little left to offer. Maybe it had something to do with being so lonely it hurt. He knew the feeling and he didn't want to hurt her. He didn't want to be hurt. Maybe if he touched her, cradled those soft, yielding curves against him and got the craving out of the way, he could end anything else that would expose him for the brittle shell he'd become.

Or maybe he was dreaming this entire scenario.

His hand started to drop, but then she rose from the chair and crossed the six feet between them to take it. Her cool fingers laced through his, and she pressed against him, her free arm encircling his naked waist. Instantly his cock surged from half-mast to full hardness, too responsive to the slightest stimulation after so long. If she noticed, she didn't say anything. She could have been coy, suggestive, doused the heat between them with some crass comment that would shine a spotlight on what this truly was—a meaningless one-night stand.

Instead, she rubbed her nose against his bare chest like a languid cat, her lips finding the hollow at the base of his throat.

"Christ," he whispered, his head listing as she placed small, tentative kisses along the side of his neck. The scent of soap and fresh shampoo filled his senses. She'd showered, left off the stockings. Her shapely legs were golden and bare.

Between them his erection pushed against the towel, against her belly, answering any questions left unvoiced and demanding much more.

Still he spoke, one last grasp at sanity. "Why are you doing this?"

"Because all we have in this world right now is each other." She pulled back to look at him, her lashes heavy, her lips parted in invitation. "Because tonight I think you're as lost as I am. And because I think you're beautiful. You're so beautiful, Jesse."

He wrapped a hand in the tousled damp mane that tumbled to her shoulders. "And so you want me to fuck you." A test.

Anna didn't flinch. "I want you to touch me. To make love with me."

"I don't know what that is anymore," he whispered, and rested his jaw against her temple where her pulse thudded a staccato rhythm. *She really is scared*. He was, too. His own heartbeat echoed hers, pounding in his throat, his chest, his engorged cock.

"It doesn't matter." Her words quavered as she caught his wrists and brought his hands up to cup her breasts. "Don't you have a wife? A girlfriend?"

"There's no one. Not in a year." He stared down at his fingers curving around the soft mounds of her breasts. Even through the velvet bodice of her dress and some stiff undergarment beneath it, her nipples poked his palms, tight little knots of arousal. He wanted to grasp the neckline and pull, tear it away from her slim body, suck and bite and lick every inch of her. She was petite; he could handle her, twist and turn and move her where he wanted her, how he wanted her, which was in every possible way. Now. *Right now*.

When Anna's gentle fingers cupped the back of his neck, the ferocity in him stilled.

Make love to me, she'd said. By God, he would remember how. She would show him.

Grasping her waist, Jesse turned her and lifted her onto the counter by the sink, putting them at eye level. She had big liquid eyes, a tender mouth that invited a sliding tongue. Pacing himself, he ducked his head, caught her lips gently, feathered his mouth across hers, once, twice, nudging his way inside with soft, non-threatening kisses, a softer probe with the tip of his tongue. Licking, flicking, meeting her tongue and darting away again, he savored the faint whiskey taste of her until her fingers dug into his back and her breathing fractured into small explosions.

It was all the encouragement he needed. His fingers slid beneath her dress and up one bare thigh to the incredible heat and dampness of her sex, where he paused, and stroked, and teased until her pelvis lifted from the counter in search of a firmer touch. Her panties were in the way, but he played her through them, driving them both higher with each stroke of his thumb, to a place where they couldn't turn back.

Groaning her frustration, Anna sought to kiss his mouth again, but Jesse was intent. He dragged her hips closer to the edge of the counter, pinning her hands to the Formica surface, and dropped to his knees before her.

"No . . ." It was half-plea, half-protest, when he grasped her legs to edge them apart and his intention became clear.

"No?" He looked up at her flushed face, at the way her hair tumbled, sleep-sexy, around her cheeks. "No, you don't want me to strip you naked and eat you until you come?"

"I don't know. I haven't . . . I don't . . ." Her eyelids fluttered open, her hand slipping from his grasp and finding its way into his hair. God, he liked the way she touched him. He wanted to feel those gentle fingers tangled and tugging for dear life while she screamed her pleasure beneath his mouth. He wanted to drive his tongue deep into her wetness and swallow her whole.

"Spread your legs for me, Anna," he whispered, and when she did, just a little, he caught the sole of her foot against his bare chest to hold her there, open to him, vulnerable.

The sultry, aroused scent of her perfume and raw desire filled his senses as he nuzzled his way up the inside of her thigh, nipping, licking through the thin barrier of her panties. The soft material was silken with her body's need as though she'd been aroused for some time.

"God, you're so wet."

Instantly her legs pressed closed. "I know, I know. Just looking at you in the convenience store made me that way." She squeezed her eyes closed at her own confession, two spots of crimson appearing high on her cheeks, but Jesse smiled and pressed a kiss of reverence against her knee.

"Anna, don't do that. You know how long I've been hard?

Maybe since you stepped foot into my motel room. Why do you think I got in the shower while you were asleep?"

"I don't know . . ."

He studied her fluttering lashes. "To jack off like some kind of desperate fool."

Her eyelids flew open and she stared down into his face, a shudder moving through her. "Did you?"

"In the end, no." He nuzzled her other knee. "Maybe some part of me was hoping you'd let me do this instead."

"Good," came the husky response, and she shifted her knees apart as though he'd uttered "Open Sesame."

"Lean back against the mirror and lift up a little." When she obliged, he drew the bikinis down to her ankles. They dangled, uselessly frilly and forgotten, from one bare foot, while he stroked the outside of her naked hips beneath the dress. Then shifting to his haunches, he pushed the hem of her dress up her shapely thighs, up, up, exposing every creamy inch of her skin, and when her neatly shaven mound came into view, he closed his eyes and gripped the counter's edge on either side of her to squelch the rush of desire that threatened to undo him.

It would be so easy to stand up, grasp her hips and pull her forward to meet his relentless thrust. To push inside her, deep, deeper, then back again, dragging through all that silky wetness, back and forth in measured lunges, setting fire to her senses, and to his own. But her request—her challenge—so brave, so shaky, echoed in his overheated mind. *Make love to me.*

And so, parting her slick folds with his thumbs, he leaned forward and with the tip of his tongue found the swollen bead of her clitoris.

"Oh!" Her entire body jerked, and his own muscles clenched in response, perspiration dampening his limbs.

He wanted to come, right then and there.

He shifted, regrouped, breathed in the clean, sexy scent of her skin and, beneath that, the perfume of her desire. Pacing himself. Reveling, for the first time in a million forevers, in beauty and pleasure. And when he was ready, he leaned forward again and let his tongue explore her, made lazy circles around and around the tiny nub at the top of her sex until she was trembling. While his fingers held her open to him, his tongue glided lower, through the moisture that slicked her flesh, savoring her salty-sweet flavor as he recalled from some sleeping part of him what made a woman sing, what made her sigh, what made her scream with pleasure.

Maybe Jesse didn't know Anna, but he'd guessed just right.

When he spread her wider with his fingertips and unexpectedly plunged his tongue into her core, she uttered a choked cry and her hands clutched his shoulders, his neck, his hair, blindly seeking to anchor herself under his tender assault. "Oh God, Oh God, Oh *God!*" Thrashing shudders lifted her pelvis and rocked her against his mouth as she climaxed under his tongue.

Still Jesse lapped and licked her, probing, stroking, until she collapsed against the mirror and her fingers loosened their death grip on his hair. Then he grasped the edge of the counter and rose on legs that quaked.

When her lashes lifted and her somnolent brown gaze locked with his, she didn't speak. No words were necessary. He helped her off the counter and drew her toward the bed a few feet away, where she sat on the edge, considering him, his naked torso, the blatant tent his erection made beneath the snug towel as he stood in front of her.

The orgasm he'd given her had apparently stripped away her inhibitions and now she sat before him, tousled, lush, vibrating with sensuous intent. This night could go so very wrong.

Or so very right.

Lost, he squeezed his eyes closed and gave himself over to her. *Make love to me, too, Anna. Make me forget everything but pleasure.*

And she did. Jesse vaguely registered the rush of cool air on his skin as she unknotted his towel and drew it away from his body, the murmur of approval she uttered as she took in the sight of his need, then her hands were clutching his naked ass and her hot, sweet mouth engulfed his cock, sucking it deep into scalding wetness.

Trembling, he let his hands find her hair and buried them in silky thick luxury. He wanted to rub those satin strands over his erection, rub and rub until he came in hard, pulsing shudders. He wanted to thrust deep into her mouth, again, again, feel the compression of her throat around him as she swallowed everything he had to give. His agony. His need. His pleasure.

There was so much he wanted, and so little time. Forcing his eyes open, he stared down at her and watched the smooth ride of his shaft pushing between her lips, then its reappearance, red-hot, impossibly harder and wet from the insistent stroke of her tongue. Despite her innate innocence, she was damned good at this. Her hands gripped his hips and guided him between her lips again, her thumbs caressing the sensitive spots inside his hipbones. Sucking him in as deep as he would go. Pulling back and playing the head of his penis with her firm, dancing tongue before taking him again in strong, hungry pulls.

"I'm going to come," he panted.

She drew back and met his eyes. "Not yet." The world tilted as she unexpectedly pulled him down with her, and he caught himself before he crushed her beneath him on the mattress. And then her thighs were riding his hips and he was moving against her, driving his hard penis against her slippery chasm, and there was so much wetness . . . from her, from him, the scent of heat and want an earthy ambrosia between them.

Jesse was frantic. Before he could stop himself, before he could think, he shoved her dress around her waist, grasped his shaft with the other and found her quivering, wet entrance with the driving tip of his cock.

"Come inside me," she breathed against his ear, giving him the permission he needed.

He thrust firm and deep within her, to the hilt. No protection in any form, not even on his heart.

"*Ah . . .*" An indecipherable sound tore from the center of his chest. A sound of agony. A sound of joy.

He was raw. "Oh God."

"It's okay, Jess, it's fine . . ." Breathing mindless encouragement, Anna pulled her knees up high to cradle his hips and took him even deeper, her hair spilled wildly beneath her, her fingers grasping at his back, his ribs, his undulating backside, then at last the crumpled bedspread, taking it with her as his fierce rhythmic thrusts drove and drove and drove her up the mattress.

"Christ, you feel . . . so . . . *good.*" He moved spasmodically, like a machine beyond his own control. This was more than fucking. The way she scalded him, enclosed him, down to the very heart of him . . . he'd never felt sensation so intense.

Release built to unbearable heights in Jesse's cock, filled it to bursting, and he tried to slow, to delay the explosion, but she was whispering hot words against his ear—"*Oh yes, oh please yes*—" thrusting back almost faster than he could plunge inside her, and then she climaxed again, her cries lost beneath the roar in his ears, and it was too late. He heard himself from a distance, groaning desperate words from a primal, universal language, months of pain and emptiness jetting inside her as he came with an intensity that detonated stars before his eyes.

It went on and on, spasms of ecstasy clenching and draining, painful and incredible and cleansing. When the stars faded, his head sagged against her shoulder, and for a moment he allowed himself to be held in warmth and what felt strangely—impossibly—like love.

"Jesse," she whispered against his cheek, and scattered light, soothing kisses over his damp shoulder. "Jess."

For an instant he lolled in the loveliness of Anna, her peace, her tenderness. Trying to remember what was wrong in his life that had brought him, ironically, to this place of joy. Because he'd forgotten. For just a second, he'd forgotten.

And then he remembered. The grief returned with a vengeance, threatening what little dignity he'd brought to this naked place. Easing off her, he rolled to his back and flung an arm over his eyes, struggling to breathe, to force the emotions back into the bottomless well he'd long feared would one day be unlocked.

He hadn't dreamed a stranger might hold the key.

He didn't know her. Hadn't wanted to. Hadn't meant for this day to become so lost and misguided, and God, where was his path to self-destruction leading him this time? The knot in his throat had nothing to do with the anger and pain that had sustained him up until now. This woman had exposed his scars with one look. *Jesus*. One touch. A little sympathy from a stranger, and he wanted to weep like some kind of idiot kid.

Quiet, Anna shifted onto her side to face him. He sensed the touch of her luminous gaze on every part of him, as though she could read the darkness etched on his heart. Her brown eyes were too probing, too aware. It was the first thing he'd noticed about her, standing beside him at the gas station coffee counter. Her velvety brown eyes, her silken soul.

"Jesse?"

When she reached out and moved his arm away from his face, he grasped her wrist to push her back . . . and failed as he registered the soft resilience of her skin, the warm, musky fragrance of a woman's desire that rose from beneath the crumpled dress. His fingers gentled to caress her, to measure the fine breadth of her wrist as he brought it to his lips and kissed the tender flesh where her pulse hammered erratically.

"You're so damned beautiful," he murmured, and that was all, because his gratitude choked anything more. She said nothing, just laid her head on her crooked elbow, watching him revel in her.

He'd wanted to touch her like this since he'd first seen her. To know the surface of her body, and beyond that, her heart. To learn the lush resilience of her mouth, the flicker of her tongue, the heat of her kiss, breathing life back into him.

A fleeting fantasy . . . yet here they were. The impossible could still happen after all.

Jesse Proffitt could still feel something besides pain.

—⟶⟵—

"Can I ask you a question?" Anna finally spoke, her voice hushed, as though the room were a sacred place. Maybe it was, she thought. They'd christened it thus.

"What is it?" He rolled to his side to meet her, and they lay nose-to-nose, elbows bent beneath their heads.

"Why aren't you married?"

It was none of her business, but she wanted something more of him to take with her when they parted. Something more than the incredible pleasure he'd given her, that they'd given each other.

He swallowed and reached out to move a wayward strand of hair from her cheek. "I used to be married. We were together eleven years. We divorced last year."

"Oh." Her gaze slid away as she assimilated the information and tried to conjure a scenario. What kind of woman had he loved enough to marry? Was she funny? Bright? Beautiful? Did she know how to touch him just right? Could he make her go all wet and weak with one look from those incredible blue eyes of his? And a really masochistic part of Anna wondered, how many times had this woman taken him inside her body and heard those magic words of desire and need whispered against her hair?

You feel so good . . . you're so damned beautiful . . .

"Did you leave her?" she asked, and winced at the sound of her own driving inquisitiveness.

"Well . . ." He rolled to his back and exhaled, one hand absently rubbing his stomach as he thought about his answer. "I guess that depends on which one of us you ask. On paper, she left me. She had justifiable reasons. I guess I drove her away. I don't know." He sighed again, his profile limned by the frail glow from the lamp. "We were happy for a while, at first. She was a real estate agent. I was a writer. We had money, a nice house. And then we had a child. A son."

Anna hesitated, sensing the shift of currents in the night. Languid arousal had slid into something dark and raw. "Where is your son now?"

"He died eighteen months ago." It was a flat statement, an offering of emotionless facts, and yet the grief behind it stole the breath from her lungs.

It explained so much, all of a sudden. This was a key to who Jesse was. And she couldn't help herself when she asked softly, "What happened to him?"

For a long time Jesse didn't answer, and Anna's cheeks warmed with each excruciating second that passed in silence. She'd crossed the invisible barrier he wore around himself like armor. Her prying had shattered all the delicious, languid intimacy between them.

Then his husky words rent the quiet. "He was hit by a drunk driver on the street in front of our house."

Anna swallowed, trying to read his features in the shadows. It was impossible. But his words bled an anguish she couldn't begin to measure.

"He was six years old."

"Oh, Jesse . . ." she scooted closer to him, her palm finding his cheek in the shadows. "I have no right to pry like this, but . . . if you want to tell me, I'll listen."

"I don't know. I haven't . . . I don't know."

"It's okay." She quickly accepted his shaken reply, moved by it into acquiescence and shame. "I'm so sorry. I shouldn't have asked."

The sheets rustled as he shifted to look at her. "Shouldn't you? Look at us, Anna. Two complete strangers. Yet I feel like I've been closer to you tonight than maybe anyone, ever. If there's anyone who I want to spill my poison with, it's you."

"Then talk to me." She cupped his face in one hand, the other tracing the somber line of his mouth. He had beautiful, sculpted lips for a man. He had a truth to tell, *poison*, as he'd called it, so potent that he carried it with him like his own secret potion. She could see the toxic anguish in his eyes, which flashed like polished stone in the gloom.

His words burst out, choked and laughing at the same time. "I thought that losing a child happened to other people. He was there every day, a part of my life, a part of me, more than my own breath. Can you imagine losing an arm or leg? How about both arms? Both legs? You can't even compare that agony to what it felt like losing Daniel."

Anna swallowed the useless words of consolation welling on her lips. Something told her that her silence was far more valuable now as he purged his truth.

"It was spring, beautiful, warm. He asked me if he could play in the yard with the other kids. Did you finish your homework, I said. Like that's even important for a kid who's just turned six." Jesse was weeping now, a flood of anguish that she met and embraced with silent strength. "He hadn't finished his homework, he needed help on the math, but I needed to write—I had an opinion column in a local paper, and if you asked me now what my oh-so-fucking-important opinion was that day, I couldn't tell you." Wiping his eyes, he uttered a short, self-effacing laugh. "I had a long way to fall to be humbled, and trust me, I'm there now. But that day—I wanted peace and quiet. I told him to go outside. And when he got there, his buddies from next door were out playing football, except their damn dog kept stealing the ball. They told me later Daniel was the only one to give chase when the dog darted out into the road. And—" He stopped, too choked, and for a moment there was only silence, while his torn breathing shattered the night, and Anna's cheeks grew wet with tears of sympathy.

"And see, there was this homeless guy, an alcoholic, who had holed up temporarily with his brother a couple of streets over. He had a few drunk driving citations under his belt, but his lawyer brother kept digging him out, and digging him out. Doing him a favor, he thought. That's what brothers do for each other. While Daniel was playing with his friends, this guy got drunk, borrowed his brother's new sports car and took it for an afternoon joyride. Down the street. Down the next street. Then down our street, going fifty miles an hour. And he didn't even remember hitting my son, later, when they caught him. He was so drunk, he didn't remember killing a child. My child."

"I'm so sorry," Anna whispered, leaning to kiss the corner of his mouth. "So, so sorry."

"Daniel was only six." Jesse's hand covered Anna's to hold it against his hot, tear-streaked face. "Six years old when he died, and I died with him. Every time I say the words aloud, I die again."

She stroked his cheek, blind in the dark, blind to who he was, only that he was Jesse, a stranger full of secrets, and perhaps he'd shared with her the biggest one.

She could share with him, too. Her sympathy. Her touch.

Herself. "Jesse," she whispered, and lifting her head, she found his trembling mouth with her kiss.

~∽∿~

So much time had passed since he'd known pleasure of any kind, much less this potent, sweet arousal flaring between them again. He tried to feel guilty for letting it dilute his grief, but desire rushed through him anew, tensing every muscle as he slid his hand up her arm and roughly pushed the dress off her shoulder. *So smooth, her skin. Like satin.*

Hot with shame, with too many tears, he started to apologize for his outburst, but she leaned closer to capture his mouth more fully, swallowing his agony, one hand stroking his hair, the other gliding over his chest to caress his stomach, to trace around his navel, then down his flank, and when he thought he'd go crazy for want of her, to firmly grasp his aching erection.

The electric contact of her fingers on his cock nearly sent him through the roof. "*Anna . . .*"

"Make love to me again," she whispered, and grasping his hands, guided them to her small, firm breasts through the lacy brassiere she still wore.

He couldn't think, couldn't rationalize, *couldn't stop*. Her dress was caught around her waist, the zipper buried beneath the drooping bodice. His shaking fingers didn't work well enough to find it, so he sat up, grasped the back of the bodice and pulled.

Anna didn't flinch at the telltale ripping sound. Scrambling to her knees beside him, she reached behind her, freed herself from the strapless bra and drew the unsalvageable dress up and over her head. The dress rustled to a forlorn heap on the floor.

Flushed, ruffled, and goddess-beautiful to his aching eyes, she met his gaze squarely and said, "Again. Please. Now."

"Ride me," he ordered, half mindless as he braced his back against the cold headboard and led her to sit astride him.

She found his shaft with a confident hand, rubbed herself against the engorged head, teasing, beckoning, and then slowly sank down on him in measured increments until they both gasped with the ecstasy of it. For a moment neither moved, then Jesse's attention shifted from her rapt features to her naked breasts, and he cupped them for the first time, gently, in reverence, filling his palms with their weight, thumbing the small nipples into turgid points.

How could he have taken her the first time without touching every part of her first? Without poring over her, learning each curve, each point of delight? She was perfect, the most desirable woman he'd ever known, and for tonight, no one and nothing else existed but them in this tiny, enchanted room.

Everything slowed then, as the anguish seeped away like swirling blood washed down a drain. He leaned forward and caught her nipple between his lips, flicked it with his tongue. Tugged a little until she shivered and arched her back. He scissored his teeth gently across it and felt the heavy, quickened drum of her pulse in response, the tiny contractions of her silken muscles around his shaft with each tug, as though an invisible string stretched between her nipple and her womb.

Anna watched him in the spellbound silence, her long brown hair fallen around them, the only sound between them the harsh seesaw of their breathing. When he lifted his head in a silent request for her kiss, she feathered her lips across his open, panting mouth. Then she rose and fell once, twice, riding his cock with a measured deliberateness that dumped every sane, human thought from his mind and sent an orgasm rushing up his shaft like fire.

"Please," he gritted. "Not yet."

"Yes," she whispered fiercely. "Now." And she cradled his head against her breasts, a strangely protective gesture that granted Jesse permission to take his pleasure without inhibition.

Biting back the wild sounds rising in his chest, he gripped her hips, pushed high and hard and exploded, every shudder of his body in rhythmic correlation to the pulsing jets he shot inside her.

And while he was still shuddering, he grasped her waist and ground her against the rigid root of his cock, all his attention focused on her pleasured face, the way she clutched his shoulders and rode him frantically in return.

There was nothing more beautiful to Jesse than the sight of her like this. *Anna.* He would remember her forever.

She cried his name when she came, her head thrown back, graceful throat flexing with the attempt to swallow the feral sounds of ecstasy. She bathed him in her essence and her peace, and drew the darkness from him.

In the aftermath, they slid down and apart and finally beneath the sheets, only to flow back together again, limbs entangled as they shared a pillow.

When Jesse could talk, he said, "Anna, Anna, Anna." A surrendering sigh. A lover's accolade.

She smiled and rubbed her lips against his still pounding heart.

"I ruined your dress," he said after another minute of floating in the healing quiet.

"Damn you," she murmured aridly.

He lifted his head to meet her sleepy cocoa eyes, noting the way she held him, with arms and legs surrounding him but not clinging, as though to say, *You can run if you need to.*

What he wanted—needed—was to stay.

"You can wear my flannel shirt and a pair of jeans I brought with me," he went on, fingering a silky strand of her hair where it lay against the pillow.

"I'll be the hit of the party, if I ever make it there." Anna stretched and smiled at him, languid and blissfully mindless of her rumpled state. He liked that about her, that lack of self-consciousness. She was innately sensuous, too. An incredible lover, and no doubt she'd show him, slower and easier, if he could get past wanting to fuck her into tomorrow. If he could stop himself from spurting the minute she touched him.

He'd just have to practice with her until he got it right.

Five

In the soft blue morning light that pierced the gap in the curtains, they dressed without speaking. After showering together to bathe away the night's desire and merely eliciting more, both were too drowsy for anything beyond long glances and tender smiles. Jesse chuckled at the sight of Anna's lithe hips swimming in his jeans. She had rolled the cuffs several times and didn't seem one bit awkward in the oversized flannel shirt he'd given her. The now-shabby velvet pumps were an interesting touch, too. Starstruck, he watched her wiggle into them with a helpless smile.

When they were packed, he dragged his knapsack and helmet off the table and stopped her before she could open the door.

"Merry Christmas, baby," he whispered, nuzzling her tousled hair.

"Merry Christmas." Her arms crept around his waist, and they stood there for a moment, each wondering if the night's storm—inside their hearts and outside in the world—had passed.

Anna turned her head to look at him as she opened the door, wondering what to say to ease the sudden unease, but Jesse was staring past her, squinting into the morning sun.

She whipped around.

The world was green and clear, the birds chirping beneath a cornflower sky.

Not a sign of white powder to be found.

Stepping out into the parking lot, she made a slow circle, her incredulous eyes taking in the utterly impossible.

Where was all the snow?

Jesse followed her, his steps slow as he looked around. "I can't believe what I'm seeing."

"There was a storm, though," Anna began, her voice trembling. "You saw it too—the drifts, the ice—there's no way it could have melted this quickly . . ."

"There was a storm," he echoed, and they lapsed into silence, staring at each other in disbelief.

Then Jesse shouldered his backpack and tucked his helmet beneath his arm. "Let's check out of the motel," he told her. "We'll ask the clerk what he saw last night."

Inside the tiny lobby, everything was the same as Anna had remembered it, except the jolly bearded guy in the suspenders was gone, replaced by a chunky teenager with ear piercings *ad nauseum* and a gleaming set of braces on her smiling, gum-snapping teeth.

"Merry Christmas," she said cheerfully. "Did y'all enjoy your stay?"

Jesse cast Anna a meaningful glance. "Absolutely."

"It was wonderful," she added, and for a second she forgot the missing snow, the broken-down Toyota, the wrecked motorcycle, the magnificent strangeness of it all. Only Jesse was there, Jesse with his blue eyes and gentle, skillful hands. A man full of shadow and light, and a fathomless grief he held close to his soul. Maybe they'd part ways forever today, but no matter what she failed to learn about him in their few remaining moments, he was no longer a stranger to her heart.

". . . And we're just curious," he was telling the clerk, his lean cheeks flushing. "Did it snow around here last night?"

The teenager laughed. "Heck, no. It's been in the seventies all week. It's enough to kill the Christmas spirit, know what I mean?"

Anna stilled. Beneath the counter, Jesse's hand closed around hers and gently squeezed.

"Well, that's funny." She recovered, keeping her voice steady when what she really wanted was to reach across the counter and shake the girl. "The old guy who checked us in last night said something about snow."

The girl leaned her elbow by the register. "What old guy? You mean here? We don't have any men working here. Martha was on duty last night."

A huff of disbelief burst from Anna's chest. "Look, we're not idiots. There *was* an old guy here behind the counter. He was bald, had a white beard and he was dressed funny, with stripes and suspenders, kind of elfish—"

"I reckon it was Santa Claus," the girl said with a laughing snort. "Serious now, only Martha was here, unless she's seein' some guy, and she'd tell me because she pretty much hates men in general, 'specially the ones 'round here, so I sure don't think that's it."

"That's it!" Anna snapped her fingers, her eyes widening.

"How do you know?" the clerk frowned at her. "Martha's a

friend of my mama's, and I can tell you if she was datin' some old guy, I would surely hear about—"

"No. I mean, what you said before—about the man who was here. He did look—and act—exactly like—" Anna glanced at Jesse in a mixture of abject embarrassment and wonder. "I-I think it was . . . Santa. And this place really must be . . ." her breath left her chest on a strangled note. *"The Holiday Inn."*

"Lady, you're turned around." The girl waved her hand, as though the conversation was perfectly viable. "This here's the Magnolia Motel. The Holiday Inn's down two exits and beyond the overpass. It's the big conference center. You can't miss it."

"But the sign out there says—"

"Magnolia Motel." Jesse's low voice broke through Anna's fog of agitation as he gazed out the window. "The sign's right there."

She stared in the direction where he pointed and shook her head. "What the hell happened here last night?"

"Maybe a little too much celebrating, if you ask me," the girl muttered.

"A visit from St. Nick," Anna whispered, meeting Jesse's eyes. "The best gift ever. Wouldn't you agree?"

"I would definitely agree." He let the curtain fall and moved toward her, both of them forgetting the invasive presence of the gawking teenaged desk clerk. When he bent his head to kiss Anna, he quietly laid the room key on the desk and slid it toward the girl.

Swiping it off the countertop, she backed away from the two crazy people in her lobby. "All righty, then. Thanks for staying at the Magnolia Motel. Y'all have a nice day." And she fled into the office.

~⊙⊙~

Neither Jesse nor Anna said a word when they found the Toyota parked in an inconspicuous spot outside the motel lobby, and a few feet beyond it, Jesse's motorcycle, unscathed.

They stood between the two vehicles for a while, bewildered, maybe a little scared.

Jesse was the first to laugh. He laughed and laughed, and after a moment an answering smile crept across Anna's face. There was no explanation for the last twenty-four hours, beyond two lost souls finding each other through an impossible storm. Finding comfort. Finding love's sweet potential. What more could one want for Christmas?

"Anna, what's your last name?" He caught her hand and pulled her, grinning helplessly, against him.

"Shea," she said.

"I'm Jesse Proffitt."

"Nice to meet you," she said, her smile widening.

"Anna Shea, do you believe in magic?"

"After last night, do you even need to ask?" She stood on tiptoe and slid her arms around his neck. "Don't you?"

"I didn't for so long." His humor faded as he gazed down into her face. "Until you showed up in a magic storm, and brought me to this magic place, and touched me with your magic hands. You made me believe in magic and so much more. Thank you." He raised her hand to his lips and kissed her knuckles. Then, "I have another question for you."

"What is it?" she asked, tears and laughter shining in her eyes.

"Tell me, Anna Shea . . . what are you doing New Year's Eve?"

Epilogue

From his perch on a kitchen chair, eight-year-old Justin Proffitt watched his mom prepare dinner, his dark brows drawn down in troubled thought. After a moment he was ready with his yearly arsenal of questions.

"Okay, so how did you meet Dad again?"

She smiled as she withdrew a bag of vegetables from the refrigerator. "Santa Claus introduced us."

Justin wasn't so sure anymore that Santa really existed. Especially because he'd recently seen his dad wrestling a large box down to the basement that looked like the racecar track he'd requested in his yearly letter to the North Pole.

"Mom, that whole thing sounds made up."

"It's true. We got lost in a snowstorm on the highway. Dad was riding a motorcycle and I was driving a car. When he slid on the ice and fell off his bike, I pulled over to help him. And soon we found out that there never was a snowstorm."

"So Santa made the snow so you guys would meet."

"Right."

He scowled, but before he could pin her down for more details, his father came downstairs from his office and stopped to kiss Justin on the head.

"How are you, kiddo? Enjoying your first day of winter break?"

"It's okay, I guess." Which meant, *I'm bored*. They hadn't seen each other all morning. Justin wasn't supposed to interrupt him while he was writing, and today had been especially difficult. Justin had awakened to a world blanketed in fluffy whiteness, which meant sledding, snowball fights, and snowman build-offs with the neighborhood kids, and no team could build as fat and tall a snowman as Justin and his dad. But today Jesse had a "deadline," which meant little to Justin except the nothing-to-dos.

The two younger boys who lived across the street laughed and made fun of the crappy snowman he'd tried to build alone. Since he wasn't allowed to leave the yard, he couldn't go across the street and punch them out the way they deserved. So he'd come in, defeated, and pulled out his art supplies to color at the kitchen table.

"Dad." He turned to watch him as Jesse set a hand on his wife's pregnant belly and leaned around her to steal a carrot from the pile of vegetables she was chopping. "Are you guys Santa Claus?"

Jesse turned to regard him with a faint smile. "Haven't we had this discussion? Like fifty times since October?"

"I guess." Justin sighed. "It's just that most of my friends' parents don't believe in him. You guys are the only ones who still act like he's real. And you don't just believe in him. You have this whole story about how he helped you meet each other." He looked down. "It's kind of embarrassing, so don't tell anyone else, okay? Nobody has to know."

"The only person we've told that story to is you," Jesse said, crossing the kitchen to sit at the table beside him. "You're the only one whose opinion matters to us. And if you don't believe in Santa Claus anymore, that's your business. But the story stays the same. We know how we met. Santa set us up."

Justin stared hard at him, waiting for him to crack a smile, but his dad just gazed back without blinking.

His mom set down the chopping knife and crossed to the refrigerator again. "We've never lied to you about anything else, have we?"

He thought for a moment, then shrugged. "I guess not." Which was good, because really he wanted to believe in Santa, even though his friends had stopped. They sure would be sorry one day if it turned out his parents were right.

"Hey, Dad." Justin poked at Jesse's hand with an unused paintbrush. "Can me and you go out in the snow for a while?"

"You and I."

"That's what I said."

"I thought you'd never ask."

"But what about your deadline?"

Jesse looked skyward and scratched his chin. "Deadline? What deadline? Last one out has to wash the dishes after dinner." Before Justin could react, his dad bolted from the chair. Justin raced after him, swerved in front of him and tried to block the entrance to the foyer, but Jesse lifted and threw him, shouting with laughter, over his shoulder like a sack of flour. "Anna, get out the lotion— Justy's going to have dishpan hands tonight!"

Father and son made a noisy exit down the stairs, leaving Anna smiling to herself in the kitchen. She turned and with a heart full of joy, watched her boys through the window over the sink.

Her beautiful, happy boys.

Once Jesse believed he would never know the love of a child again, the sound of his own boy's laughter, the way a father felt when his son walked tall in his wake. Now he had it all in spades, because he was as much Justin's world as Justin was his. And the best part was that Jesse hadn't been afraid to love again when his second son was placed in his arms, or to remember—and cherish—the sweet, lost boy of his shattered past.

How far Jesse and Anna had come together. She'd never thought she wanted children until she met him. He made her believe anything was not only possible, but well deserved. He was her rock, upon which she'd built a life of happiness. And she was his. A risky prospect, placing one's heart in the hands of such an infallible creature as another human being. Such was love— sometimes frightening, sometimes perilous, and always, *always* magnificent.

She absently caressed her hard, rounded belly as she studied her family through the window. Only three more weeks, and then there would be four.

"Yes, Katie Proffitt," she assured her unborn little girl, the first of many times to come. "There really is a Santa Claus. Let me tell you how I know . . ."

$\mathcal{U}$NWRAPPED

LACEY ALEXANDER

This story is dedicated to my readers.
Your support means the world to me!

December 1

Simon's skilled hand eased beneath the sheet—and then between Emily's thighs. She parted them, whispering, "I love you."

"I love you, too, sugarplum," he said, his voice both sexy and teasing. He'd called her that ever since they'd met, three years ago, at a mutual friend's Christmas party. When they'd said goodbye that first night, he'd told her visions of sugarplums would be dancing in his head, and the pet name had been born. Then again, she'd always thought his Australian accent made *everything* he said sound sexy.

"Move against my fingers," he instructed her, the words coming low and throaty.

His touch felt *so* good, radiating through her in ribbons of heat, but she *wasn't* moving against his hand, at least not automatically, like she supposed most women would. She never had.

She could scarcely understand it. She *adored* being close to Simon, yet . . . sex always embarrassed her to a large degree. She'd never been able to completely let herself go.

Now, she tried to lift her pelvis against his touch.

His fingers stroked deeper and the sensation spread outward, through her rear, her legs, the small of her back. Oh God, it felt so wonderful, beginning to take her over, own her. *Yes, oh yes. Touch me, Simon.*

"That's right, my sugarplum girl. Fuck my fingers."

Emily sucked in her breath as her muscles tightened instinctively.

Oh damn. Why? Why, when he talked like that, did it at once arouse her and yet stop her dead in her tracks? In most other ways, she saw herself as a smart, confident woman, yet sex consistently filled her with conflicting emotions she didn't know how to fight.

She went still—and Simon sighed. "Sorry," he said, but his tone echoed his frustration. Which, in turn, made her feel guilty and inadequate. A familiar pattern.

She answered his sigh with one of her own. "I'm sorry, too, Simon. I don't mean to be this way—you know I don't."

He peered at her through the darkness—she always made a point of turning out the lights for sex—his handsome face somber in the shadows. "It's not your fault if I don't excite you." Then he rolled to his back in the bed and, despite her qualms, she missed having his hand between her legs.

Her chest had hollowed at his words, so she turned on her side to press her palm to his bare shoulder, instantly needing to assure him. "Simon, it's not you—it's me."

A fact they both knew very well. She'd been a virgin at the ripe old age of twenty-three when they'd met. And he'd been so tender and gentle, slowly coaxing her desires free. When they'd finally made love nearly a year after meeting, it had been the sweetest, most profound experience of Emily's life. And she'd been so thankful to find a man so patient, so caring—caring enough to wait, and caring enough to put up with her inexperience and nervousness.

In short, Simon was amazing.

And she was a letdown.

Now, two years after giving him her virginity, and a year after moving in together, she just wasn't getting any better at sex. And it wasn't that she didn't want it—her body *burned* for him. It was simply that she'd been raised by very old-fashioned parents who had taught her she had to be a good girl . . . or else.

She wasn't sure what came after the "or else," what would happen if she *wasn't* a good girl—she'd never deigned to find out. But it was ingrained in her soul-deep, always had been. And even if her body *begged* her to move against Simon's hand, even if something deep inside her sparked to dirty life when he said the word "fuck," there remained a large part of her that simply couldn't seem to let go of being a good girl at the core.

And now she was afraid she would lose him.

Out of bed, they got along fabulously and were everyone's favorite couple. They shared a passion for hiking and long drives in the country and quaint little bed-and-breakfast hideaways, and they'd taken a fabulous road trip across the country—all the way from their home in Cincinnati to San Francisco—last summer. He supported the work she did as an advocate for the homeless, even though she didn't make much money, and she was proud of the way he was swiftly moving up the ranks of his prestigious downtown accounting firm. She'd even learned to enjoy soccer and basketball, his favorite sports. She remained thrilled to be the woman on his arm for any event, be it a fancy company banquet with his coworkers at Crain and Wilborn or a charity auction she had organized through *her* work.

But sex mattered. She knew that. Sex was important to men, plain and simple.

And really, it was important to her, too—she just . . . hadn't quite been able to express that. It was as if a vixen lay trapped in the body of a nun, struggling—unsuccessfully—to get out.

She kissed his chest, once, twice. Soaked up the warmth of his skin. As his arms closed back around her, she relished his strength and felt her body surge with the moisture of wanting him. "I'll try harder," she whispered, and she meant it.

Normally, Simon would argue now, tell her that she didn't *have* to try harder, that he loved her just as she was, that their sex was fine.

Yet this time he stayed quiet—and it didn't even hurt, because she knew he was entitled to more than she gave.

Maybe he even senses it—the way I want to be, the vixen lurking inside me. Oh God, I wish I could be the lover he deserves.

Now, she supposed, was her chance to try.

As she kissed her way down his chest, onto his stomach, a fresh yearning grew. Especially when her arm brushed over his erection under the covers. *Oh.* He was so hard for her, so big. He felt so good when he was inside her, and she wanted him there now. *Tell him that. Just say it. He'd love it, and it would be a good start.*

Yet she couldn't—the words felt locked inside her.

Above her, though, Simon's breath grew soft, ragged. Because she was moving lower. And lower.

She'd kissed him there before, at his urging. On his cock. She could *think* of it that way, but she just couldn't *say* it, damn it. *Why, why, why?*

Don't worry about that now. Just go down on him. That's how he would phrase it—he'd ask her to go down on him.

Kissing lower, she finally reached it—his cock. She said it again in her mind, trying as hard as she could to desensitize herself to the word. *Cock, cock, cock.* She studied it in the shadowy darkness, trying to meld both her gut responses, even though they seemed at odds with one another—that his erection was at once beautiful . . . and utterly sinful. His shaft jutted so big, so prominent, so very close to her face.

But it's not sinful, she argued with herself. *He's a man, and that's what men have, and there wouldn't be babies if they didn't.* And it *was* definitely beautiful. She grazed her palm down its length, her chest tightening with pleasure when he moaned. She *loved* to make Simon moan.

"Feels so good, baby," he breathed, further exciting her.

I can do this, I can use my mouth on him.

She lowered one soft kiss to his arcing length. So hard against her soft lips, like kissing warm steel. The heat from it pooled low in her belly, spreading down between her legs. *Mmm, yes. I can do this.*

She kissed him again and again—soft, sweet and impassioned—edging upward on his shaft toward the head. She ran her fingers gingerly over the tip, wiping away the thick dot of moisture there—and listened to Simon's throaty plea waft over her. "Suck me, baby. Suck my cock."

Inside her, just like before, everything tightened. Simon was rubbing her bottom now as she bent over him from the side, the sensation radiating inward, but her age-old enemies were setting in. Nervousness. Awkwardness. Fear.

She let out a sigh. She wanted to take him in her mouth—but she couldn't, just couldn't, for reasons that ran too deep for her to understand.

Oh God. Why am I like this? Why can't I be a good lover?

She found herself backing away then, her whole body stiffening, until she lay beside him, wishing she were anywhere else besides in bed with a man whose desires she couldn't fulfill.

"I'm so sorry, Simon," she whispered. "Forgive me."

"Of course," he said, voice quiet, strained.

He's lying. He doesn't forgive me.

"I want you," she said.

"It doesn't feel that way."

"I do. I swear." It was true. Unbelievable to him, probably, but so true.

"Please," she said, rolling to touch his chest again. "Please—I want you inside me. I love you so much."

Simon looked at her in the shadows, but she couldn't read his expression. A certain darkness lingered there. Heated desire? Or disgust with her flip-flopping routine?

Either way, he rolled over onto her, situating himself between her parted legs. He kissed her neck, and as always when he did that, passion fluttered inside her once more. She did want him, she truly did. And as he pushed his way into her body, filling her, she groaned with the wonderful intrusion, reaching to meet his lush mouth with her own.

Things were different—so much more effortless—when he was on top of her, when he asked nothing of her, expected nothing.

Maybe it just meant she was a selfish lover, she didn't know. But now that he was inside, she felt his renewed heat and saw it burning in his eyes. Now that he was inside, he was hot for her again, and *she* was hot for *him*, and the world was suddenly perfect.

"I love you, baby," she whispered.

"I love you, too. I want to make you come."

Could any man be better than Simon? All this, and still he cared about her pleasure. More than she did, possibly, because . . . well, she didn't always climax, not even when he touched her there. His touch was scintillating, but she knew she thought too much, let her nervousness get in the way.

As was their routine—the only one she'd ever really allowed them to fall into—Simon eased back, still inside her but upright, onto his knees. Using his thumb, he found her clitoris and began to stroke. "Want to make you feel so good, my sugarplum girl," he murmured over her deeply, sweetly. "So, so good."

His soothing voice combined with the darkness to help her slip away to somewhere else completely. In her fantasy, Simon held her down, gave her no choice, *made* her feel the pleasure. They were in a different time, a different world, where it was okay for her to feel dirty, to feel the slick way his thumbs stroked through her wetness even as his cock slid just as slick into her opening, to relish the hot pressure that rose in her, the fullness, the pleasure, the—*oh God!* "Unh!"

Despite herself, she cried out as the orgasm broke over her quickly, heard her own high sobs as the pulses pounded through her body, until finally she was dropped back in the bed, back to here, back to now—torn between that weird sense of guilt and the joy of having let go, even if just for a moment.

"So sweet, baby," he purred over her, then kissed her, once, twice, his tongue mingling with hers—but then, short seconds later, he began pounding into her, hard, harder.

Yes, oh yes! She loved his power, loved the way his thrusts echoed through her whole being. Now that her climax had passed and she'd come back to herself, she could no longer yell her pleasure aloud, but inside, her screams were deafening.

"Watching you come," Simon said on a heavy breath, still driving his cock deep, "gets me so hot . . . I can't hold back."

As he exploded inside her, she absorbed the hard plunges, filled with warmth to know she'd taken him there—although to her way of thinking, it was amazing she even aroused him at all, given her behavior. So she hugged him tight, thankful she'd made it through one more night of these weird, contradictory desires and could now simply hold her man while he recovered in her arms.

Please don't give up on me, Simon. I love you so much.

December 6

Simon looked up over his plate of hors d'oeuvres, his cock responding at the mere sight of Emily walking into his office Christmas party. Her dress was simple, black with thin straps at the shoulders, but it showed plenty of gorgeous cleavage and hugged her sumptuous curves. Her dark hair was piled on top of her head in a glamorous yet messy style he thought worthy of a red carpet, baring her beautiful neck.

Most men, he supposed, wouldn't get a hard-on just from watching their girlfriends walk into a room. Most men, though, didn't have the conundrum that was Emily in their lives. Funny, smart, sexy and more than a little easy on the eyes, his Emily. But get her in bed and she was like a deer in headlights.

He had no idea why, other than what she'd explained to him about being raised to be prim and proper. He couldn't seem to get it through her head that when you loved somebody, all that shit went out the window. Or it should, anyway. He swallowed back the little dart of disappointment that pierced his heart at the thought. They were perfect together—if he didn't count how much she seemed to dislike having sex with him.

Elegant jazz versions of favorite Christmas classics provided the background to the party. The lavish, oversize lobby of Crain and Wilborn had been draped in sparkling red and gold, the large tree in the corner done in the same color scheme and sporting elegant glass ornaments. People sipped wine and mixed drinks and held paper plates festooned with holly leaves. As Christmas parties went, it was pretty boring. Which might explain why every eye in the place turned toward his sugarplum as she crossed the floor toward him. She had no idea what a knockout she was.

"Sorry I'm late." She smiled up at him, then helped herself to a shrimp puff from his plate.

He leaned down to kiss her. "You look incredible. Glad you're here."

She gave him a once-over that stiffened his cock a little more. "You look pretty incredible yourself."

He shrugged, but appreciated the compliment. "Just my everyday work attire, sugarplum." A crisp black Armani suit with a red tie, chosen that morning with the holiday in mind.

"But you wear it so well," she said.

And damn, if he didn't know better, the look in her pale blue eyes would make him think she was feeling hot, seductive.

His gaze dropped to her breasts, their rounded inner curves revealed by the clingy dress. He wanted to slide his cock into that perfect valley. He was tempted to tell her that. With most women, after three years together, he'd be able to say that if he wanted, whisper it in her ear, a promise for later. But with Emily, he bit his tongue. She'd probably faint if he told her what he wanted to do with her breasts right now. At the very least, she'd turn fifty shades of red.

Just then, his colleague, Mark Wagner, sauntered up. Tall and lean like Simon, but olive-skinned with darker hair, Mark was a handsome flirt, and half drunk from the looks of him. "Long time, no see, Em," he said, then planted a palm firmly at her hip, leaning in for a slightly-too-long kiss on the cheek.

Damn. Even watching some other guy put the moves on his girl added to the stiffness in Simon's pants.

"Hi, Mark—how are you? Is Carolyn coming? Or are the twins keeping her too busy?"

Simon smiled. *Nice move, sugarplum.* She'd asked the questions in a completely sweet, confident tone, but they'd struck home, reminding Mark she knew exactly how much of a family man he was and that he should probably be keeping his hands and lips to himself.

Mark straightened, looking slightly cowed. "Yeah, Carolyn should be here any time now—had to drop the girls at her mom's first."

"Good—I look forward to seeing her," Emily said.

Simon forgave himself for having dirty thoughts about his coworker's hands on her since, hell, their sex life was so bland and dry and awkward that he figured pretty much *anything* would arouse him at this point. He knew Emily was as troubled by their different tastes in sex as he was, but it was wearing on him lately.

Just then, his boss and friend, Cal Hanson, walked up and slapped him on the back. "Drink up, buddy—life doesn't offer an open bar just every day."

Simon laughed. Cal, unlike him, possessed a sex life to be envied—and he liked to tell Simon about it, forcing him to suffer through tale after tale of seduction and debauchery.

Single and thirty, the same age as Simon, Cal had a knack for finding girls with sexual appetites and whims toward the kinky that Simon could only dream of. One of Cal's many girlfriends had recently dressed up in a French maid costume and cleaned his condo in between fucking his brains out. And it hadn't even been Halloween.

Nope, on Halloween Cal had gone to a wild party dressed as a sheik and come home with not one, but two hot harem girls who had taken turns pleasuring him, and each other, all night long.

Simon didn't care about conquests or anyone cleaning for him—but he'd love to have a girl who was that wild and free. Was it possible to have a great relationship like what he shared with Emily and also have a wild, crazy, no-holds-barred sex life? Was he asking too much? Hell, he'd settle for *less* than wild and crazy—he'd be thrilled out of his mind if Emily just gave him a blowjob, or let him eat her pussy. He'd gone down on her a couple of times, but she'd gotten all stiff and quiet on him and he'd known that instead of turning her on the exact opposite was happening.

Now he looked at the woman next to him who was expertly chatting up his boss, clearly the envy of every other female in the office lobby. How could she be so very vibrant and exuberant— yet so distant and unhappy when they got naked together? It made no sense.

And the truth was, he wanted to take their relationship further—he and Emily had a great time together, they understood and respected each other, and in most ways, she embodied every- thing he could want in a woman. But sex—or the lack of it—was an issue for him. Maybe that made him shallow, but he couldn't deny that it put a damper on what they shared. Could he really be happy tying himself for life to someone who didn't enjoy sex?

He shook his head, banishing the thought for now.

Cal had just dragged Emily to the nearby bar, insisting she needed a drink—Simon heard him bellowing about the open bar again. So Simon took Cal's advice and drained his scotch and Coke, ready to get another himself—when Dana Landers grabbed his arm.

He looked into her dark eyes, but his gaze automatically dropped farther, to the deep V of the red cocktail dress she wore. Her large breasts were very much on display, and whether he liked it or not, it added to his erection. He hoped like hell his reaction didn't show on his face. "Hi, Dana—having a good time?"

She tilted her head, her expression playful and seductive. Dana had been flirting with him since she'd started working at Crain and Wilborn six months ago. Now, she rubbed his arm through his suit. "Kind of. But to tell you the truth, I'm in the mood for another kind of party altogether."

He slanted her a wary grin. "What kind of party is that?"

She let out an enticing sigh, her breasts heaving with the gesture. "The private kind. Cerise and I"—she motioned to another girl from the office, a recent college grad and blond beauty who he knew was also a cheerleader for the Bengals—"were thinking of heading back to my place and we were hoping you might want to come with."

Simon peered down into her eyes and took in the scope of the invitation. As starved as he felt for hot, no-inhibitions sex... Well, he'd never done the threesome thing himself, but if he didn't have Emily, he knew he'd be doing it tonight. Both girls were majorly hot and his cock now officially throbbed with the dirty visions entering his mind of him with two sexy babes who knew how to have fun in bed.

But he *did* have Emily, and even if she hadn't stood just a stone's throw away, he wasn't a cheater. He spoke kindly, though. "Dana, you know I have a girlfriend." He punctuated the comment with a lift of his eyebrows and a scolding grin.

She smiled boldly, unashamed. "We don't mind."

"But I do, I'm afraid. And besides, she's here tonight." He found himself pointing Emily out, still at the bar. "Black dress, talking to Cal."

Dana studied her. "Wow, she's hot." Then she lowered her chin provocatively. "She could come along, you know. Cerise and I aren't greedy."

At this, Simon just laughed. Both at Dana's flexibility and how much Emily would freak out if he even told her about the suggestion.

But then a picture entered his head. Him and Emily sitting on a sofa at Dana's place, watching Dana and Cerise fool around. Would that excite her? In the little fantasy in his head, it would turn Emily crazed with need. She would be so aroused that she'd lift her dress, straddle him, and fuck him, right in front of the other girls. She'd pant and moan and ride him hard, and she'd be so fucking beautiful doing it that he'd probably drop to his knees and beg her to marry him right on the spot.

Sweat broke out on his brow, but not exactly from excitement. Shit, how had his hot fantasy led to ideas about a *marriage proposal?*

He sighed. Probably because it had been on his mind lately.

He really wanted to spend his life with Emily—if only she liked fucking him more.

He blew out a heavy breath as he refocused on Dana and her inviting cleavage. "Tempting, honey, but afraid we'll have to pass." Then he bent closer. "Here's a tip, though. Try Cal. He's into that kind of partying."

Dana looked disappointed. "It's really *you* I wanted."

He—and his dick—couldn't help being flattered, but . . . "Sorry, Dana—afraid that's just not our scene."

No, our scene is to do it in the dark, in the missionary position, once every couple of weeks or so.

He couldn't help thinking Dana would be *really* disappointed if she knew *that*.

"Well then," she said, "I guess I'll go see if you're right about Cal."

Ah, way to be a trouper, honey. "Don't worry, I am."

An hour later, Cal and the two girls had departed, and Emily and Simon had chatted with most of his coworkers. Music still played and alcohol still flowed. Emily always charmed anyone she came into contact with and this gathering was no exception.

Unfortunately for Simon, though, just watching his sugarplum charm people was enough to keep him aroused. Good thing he had his suit jacket on and buttoned, or everyone would know he wanted to take her, right in the middle of the red and gold lobby and expensive snacks. He wanted to start by kissing that long, slender neck. Then he wanted to lean into her from behind, let her feel his cock pressing into her ass as he reached around to cup her soft breasts. He wanted to push up that sexy little dress and drive his erection deep into her sweet, hot cunt.

Which was almost always wet for him. That's what stumped

him. She was always wet, always ready—even when she was shy-
ing away from anything beyond that damn missionary position.
If she was so disinterested in sex, why was she always so nice and
moist when he reached inside her panties?

He looked at her now as she spoke with Mark Wagner's wife,
who apparently wanted to donate some money to help the homeless and had asked Emily for advice on the best route to take.
Finishing another scotch and Coke, he asked Emily if she'd like
another glass of wine. She looked up, drawn from her conversation. "Oh—yes, Simon, thanks."

So off to the bar he went, thinking to drown his sorrows. *If I
were a worse sort of guy, I could be sandwiched between two naughty girls right
now*. A jazz version of "Santa Claus is Coming to Town" played
overhead, reminding him 'twas the season to be deemed naughty
or nice. Just his luck to fall for the nice girl.

On the way back from the bar, he realized Emily was nowhere
in sight. "Where'd she go?" he asked Carolyn Wagner.

Mark's wife pointed. "That way—looking for the restroom.
Only, after she'd gone, I realized it's—"

"In the other direction," Simon finished for her with an easy
grin. "Don't worry, I'll track her down. Watch these for me?"

"Sure," she said as he lowered their drinks to the table where
she sat.

Pushing through the door that led to the firm's offices, he spotted Emily walking toward him, looking pretty—and a bit tipsy from
wine consumption. "There are no bathrooms back here," she said,
motioning vaguely over her shoulder as a short giggle escaped her.

He couldn't help smiling. "No, sugarplum. But look what's
right *here*."

He moved forward to meet her next to Dana's office doorway, where a sprig of greenery and white berries hung. Emily glanced up. "Is that mistletoe or something?"

He gave her a playfully scolding look. "Of course it's mistletoe. Do you mean to tell me you've never seen mistletoe before?"

"I guess not."

"Well, you at least know what it's for, I hope."

She nodded invitingly. One thing about Emily—she might not like sex, but she loved to kiss.

At that, Simon slid his arms around her waist and stepped up close to her.

"Is that a Christmas present in your pocket or are you just happy to see me?"

He laughed, but gazing down into her eyes turned him serious just as fast. "The latter."

"Mmm," she purred as he molded his mouth to hers, easing his tongue inside. Her arms curved around his neck as their bodies settled closer together, his erection pressing to the juncture of her thighs.

One kiss turned into two, then more, as their tongues lazily sparred. He kneaded her hips, then her sweet round ass full in his palms, and wondered if she could feel his cock getting harder and harder against her. He'd been so damn aroused all evening, all week—hell, for the last three years—that he wanted her madly, wanted to make his little office party fantasy come true here in the privacy of the hallway.

Would she let him? Or would she bring their passion to a grinding halt as usual? Only one way to find out.

He let his kisses drop to the pale expanse of her neck, pleased when she leaned her head to one side, offering him easier access.

"So pretty, my girl," he breathed in her ear. "Hot and beautiful. You make me the envy of every man here."

She bit her lip, turning to gaze up into his eyes. "Really?"

He nodded. "You're a gorgeous woman, Em. And I'm a lucky, lucky man."

And if there's any justice in the world, about to get luckier. He eased one palm to gently cup her breast through the dress, listening to her heated sigh. Slowly massaging the weight of it in his hand, he stroked his thumb over her beautifully beaded nipple.

She gasped—but it wasn't her "stop" gasp. No, this was more of an "oh yeah" kind of gasp. So he passed his thumb over that sweet, hard peak again, this time catching it between thumb and forefinger as he deepened their kiss, easing his tongue more fully into her mouth. She responded, arching, thrusting her breast into his grasp.

There were a million things Simon wanted to do to her right now while she was so heated up, so willing. He wanted to lean her against the wall, push her dress to her waist, drop to his knees and lick her damp slit. He wanted to urge *her* knees to the carpet and slide his cock into her warm mouth. He wanted to take her into Mr. Crain's corner office at the end of the hall and fuck her on the CEO's desk with her ankles locked around his neck, her high heels clicking together each time he pounded into her.

But he had to take this slow. Any progress he ever made with Emily and sex was always a result of going slow.

"I love you," he reminded her, his voice coming raspy.

She whimpered through her pleasure that she loved him, too.

"And I want so much more of you, my baby."

No answer, but when he reached to pull the slinky strap of her dress off her shoulder, she didn't protest. The thin strap of her black bra came with it until he was reaching inside the cup to lift her breast free.

Another hot sigh echoed from his sugarplum's lush lips, but she didn't stop him, only watched as he lowered his mouth there, taking the erect pink peak in his mouth. Ah, damn, he loved being able to see her—her full, round breast, the deep mauve shade of her distended nipple, the passion on her face—loved the simple fact that they weren't in a dark room. He suckled her gently at first, then deeper, deeper, relishing the hardness on his tongue, wondering if she felt the sensation between her thighs. She moaned her pleasure and he used both tongue and lips on her, drawing, sucking, as if the taut pink bud were a little straw that stretched all the way to her cunt.

He kept waiting for her to say no, but she didn't. And his hands moved without thought or decision—massaging her ass, then gathering the silky black fabric in his fists until he could reach underneath. And then—oh God, yeah—he found her bare flesh in his hands and remembered how she wore thigh-high stockings with dresses because they were more comfortable, and thongs with clothes she feared might show a panty line. She was so fucking sexy and didn't even realize it.

Of course, the thong made it easy. Too tempting to resist. He eased his fingertips down the valley of her ass overtop the lace strip residing there, then eased two underneath and into her warm, drenching folds. She let out another hot gasp as he whispered deeply, "Wet like always for me, sugarplum. So fucking wet."

He pushed two fingers up into her, listening to her soft sob, feeling the way she moved, rubbing against his cock in front, fucking his fingers in back. Yeah, oh yeah—it was finally happening.

She was letting herself feel good. She was letting him make it happen. He fucked her deeper with his fingers, harder, and the only sound was their breath, ragged and raspy in rhythm with their movements. And then, soon, came the *noise* of his fingers, of her drenching wetness as he thrust up into her sweet pussy. Ah God— that new sound was enough to make him tremble, nearly enough to push him over the edge. He had to get inside her—now.

That's when she grabbed his shoulders and spoke throatily. "Simon, we should stop. Someone could walk back here anytime."

True enough—only one door stood between them and the party, and a big band rendition of "Jingle Bell Rock" echoed through, albeit muted. But Simon couldn't have cared less. He just wanted to fuck her. He wanted it more than he'd ever wanted anything in his life. He had to have her, had to sink his aching cock into her welcoming flesh. "I don't care," he told her. "This is too damn good."

"But . . ."

He eased her back through the doorway of Dana's office. "In here. This will be more private."

"But I can't," she said. And she still moved against him, on his fingers, but . . . those movements were decidedly slower now, more stilted.

Oh fuck. Fuck, fuck, fuck. She was going cold on him. Just when he'd been stupid enough to think . . . Just when he'd believed she might really . . . *Shit.*

A few months ago, in this same position, he might have tried to cajole her, convince her, continue to excite and persuade her. But something had just clicked inside him. He'd had enough.

And it wasn't just because she wouldn't fuck him here. He

knew some women would go for that and some wouldn't, and not going for it wasn't a crime. It was *everything*—the whole fucking three years that he'd tried to be patient, tried to teach her, tried to make her want him, want more from their sex. It was that she'd just taken him so deep into arousal before pulling the plug on it that his cock physically hurt now.

He backed away from her, swearing under his breath.

"Simon, I'm sorry. But right here . . . it's too . . ."

He simply shook his head. He couldn't even talk to her right now, couldn't explain. His frustration ran too deep. "I'm leaving," he said.

"But—"

"I'll see you at home," he snapped, then turned and walked out through the door that led to the lobby.

He'd just left her standing there, and he didn't care. Maybe that made him a lousy guy, but he felt like he'd been teased, led on. One too many times. And he was damn tired of it.

If he had half a brain, he'd find out where Dana lived, get in his car and go *there*. Emily would never have to know. Or, hell, maybe he should do it and *then* tell her about it, when he was breaking up with her.

He loved Emily, but he loved sex, too, and he didn't know how much more rejection he was supposed to take.

Without another word to anyone milling about drinking their drinks and listening to their Christmas music, he strode through the lobby and out the glass doors toward the elevators, ready to quit being the good guy for a change.

Merry-fucking-Christmas to me.

December 12

Emily trudged along, shopping bags in hand, trying to wade through the crowd. She loved Christmas, had always loved all the traditions and festivities that came along with it, but massive gridlock in the mall she could live without.

As she turned a corner, a teenage boy moving at a jog completely sideswiped her without looking back.

"Excuse you!" she snapped over her shoulder.

Sheesh. She was more than a little grouchy.

And if she was honest with herself, she probably couldn't blame it solely on the holiday rush.

She was upset and worried about Simon. His office party had been almost a week ago, and they'd smoothed things over and made up, but the intensity of the argument still ate at her. She'd driven her own car to work the morning of the party, just as he had, and met him there after, so they'd have driven home separately anyway—but it was still hard to believe he'd just walked out on her, at *his* event. It wasn't like him.

He'd acknowledged as much when she'd gotten home, and they'd talked about his frustration, about her confusion over why she just couldn't enjoy anything but simple guy-on-top, girl-on-bottom sex—and sometimes even *that* was tense for her.

She wanted to believe the talk had helped—but they'd had the same discussion before. And Simon had seemed rather wooden ever since the party, coming home late and going to bed early most nights—basically, just avoiding her.

Trudging on through the mall, she remembered the first time she'd met Simon. Harry Connick, Jr. had been singing "I'll Be Home for Christmas" in the background, and Simon had been wearing a red and white Santa hat, clearly a little drunk and flirtatious as he handed out small gifts their party host had gotten for every guest. "You must be Emily," he'd said in that fabulous accent. "Which means this one"—he held out a small silver box—"is for you."

Their hands had brushed as she'd taken the gift and the sensation had fluttered down her thighs. "How did you know my name?"

"I was told Emily was the most stunning girl in the room. So that has to be you." Tall, lean, with brown professional-yet-stylishly-cut hair, Simon's confidence was evident and attractive. His crooked smile had given away his tipsiness, but his eyes had held the sexiest gleam she'd ever seen.

Maybe that was the problem. Simon was so sexual. You could see that in him instinctively. It had drawn her, in an animal way, from the start. Only later, she'd remembered, realized, that even with him, she just wasn't an animal. She didn't know *how* to be. A couple of weeks ago, she'd thought of herself as a vixen inside a nun's body—now another analogy struck her and she thought of herself as a tigress inside a staid housecat. She knew how to purr and rub up against Simon, but she didn't know how to claw or growl or be wild.

And if all this wasn't dire enough, she had no idea what to get him for Christmas. Almost every other person on her shopping list was finished, but not Simon. And he was easy to shop for—he loved nice clothes, had flexible taste in music and enjoyed popular fiction. But this year, with all the stress and strife between them, she wanted to give him something special, different, unique. She wanted to find a gift that truly reflected the measure of her love for him—since she couldn't seem to show him in the normal way.

Oh God, I'm losing him. I'm really going to lose him. Because I have sexual hang-ups and can't get past them.

She let out a big whoosh of breath and realized she'd stopped walking to lean against a glass wall that fronted one of the stores. The deep realization that she was going to lose the man she was in love with had struck hard and made her feel as weak . . . as a kitten.

Just then, she felt a soft touch on her arm and glanced up.

"Dawn?" Before her stood an old friend from college who looked just as gorgeous as Emily remembered. Auburn hair still fell long and flowing over her shoulders, and a fitted top and jeans showed she still possessed a killer shape. Midnight-blue eyeliner made her green eyes look large and smoky. Dawn had always been very different from her—a wild child who, even back then, could have filled a book with her sexual exploits—but they'd been in the same dorm through all four years at the University of Cincinnati and had always gotten along well.

"Emily? I thought that was you. Are you okay?"

Caught off guard by the meeting, Emily straightened, tried to take control of herself. "Yeah—yes. I'm fine."

Dawn didn't appear convinced. "You looked like you might faint or something. Maybe it's too crowded for you in here."

Emily just nodded. "Could be." But then she sighed.

And Dawn's eyes narrowed. She'd always been especially perceptive. "Something else is wrong. What is it? Maybe I can help."

Emily gave her head a quick shake. She hadn't seen Dawn in years, and though they'd once been fairly good friends, she couldn't just spout out the trouble with her love life.

Except . . . the stress must have been worse than she even realized, because she heard herself doing it anyway. "I'm afraid my boyfriend is going to leave me."

Dawn's feminine hands closed on her upper arms. "Oh, *honey*," she said, her voice filled with compassion.

Emily rolled her eyes. "My God, I can't believe I just told you that. I haven't even said 'How are you?' yet."

But Dawn simply laughed, her heart-shaped lips widening into a smile. "Don't worry about it. And I'm fine—better than you are, apparently." She shifted from one platform heel to the other. "Listen, why don't we get out of here. Go to my place. I'd love to catch up. And you can tell me all about this guy of yours and what the problem is—and who knows, maybe talking about it will do some good."

❧

Dawn lived in the trendy neighborhood of Mt. Adams, in a condo atop a three-story building that overlooked the city through a wall of windows. The place was decorated in lavish fabrics and jewel tones, a purple velvet chaise draped with a red chenille throw serving as one of the most outstanding pieces of furniture in the large living room. Dark wood trim and a fireplace added to the warm feel of the space, in which the only holiday decoration was a small, unobtrusive tree in one corner done in matching jewel tone ornaments. Emily couldn't help thinking it would be a great room to have sex with Simon in.

Which confused her, all things considered. Then again, she figured the thought blended with her usual state of sexual turmoil.

Over hot chocolate laced with brandy to warm them up after coming in from the cold, Emily found herself telling Dawn about Simon, and about her problems in bed. She didn't know why she found Dawn so easy to talk to, but her old friend had always had a way of gently coaxing honesty from her. Of course, maybe the brandy helped, too. Either way, she heard herself telling Dawn things that, for some reason, she hadn't quite been able to tell Simon.

"It's like . . . my body is just teeming with all this desire, but my brain tries to turn it off—and usually succeeds."

Dawn leaned forward on the leather sofa they shared to touch Emily's knee. "Is it *fear* you feel when he urges you to try new things? Or some kind of *shame?*"

Emily swallowed, thinking it over—wanting desperately to figure it out, finally. Something about Dawn's soothing voice, the comfort of her touch, the cozy setting—plus the brandy's ability to relax her—made her feel close, so very close, to finally digging beneath the surface of her troubles and really reaching an answer.

"Fear of the unknown is definitely a part of it. And yet, another, wilder part of me that I can't quite reach really *wants* to try these things, really wants to learn."

Dawn flashed a sympathetic expression. "So you've *really* never given a guy a blowjob? Or had sex in any position besides missionary?"

Emily didn't feel embarrassed by Dawn's surprise over the secrets she'd already shared—just sad. "No, never. I really *want* to—just thinking about it excites me inside. But when I try to actually do it, I just freeze up. I guess . . . I guess maybe it *is* some kind of shame—although I never thought of it like that before. It just feels . . . wrong somehow. Not inside my heart, but in my head."

Dawn lowered her chin and widened her eyes, looking inquisitive. "Just how strict *were* your parents, honey?"

Emily bit her lip, remembering. She didn't particularly like thinking about it. "They were *very* strict when it came to boys. I couldn't date until I was seventeen, and even then, they filled me with terror about letting a guy touch me at all, or kiss me. I remember being a nervous wreck. Even before that, though, if we were watching TV and anything at all sexual came on, my mother changed the channel. We just never talked about sex in our house, unless I was being warned not to do it. Even the *topic* embarrassed me at the time because it seemed so taboo."

"And you were an only child, right?"

Emily nodded. "So I didn't have anyone to talk to about this stuff. Girlfriends, sure, but no one really understood why the very idea of sex freaked me out so much, because they didn't see what it was like to live with my mom and dad."

"Was it . . . a religious thing for them?"

"Not really. We went to church, but . . . well, I think maybe my mom was sexually abused when she was younger. She's never said so—but once my aunt told me I had no idea what my mother had been through and that I just had to be patient about not being allowed to date. Since we didn't talk openly about anything like that, I never asked her. But whatever the reason, she and my dad both definitely wanted to shield me from anything sexual."

Next to her, Dawn swallowed a sip of her hot chocolate and sighed. "This is making more sense to me now. Some people who are abused handle it well and raise their kids in a sexually healthy way. But some don't."

Emily widened her eyes. Dawn sounded so . . . knowledgeable. "And you know this how?"

Dawn smiled. "I should have told you this already, but I didn't want to intimidate you. We kind of moved right past the normal chitchat today, so it didn't come up, but . . . I'm a sex therapist, Emily."

Emily held in her gasp. Although maybe she shouldn't have been surprised, given Dawn's affinity for sex when they were younger. "Wow. What does a sex therapist do, exactly?"

"What you would expect, mostly. I counsel couples and individuals who are having sexual problems. We try to get to the root of the problem and then see if we can find solutions or at least ways to improve the situation." Then a coy smile formed on her pretty face. "And since I'm getting a little drunk on the brandy here, and since we're old friends, I'll tell you that I have, on occasion, served as a sexual surrogate, too."

Emily blinked, but tried not to look too shocked. "Meaning you . . ."

"Have sex with someone who needs the kind of help that only direct, personal instruction can provide."

"With men," Emily said, to clarify, although she had no idea why.

Dawn quirked a sexy grin in her direction. "Women, too, sometimes."

"Oh." Her voice fluttered.

Dawn touched her knee again. "Don't worry. I wasn't suggesting I'd do that with *you*." She spoke slower then. "Although I would. If you wanted me to."

Emily immediately shook her head and looked down, suddenly unable to make eye contact. "Oh, no. I would never, could never . . ." Her heart beat too fast.

Facing her on the sofa, Dawn lifted Emily's chin with her fingertips and looked deep into her eyes. "Listen to me. This is lesson number one. You have to quit being embarrassed about sex. You have to maintain eye contact. It's *just* sex. Just how people show their affection for one another. It's both natural and normal."

Emily swallowed, intensely aware of Dawn's soft touch beneath her chin, and worked to keep looking into her shadowy green eyes. After a few seconds, it got easier.

"See?" Dawn's voice remained *so* soothing. "It's not so hard to look at me, is it? It's not so hard to talk about."

Emily let out a trembling breath. She wished she hadn't just gotten so nervous—she *hated* that feeling. She reminded herself that this was just Dawn, her old friend.

Of course, now she knew Dawn had sex with women. But even so, she was still Dawn, and Emily was comfortable with her. "No. You're right."

Dawn smiled. "Good. Now take another drink. Let it relax you."

Emily complied, and the brandy warmed her chest as she emptied her mug.

"And now, keep looking at me, Em, and tell me you want to talk about sex."

"I want to talk about sex." Okay. That was easy.

"Tell me you want to learn how to please your man."

Easy again, because it was so true. "I want to learn how to please my man."

"Tell me you want to be totally at ease with him."

"I want to be totally at ease with him." She was getting good at this, maintaining eye contact, *feeling* the words as she said them.

"When he touches you," Dawn said, clearly intending Emily to keep repeating.

"When he touches me."

"When he fucks you."

Emily drew in her breath, shut her eyes. Then opened them. "Words like that . . . I can't seem to say."

Dawn's mouth made a straight line across her face, but she didn't look surprised. Maybe she'd encountered this before. "They're only words, Emily. Sounds. Letters put together."

"They're . . . dirty to me."

"Dirty can be a very good thing."

Emily understood that on some level, understood in those brief moments when she let herself feel naughty that she also felt . . . alive, free, wild, wonderful, in a way she never had before. "Maybe so, but . . ."

"Say *fuck* for me."

When Emily didn't do it, Dawn persisted. "Say it. Just say it. It's only a word. It can't hurt you."

Emily swallowed nervously. "Fuck," she whispered.

"Was there anything horrible about that?"

She sighed. "No. No, not really."

"No, of course not." Her friend spoke gently. "But there *can* be something very good about it. Simon will love it when you ask him to fuck you, I promise. Words can excite and please a man *so* much. They show him you want the same things he does, with the same force, the same deep need. Now, say it again. But in a sentence. Say *fuck me*."

Emily drew in her breath. "Fuck me."

She was looking right at Dawn as she spoke, brutally aware that it sounded as if she were making the demand to her friend. But Dawn only smiled. "Very good. Now, *fuck me, Simon*."

Emily's chest burned with trepidation and a strange heat. Her throat felt heavy, thick. She said the words slowly, her voice low, and felt them in her soul. "Fuck me, Simon."

Dawn nodded, and Emily's chest tightened. "Mmm, yes. That's nice," Dawn said.

Oh God, was she crazy or did her friend actually appear kind of aroused? Emily's heart beat harder and her breasts tingled.

But then, thankfully, Dawn's intense gaze dropped to the empty mug Emily still held. "More?"

More brandy? Probably a good idea. "Yes. Thanks." Or at least she *thought* it was.

As Dawn moved to the open kitchen flanking the living room, an area filled with equally warm colors of dark yellow-gold and burgundy, she said, "I want you to practice after we've parted. Practice saying *fuck*. Practice saying *pussy*. Practice saying *cock*."

"I've been practicing *that* one a little already," she admitted. *At least in my head.*

Dawn giggled throatily. "Good." She went about heating the hot chocolate in the microwave, then adding quick splashes of brandy into the two steaming mugs. "Work on them in sentences, too. Become comfortable with them. Being comfortable with words gives you power, control."

She returned to the leather sofa, passing Emily's mug. Emily blew on the chocolate as the ceramic warmed her palms, and she told herself she could do this—she could learn to talk dirty for Simon.

She looked up, surprised to see Dawn lower her cup to a coaster, then promptly disappeared through a nearby doorway. "Be back in just a minute," she said over her shoulder. "Get ready for lesson two."

"Which is?" Emily called.

"Touching."

Emily gulped, her body seemed to deflate a little from shock. "Um, touching?" Was Dawn going to . . . touch her? Or expect her to return the favor? Every fiber of her body recoiled instantly at the thought. Except . . . for maybe one or two.

Whoa. Oh *God.*

The *awareness* of those one or two more adventurous fibers, arriving with a tiny hint of curiosity that made the crux of her thighs pulse, shocked her more than anything in her life had up to now and made her breath hitch. Could she? Could she want that?

"I'm going to show you the joys of touching yourself," Dawn

said, appearing in the doorway in a sexy bra and panties a moment later. Made of red lace with black ribbon trim, they hugged her snugly—thin black bows at both hips held the panties on. The tight bra barely concealed her nipples and revealed exactly how large and round and smooth Dawn's breasts were.

"Um . . ." Emily began, lost. The truth was, her whole *body* was tingling now—with excitement. She didn't like it, but she couldn't control it. At least Dawn wasn't suggesting they touch *each other*, but Emily's flesh still felt strangely supercharged, sensually energized in a way it never had before.

Dawn calmly smiled. "Here's where you work on relaxing again. Sip your drink. And don't look away from me. Get comfortable with things that are sexual." She moved in long, graceful strides to a plush red chair across from the couch where Emily sat sipping her hot chocolate madly. "Nothing turns a guy on more than watching a woman touch herself. It's the ultimate erotic act for them."

Emily drew the mug down from her lips. "Then, um, shouldn't we start with something a little tamer?"

A thick laugh escaped Dawn's throat and Emily wondered if her nipples were showing through her sweater. "No," Dawn answered. "Because once you've mastered *this*, the rest is easy. Get comfortable with touching yourself intimately and it will be easy to touch Simon that way, too. Learn to understand what your body needs and it will be easier to get it." She grinned. "Now, sit back, relax and watch. Don't be afraid, or embarrassed. Pretend you're just watching this on a screen, by yourself, in the privacy of your own home. Then, later, you're going to go home and do this yourself, okay?"

Fat chance. But Emily was numb. "Okay."

Sitting down in the soft red chair, Dawn spread her legs wide and ran her palms sensually up her inner thighs, then lifted one shapely leg to drape over the arm of the chair. Emily drank her hot chocolate, then bit her lip. The spot between *her* legs throbbed still more now, and when she felt the urge to look away, she took another drink instead and forced herself to keep watching.

Dawn smoothed splayed fingers up over her lace undies, then her silky, white stomach and onto her ample breasts. As she slowly kneaded, massaging them, she leaned back her head and sighed. Her eyes fell shut, her mouth went lax. And Emily's chest turned heavy, warm.

Opening her eyes again to peer over at Emily, Dawn reached behind her with both hands and, a second later, the bra loosened around her. Emily held her breath, for the first time in her life curious to see another woman's breasts.

The lace dropped away to reveal perfect round orbs, large and beautiful, that Emily thought might have been augmented. When Dawn met Emily's gaze, then took her bared breasts back in her hands, tweaking the dusky nipples between thumb and forefinger, Emily's *own* breasts seemed to swell within the confines of her sweater. At this point, she *couldn't* look away—she hadn't the power. She watched, transfixed. Aroused, curious, wondering if she could possibly ever touch *herself* that way, and if she could, could she do it in front of Simon? Did it feel good? Was Dawn's body humming right now, as Emily's was? Was it as arousing to touch yourself while someone watched as it was to be the one watching?

From there, Dawn dropped her hands to one hip. Sensually

licking her upper lip, she slowly, teasingly pulled the black ribbon tied there. The panties loosened and Emily waited impatiently as her friend reached toward the other side. When the lace fell, revealing Dawn's vagina, Emily sucked in her breath. All the hair had been removed! It was so very on display! Pink flesh surrounded her soft, white skin.

"Do you ever touch your pussy, Emily?"

Oh damn, she was supposed to be thinking of it that way—as a pussy, not a vagina. "Um, no." Her gaze remained riveted on Dawn.

"You have to. Tonight. As soon as you leave here and go home. Promise me you will."

She let out a heavy sigh. "Um . . . okay." *But I don't really know how. Like Simon touches me?*

Only she need not have worried—she should have known Dawn was about to show her.

Her friend slowly dragged her middle finger, tipped with a bright red nail, through the damp pink folds at her center. "Mmm," she purred.

Then she used *two* fingers, gently stroking, stroking, before concentrating her attention at the top of the open slit, on the clitoris. The clit, Dawn would surely call it, though. Emily tried to think of it that way, too.

Dawn rubbed two fingertips in rhythmic circles over her swollen clit and Emily found her own pussy burning more and more anxiously now and wished she could touch herself, too. She couldn't, of course—but at least she'd just thought of that part of herself as her pussy, so that was progress.

She watched raptly as Dawn continued to finger herself, her

eyes falling shut again as she let out a low moan. Before long, she clenched her teeth, her self-caresses turning more fevered. Emily took a long chocolaty gulp of her drink, aware that the heady feeling of intoxication was making it much easier to watch, and to feel. Her pussy throbbed against the heavy seam of her blue jeans and she just barely resisted the urge to move around in her seat.

Dawn's breath came heavy, hot, the only sound in the room— and Emily's entire body felt imbued with still more of that new energy, an arousal unlike any she'd ever experienced.

"I'm gonna come," Dawn informed her, still breathing heatedly. "I'm gonna come hard."

And then she cried out—a short, loud sob followed by a series of low moans that made Emily's stomach contract with the intimacy she'd just unwittingly shared with Dawn. "Oh my God," she whispered, taken aback by it all. Such a private act, and yet she'd been there, witnessing it, getting excited by it.

Slowly, Dawn's body seemed to relax, until she finally opened her eyes and refocused on Emily with a smile. "Was it good for *you?*"

"*Amazing,*" Emily uttered.

"So you see how incredible it feels to watch. Just think of *Simon* feeling that way, watching *you.*"

"Oh, I *want* that for him, because . . . wow, it *did* feel incredible. So hot and intoxicating and . . ." She trailed off, realizing she was gushing about how great it had been to watch Dawn climax. Dear God. She was *so* not a lesbian—what was happening to her? "Only, I mean . . ."

Dawn tilted her head, looking relaxed, happy, indulgent. "What *do* you mean?"

"Just that I'm . . . not into girls . . . that way." She was shaking her head.

As usual, though, Dawn simply laughed. "Doesn't matter. Sex is sex. You can't choose what arouses you. People work way too hard defining things like that, trying to analyze what every sexual reaction means—and fearing them. When they *should* just be enjoying themselves."

Emily sighed. "I wish I could be so . . . free about it all. Even *half* as free."

Naked, Dawn rose and walked to the sofa, kneeling on the carpet to place both hands on Emily's knee. "Tonight you'll go home, get yourself off, and realize how wonderful it is, and you'll be a big step closer to sexual freedom."

Emily looked down into Dawn's green eyes, and more honesty erupted. "I . . . I'm not sure I *can*. Make myself come, I mean."

"Weren't you paying attention? I hope you were watching exactly what I was doing with my fingers—both for your sake and for Simon's."

"I was." *I definitely was.* "I just . . . don't always have orgasms very easily. Sometimes, sure—but other times, I just . . . can't quite get there." When Simon had made her come that night a couple of weeks ago, the speed and ferocity of it had been downright shocking—and that wasn't the norm.

Dawn drew back slightly. "The same old trouble? Feelings of it somehow being wrong?"

Emily tried to examine what she so commonly felt. "Something like that. Sometimes Simon touches me and I climax and it's great. But other times . . . I just can't feel what I'm supposed to. And the harder I try, the worse it gets. And I guess, yeah, it feels . . . shameful or something to . . . to become so . . . heated, to . . . lose myself that way, even for just a few minutes."

Dawn squeezed Emily's knee and the sensation shot to the crux of her thighs. "Poor baby," she said, looking truly sad for her. "You just have to change your mind-set. You have to know that there's nothing shameful in sex, or in getting off. You have to teach yourself that. You have to pretend you're learning about sex and orgasm for the very first time and then form new opinions, new feelings about it. Do you think you can do that?"

"I . . . can try." Given what she'd just let herself sit and watch, maybe she *could* do things she'd never thought she could before. She let out a sigh, though, still thinking of orgasms. What if she gathered the courage to touch herself in front of Simon, but then couldn't come? It would feel like the ultimate defeat to get that far and not be able to go all the way. "I'm still . . . worried about coming, though. Or . . . *not* coming, as the case may be."

Dawn pursed her lips thoughtfully. Then she reached up to take the warm mug still in Emily's grasp, lowering it to the coffee table next to her own. "Tell you what, honey. You go lie down on the chaise, okay?" Dawn pushed to her feet, taking Emily's hands in her own.

"Why?" Emily murmured, letting herself be drawn up from the sofa.

"I'm going to go throw something on and I'll be right back. Then we're going to work on relaxing you."

Emily nodded. Relaxing was good. And surely easier than watching Dawn masturbate.

So she pushed to her feet and meandered to the velvet lounge. Lying back, she took in the view of the city and the Ohio River beyond. A stark winter-white sky turned the whole scene slate-like, pale and cold, making her all the more relaxed by the warm atmosphere of the room.

When Dawn came back, she hadn't put *much* on—a short, slinky red kimono tied in front and stopping high on her thighs. She smiled. "Relaxed?"

"Trying to be."

Really, she thought she *was* beginning to calm down inside. Sure, she remained a little aroused by what she'd just observed so unexpectedly, and all this talk of sex and thoughts of being naughty with Simon—but the brandy was making it all too easy to sink fully into the luxurious chaise.

"Good." As Dawn stepped behind the plush lounge, her voice became even more soothing than usual. "Now close your eyes, Emily, and hear my voice. Concentrate on my words, nothing else." With that, she began to slowly, deeply massage Emily's neck and shoulders. The kneading sensation echoed through her like fingers of heat.

"Oh, that feels good," she moaned. Her muscles were stiff lately from too much time at the computer combined with toting heavy shopping bags and wrapping gifts.

"Like we discussed before, we need to teach you to relax and just feel, not think. Just let your body take in the sensations being delivered to it. Just let yourself do what feels good." Her voice dropped a bit lower then. "Watching me, for instance. Watching me touch myself felt good to you. Being able to see it, see my body, my expressions, my actions." Emily had admitted early in their conversation that she always turned the lights out for sex. "Visual stimulation is an important factor in arousal, Emily. The body is a beautiful thing, both the man's and the woman's. Again, there's nothing wrong with letting your body feel what it wants to feel. Especially if you have a sexy guy you love to do it with."

Emily voiced the thought that broke through her semi-relaxed state. "The problem is, I guess I'm afraid that . . . he has this idea of who I am now, and what if he doesn't like me as a wild, sexual woman?"

Dawn's chuckle flowed over Emily warm and confident. "Honey, I've yet to meet the man who doesn't like a wild, sexual woman." Then she paused before adding, "Do you remember, in *Grease*, when Sandy changed into a bad girl at the end? You still liked her, didn't you?"

"Actually, I thought she was abandoning her true self to please a guy."

Dawn laughed again, a more full-bodied sound this time. "Okay, fair enough. But the difference here is—you *want* to be sexual. It's *in* you. You've told me so. And just remember the look on Danny's face when he saw the new Sandy. He was thrilled—finally, she was everything he needed her to be. And if deep inside, you're *already* everything Simon needs you to be, you have to let that out. You can't waste another minute that you could be having hot fun with him, making him happy and growing closer all at the same time." Dawn's fingers still moved rhythmically over Emily's shoulders, her touch beginning to stretch down over her collarbone.

"You make this sound easy."

"Given where you're coming from, no, it's not easy at all. But it's worth it. If you don't open yourself up, you might never really be happy."

Emily let out a long, heavy sigh. Dawn's last words had just hit her square in the gut. Not just because she'd lose Simon if she didn't open up, but because she'd never really get to know her true desires, the things she really wanted. She'd never be the whole woman she could be. "You're right, Dawn—you're so right. I want to let go of all this silly baggage. I want to pleasure Simon. And I'm going to."

Just then, Dawn's kneading fingertips stretched farther, onto the tops of Emily's sensitized breasts. She felt the touch everywhere.

And her voice went softer. "I'm going to."

"That's so good, honey," Dawn said, her tone sweet, comforting. "Now . . . no more talking. Just feel. Just imagine my hands are *Simon's* hands. Just imagine you're alone with him, and afraid of nothing, letting your body do what it wants."

When Dawn's hands slipped down over both her breasts, Emily thought to protest, but she didn't. She was supposed to just feel. To teach herself it was okay. No more talking, Dawn had said. *Just feel. Just feel.* If she wanted to save her relationship with Simon . . . she had to just feel.

She clenched her teeth as pleasure spread through her chest and outward, downward. She tried to keep her breathing even, tried not to sigh with how good it felt. *This is Dawn, your friend, a woman, touching you sexually!* The thought rushed through her brain, but she held it at bay. *She's a sex therapist. She's helping you. Be quiet. Just feel.*

"Think of Simon," Dawn whispered, her voice barely audible. Emily's eyes remained shut, but she sensed Dawn moving around to the side of the chaise. Once there, she resumed gently kneading Emily's breasts, her soft touch drifting down to caress her stomach, too. "Think of pleasing your man. The hands on you right now are his. Think of his cock, Emily. Think of it big and hard, just for you. Think of taking it in your mouth, wanting it there, letting it fill you. Hear his moans when you slide your lips up and down, feel his fingers in your hair." At this, one hand left Emily's breast and threaded back through the hair at her temple, making her sigh.

"You want to please him so much, and you want to let him pleasure you, too. Think of him parting your legs with his hands." Dawn did that then, gently parted Emily's legs. "Think of him licking your pussy." She ran one finger smoothly up the center seam of Emily's jeans between her thighs. "Think of his mouth on you, giving you such raw pleasure." Dawn began to rub then, rub Emily's mound through the jeans. "Think of him licking and sucking your clit deep into his mouth . . . until you come for him, so hard."

When Emily felt the urge to lift against Dawn's touch, she didn't fight it. For once in her life, she didn't fight something that felt wild, crazy, a true act of hedonism. She wasn't into girls. She only knew it felt good. Like electricity zipping through her. She had to go with it, let it happen. Quit analyzing.

She followed Dawn's instructions—she thought of Simon. For the first time, the idea of his face between her legs didn't feel dirty or strange or wrong. She parted them wider, imagining his mouth on her, taking in as much of her pink flesh as he could. She thrust gently, her body swallowing the rhythmic pleasure—getting lost in it, not thinking, only feeling.

So good. So good. Oh, how she wanted Simon. She wanted to

throw herself on him. Suck his cock. Then ride it. She wanted to touch her breasts for him—and so she let her hands glide upward, onto them, to gently squeeze. Her own nipples pushed through her bra and top into her palms. She thrust her pussy harder. She licked her upper lip. She held her breasts tighter. She didn't think, just felt, just moved, just reached—and then she came. It broke over her in startling waves of heat and light that devoured every other thought or sensation but all-encompassing pleasure. It moved through her like wildfire and nothing else existed. There was no shame, no guilt, no thought—only orgasm.

When finally it faded, she waited—for the guilt. Surely it would wash over her now, hard and heavy. After all—my God!— she'd just fooled around with a woman.

Only, the guilt didn't come. Dawn had somehow made all this seem perfectly normal, and simply therapeutic.

She opened her eyes and met Dawn's gaze. "I can't believe I did that."

Dawn only smiled. "I can. And my prognosis for you is that you're going to be just fine. So long as you let yourself."

When Emily left Dawn's condo a little while later, she felt a new kick in her step as she made her way to her car parked along the curb in front. Maybe after today she could do this. Maybe she could be what Simon *needed* her to be, what *she* needed her to be. She'd have to practice, have to teach herself, like Dawn said—she'd have to truly let go of the unhealthy sexual ideas her parents had ground into her and accept herself as the sexual being she was. But maybe she could do it. Hell, maybe she could even do it by Christmas if she worked really hard.

She glanced up at Dawn's front window with a smile, thinking, *Thank you*. And as she got in the car and pulled away, heading home, she had a feeling she knew what to get Simon for Christmas now.

Her, unwrapped.

December 18

Simon wandered out of a jewelry store into the madness of the mall, where he'd been shopping for a gift for Emily without success. Harried shoppers rushed to and fro all around him and Gene Autry sang "Rudolph the Red-Nosed Reindeer" overhead through hidden speakers. He usually *liked* Christmas. This year, though, not so much.

It was Emily. She'd seemed happy enough the last week or so, busy wrapping gifts and baking cookies and reminding him to wear the reindeer tie his mother had bought him last year—which he kept purposefully forgetting, since he liked the song okay, but just didn't think reindeer made a good fashion statement.

For her, it seemed as if that night at his office party had never happened. He only wished he could feel the same way. But he remained torn. He loved her, yet he just couldn't seem to move past their problems this time. And he knew it wasn't her fault—he knew this was all about the way her parents had raised her in a little farming community a few hours north of the city—but he also had grave doubts about whether they could truly be happy in the long-term when they felt so differently about something as big as sex.

Ahead, he spotted the big Santa display in the middle of the mall. Santa Claus sat in a large throne-like chair on a platform with mechanical reindeer scattered about and enormous round peppermint candies suspended on long cords from the ceiling far above. The little girl perched on Santa's lap cried while her mother made silly faces at her from behind the photographer.

Despite himself, the sight reminded Simon of the dream he'd had last night.

Like so many dreams, it was somewhat nonsensical—but he'd definitely liked it.

He'd been dressed up, playing a department store Santa himself. He'd never done that or had any urge to, but in the dream, it seemed normal. He sat atop a throne similar to the one before him now, but he'd been surrounded by a cottony, glittery winter wonderland scene—which he thought he should tell the mall personnel about, since he'd found it much more appealing than the plastic reindeer and oversize candy.

Other major differences between his dream and this reality: There had been no crowd in the dream, no one else around but the girl perched in his lap. And that girl hadn't been a child. She'd been Emily, wearing a red, see-through baby doll nightie and carrying a matching lollipop. She'd squirmed flirtatiously in his lap, sucking provocatively on the candy.

"Are you naughty or nice, little girl?" he'd asked in a deep Santa voice.

"Oh, definitely naughty," she'd assured him in a sexy tone he'd never had the pleasure of hearing Emily use.

And then the damn alarm had gone off, and he'd awakened to find one of Em's legs looped over his, which was both comforting and . . . frustrating. Given the dream. And the fact that he didn't have the luxury of rolling over and initiating some nice morning sex with her as he would have with most women.

She'd smiled at him, having no idea of his thoughts, or that his dick was hard. Happy as a clam these past days, his Em, and he had no idea why. The holiday spirit, maybe? He knew she was looking forward to the big dinner she hosted every Christmas Eve at one of the large local shelters—since Christmas was an especially tough time for the homeless, she liked knowing they had somewhere welcoming to go on that particular night. *And* it gave her an opportunity to convince newcomers to *stay* at the shelter, where maybe her agency could help them get back on their feet.

He'd gone with her to the dinner the past two years and would this year, too. He loved watching her do her job—she was no less than amazing with the people who wandered into the shelter looking emotionally battered, lost, afraid. Each time he saw her at work it made him fall in love with her a little more.

Although maybe he shouldn't go this year, now that he thought about it. Loving her more would hardly help this situation, which, for him, was growing dire.

"Morning, honey," she'd said.

"Morning, Em." He'd glanced over at her. She was the sort of woman who looked good first thing upon waking, sans makeup, hair tousled.

"I'll be late tonight. Cookie exchange at Lisa's after work." A neighbor friend.

He'd nodded against his pillow. "Maybe I'll do some shopping then."

But so far, he'd managed to buy nothing for her—no gift he could find seemed "right" for right now.

Maybe, he thought then, the idea just striking him as he walked past Victoria's Secret, he should seek out a baby doll nightie like the one in his dream. She'd look gorgeous in something like that.

But then he'd have to beg her to even wear it, and it wouldn't be worth the trouble.

With a sigh—and empty hands—he gave up and headed outside, where it was just beginning to snow.

December 24

"I'm going to take a quick shower, sugarplum," Simon said. They'd just gotten home from the annual Christmas Eve dinner at the shelter, where they'd helped serve two hundred and fifty-two homeless people a decent meal. Emily had talked personally to as many as she could, handing out brochures and encouraging them to stay afterward. She would be lucky—and thankful—if thirty or forty took her advice, but if that many people had a better night, and maybe a few of them a better future, that made her efforts more than worthwhile.

And she was fairly exhausted, but not too exhausted to follow through on her plan now that they were home. She and Simon had already developed a few little holiday traditions—and among them was serving dinner to the homeless on Christmas Eve, then coming home and exchanging their gifts to each other. "Okay," she replied. "I'll . . . meet you in the living room in a few. With your present."

She smiled, and he did, too, leaning in to kiss her forehead.

But that didn't change how strange things had been between them lately. As she watched Simon disappear behind the bathroom door, her heart hurt remembering how unhappy he'd continued to seem these past couple of weeks. In fact, she had the distinct feeling that he was "sticking it out" with her until the holidays were over and then might very well be planning to break up.

Every time that thought hit her, it was like a physical blow. And now, with *that* horrible pressure weighing her down, she had to give him the gift she'd been planning—and hope it wasn't too late to save what they had.

She'd followed Dawn's advice to the letter—she'd practiced touching herself, once even doing it in front of the mirror, so she could see what *Simon* would see. She'd grown comfortable with the feel of her own breasts, and even her pussy. She could say that now, and lots of other naughty words, without flinching. Because she'd practiced that, too—dirty talk—also in front of the mirror.

She'd thought herself pretty resourceful when she'd bought Popsicles to simulate sucking Simon's cock. Of course, they were much smaller than what she'd be putting in her mouth tonight, and cold, too—but it had at least allowed her to develop some techniques, and she figured it was better than nothing. And she'd actually reached a place where the idea of taking his shaft between her lips held some appeal for her, some true desire.

So she was as ready as she *could* be.

But she also knew that putting her plans and practice into action would be an entirely different and more complex endeavor. So even though she'd gone through the last two weeks with a smile on her face—at some points truly happy about her new self-discoveries and plans for Simon, at others stressed out and just trying to keep the peace with him until she could complete her "self-education"—her stomach churned and her hands trembled as she went to the bureau to pull out the naughty little outfit she'd bought for this evening.

The shower still ran behind a closed door when Emily once again found herself before a mirror, looking like a December centerfold. Or at least she *hoped* that's how she looked.

She wore a red velvet shelf bra sporting white fur along the top edge, the naughty lingerie built to support her breasts but not to conceal them, so her nipples were fully on display and hard with excitement. Below that, a very short, flouncy, red velvet skirt with more white fur at the hem—and no panties underneath, which had the desired effect of making her feel positively wicked, in a *good* way. Black boots came to her knees and a Santa hat sat perched on her head. *Mrs. Santa Gone Bad.*

She quivered a bit at the sight of herself, with both nervousness and excitement, imagining Simon's surprise at finding his gift already unwrapped and ready to be played with.

—⊂∞⊃—

Simon ran a towel through his mostly dry hair, then stepped into a pair of underwear and the flannel pants Emily had laid out on the bed for him. Of course, they were dotted with tiny reindeer, ornaments hanging from their antlers. She'd given them to him last Christmas. Why were reindeer becoming such a theme in his wardrobe? But for Emily, he would wear them.

As usual, she'd blown him away at the dinner, and he had, indeed, fallen for her even harder. Maybe it was a foregone conclusion in his life that he was destined to love a woman who hated sex. Starting toward the living room, he let out a sigh. *Why me?*

When he walked through the doorway, Elvis's bluesy, sexy

"Merry Christmas, Baby" played low on the stereo, and the room was aglow with candles and the tiny colored lights of the Christmas tree, as well as the low flames burning in the fireplace.

He didn't see Emily—at first.

But when he did, he swallowed. Hard.

What the hell?

She lay stretched provocatively before the decorated tree, amid the gifts, legs slightly bent, back arched, propped on her elbows. Her hands cupped fur-lined breasts, the nipples beaded and shadowy in the dim lighting. *Jesus.* He went hard in an instant.

A big red bow was wrapped around her bared tummy, and her eyes shone on him—Holy Mother of God—with wild intent. He stood before her numb, speechless.

"Do you like your present?" she asked, her voice silky, sensuous—new.

He still couldn't find any words, so simply swallowed again as he nodded.

"Good. Because this is only the beginning."

"Unh," he eloquently managed to reply. His whole body had gone rigid with arousal, but his jaw had dropped and he seemed unable to raise it back up.

Keeping her suddenly sexy eyes on his, she eased both hands up through the fur on her bra to gently tweak the beautifully erect peaks of her breasts. He felt her sensual moves in his cock, yet still wondered just what the hell was going on, what had happened to her. He almost wondered if he was having another dirty dream.

She smoothed her palms over the lovely curves of her velvet-bound breasts and onto her pale torso, where she used her middle finger and thumb to slowly, gracefully pull at the ribbon tied around her waist. He watched, amazed, dumbfounded, as the thick red ribbon gently fell away, giving him the sense that the simple gesture somehow *opened* her to him.

That's when he forgot to keep wondering what was going on and stepped toward her, his feet moving on pure instinct, his body ready to have his way with her—and to hope this was real.

"Stop," she said then, gentle but firm.

He did, but the command caught him off guard.

"Sit." She pointed to the sofa.

"Why?" The first word he'd managed to utter since walking into the room.

She bit her lip, looked slightly pensive for half a second, but then turned all the way sexy again. "I have more to give you, baby. More of *me*."

Once again, Simon swallowed. Emily had always been a beautiful woman, but when—*how*—had she gotten so fucking *hot*? "All right," he said lightly, then did as she instructed, wondering what on earth awaited him.

He watched as she rolled smoothly up onto her knees, then began to crawl in long, sensual strides toward a small ottoman in front of an easy chair situated across from him. The long lines of her legs as she moved so sleekly, the curve of her back, the plump roundness of her breasts, all served to tighten his cock within his pants that much more, and it was all he could do not to bound across the coffee table and ravish her—but he stayed in place, still in wonderment over her gift to him.

She moved lithely up onto the ottoman, facing him, her eyes filled with . . . he could only read it as the deepest passion he'd ever witnessed from her. It wasn't just about *this*, about *sex*. He thought it was about *sex* and *him* and *her* and every moment they'd ever shared together, good and bad.

Then she parted her legs.

He drew in his breath at the erotic vision she made. But only when she reached down, lifting her little skirt to reveal nothing underneath—nothing but the smooth flesh of her shockingly denuded pussy and the pink folds at its center—did a low groan escape him.

"Do you want me to touch myself for you, Simon?"

He nearly fainted. Jesus Christ. "God, yes," he managed on a ragged breath.

Sliding her tongue sensually across her upper lip, and looking coquettish as hell, she reached one long, tapered middle finger down into her glistening cunt. As she raked her fingertip upward through the valley of pink, they both sighed. He'd never seen a more arousing sight in his life.

"More," he whispered without planning it. That's what he wanted, needed, with his whole soul in that moment. *More*.

Emily complied with his request, her body on fire. She was *doing* this, really doing it, and Simon appeared just as riveted as Dawn had promised he would be. Reaching down, she stroked through her moist flesh for him again and again—each pass drawing another hot sigh or moan from her man even as her own arousal grew.

Having his eyes on her while she did this was more powerful than she'd even imagined. That first stroke had been hard—truly letting go of her lifelong fears about sex was complicated—but now, it was becoming easier, slowly easier, with each swipe of her finger through her moist slit.

Glancing down, she saw how open she was, how excited and ready, and she was reminded of the raw, blatant view she was giving her man. A last ounce of that awful, hideous sense of shame bit at her—but then she forced it away. *This is okay. More than okay. This is good. Pleasuring yourself while you pleasure your lover. This is . . . pretty freaking amazing, in fact.* And then the shame was gone, and she was free. Free to be the woman she wanted to be for Simon.

"You're so hot, my sugarplum girl," Simon cooed to her, his lids heavy now, eyes shaded with desire.

"Do you like this? Like watching me rub my pussy for you?" Her voice came breathy, because it was another step, and felt huge, but she wanted it, wanted to arouse him with her words as much as with her body.

Simon actually looked weak with passion. "Oh my God, baby, *yes*. Rub it for me. Rub your beautiful cunt for me."

She sucked in her breath, more aroused than bothered by the word. Which made a soft smile steal over her face. And gave her even more courage—the courage to follow a whim.

Sensually biting her lip, she reached to a nearby table where a decorative snowman mug held a handful of red-and-white-striped candy canes. She snatched one out, grabbing on to the curve at the end, and slid the length of it slowly through her lips, one side to the other, the taste of the peppermint on her tongue somehow arousing her even more. Then she slowly eased the stick of candy down, down into the folds of her pussy, using it like a finger, surprised when something in the mint made her tingle even more than she already was.

"Aw . . ." Simon moaned, his mouth going slack at the sight.

Emily rolled the peppermint cane slowly across her parted flesh while he watched—before beginning to slide it up and down.

"Oh, baby, that's so fucking hot."

She licked her upper lip, fully into it now, pleasing herself, pleasing Simon. And then she followed another wild whim, letting the tip of the candy cane sink lower, lower, until she held it poised at the opening of her passage. Simon's gaze was glued to her cunt. She eased the length of the candy inside.

Simon's moan cut through the low music that still played, fueling her pleasure, and she followed the instinct to move the thin stick of candy in and out, in and out, pushing it all the way to the crook of the cane, then easing it slowly back for Simon's hungry eyes. She was fucking herself with a *candy cane*. She couldn't quite believe it, but she was fucking herself with a candy cane—and it was good.

So good—the audacity of it, the raw sex of it, the heat that shone in Simon's expression—that she didn't fight the urge to reach her free hand down, using the first two fingers to caress lazy circles over her clit. Mmm, it was swollen now, sensitive and hot—it felt huge beneath her fingers. She moaned in response as the pleasure stretched through her, magnified and multiplied by the motions of the candy cane below and by Simon's rapt attention.

"Make yourself come for me, baby," Simon demanded. And for the first time in her life, she relished a sexual command, feeling the heat of it, the desire it sent spreading through both of them.

She rubbed her clit harder, the circles her fingers made growing faster and more intense, matching the rhythm of the stick of candy she thrust in herself below. "*Mmm*," she sighed, her pleasure rising, rising.

"Oh yeah, baby. Get yourself off for me. Be my naughty girl." Simon's voice was a low rasp.

Which made her rub herself even harder, quicker. "Mmm, yes," she heard herself purr. *"Yesss."* So close, so close. *Get there, get there, come for him.*

And just when she began to worry that her fears might come true, that she might not be able to make herself climax—she reached that glorious threshold, that few seconds where she knew she was safe, the orgasm was coming, a heartbeat away.

And then it washed through her, *hard, hard, hard,* in waves of jolting heat that made her clench her teeth and cry out—again, again.

When the waves settled and she came back to herself, she was acutely aware that she was sitting before Simon with a candy cane in her vagina and her fingers wet with her own juices. Now that she'd come, would this all still seem okay?

She met his eyes, wondering if her fear showed as she waited—for his reaction, and for *hers.*

"You," he began, almost seeming at a loss for words, "are *so* fucking incredible."

Her chest heaved slightly with her renewed nervousness. "I am?"

He tilted his head, looking as if she were crazy to ask. "Oh, *baby,*" he said. "Come to me. Come to me and let me *show* you how incredible you are."

And that's when Emily knew. It was still all right. She was still excited, even after the orgasm had faded. And she was going to go to him, all right. Only . . .

"No," she said softly, getting to her feet, clutching the freshly extracted candy cane in her hand even as she rounded the coffee table. "There's still more *I* want to show *you*, give *you*. More of my gift to you."

She saw more than heard his sigh as she abandoned the candy on the table, then dropped to her knees between his legs, firmly parting them.

She gazed up at his handsome face. "I want to take you to heaven, Simon." Then she ran the flat of her palm up over the stiff erection making a clear tent in his pants, for the first time *fully* enjoying how hard he was, how big, and that it was all for her. She wanted it.

She wasted no time undoing the drawstring of his pants, pulling them loose, then pulling them down, along with his white boxer briefs. And—*oh*! Talk about *incredible*. *He* was incredible. She'd never felt such a response to seeing his big, beautiful cock before, but now the mere vision of it ricocheted all through her.

Pulling in her breath, she leaned low, near enough to kiss it, then gazed up at him.

His voice sounded a little choked. "Baby, are you gonna . . . ? Finally?"

"Yes," she whispered, then licked a long path from the base of his shaft to the tip.

He shuddered, and she loved it—but loved even more knowing that she was going to give him what he'd waited for for so long. Although she felt the need to say, "I may not be any good at it."

He let out a cynical laugh, as if she were nuts, and his eyes looked glassy as he peered down at her. "You *can't* be bad at it, honey. It's not possible. You're going to be *perfect*."

The words echoed through her, giving her the courage she

needed, and God knew that the *desire* was suddenly there, suddenly urging her to go down on him, so she didn't hesitate any longer. Taking his cock firmly in her grasp, she swirled her tongue sensually around the head, licking away the moisture there, then she lowered her mouth over him.

Her first thought was—*how do people do this?* It felt immeasurably *huge* filling her mouth. But her second, more pleasant thought was—*oh God, I like it.*

She liked the hot, thready moans that wafted down over her, she liked the feel of such immense hardness on her tongue, her lips, the inner walls of her mouth. She liked the power she felt there—the power in his cock, and the power *she* held by pleasuring it.

She liked the way his large fingers threaded through her hair, holding it back—just as Dawn had promised. She liked feeling his eyes on her, just as she had when she'd been touching herself for him.

And as she slowly began to experiment, to move up and down, she grew more bold, took him deeper, moved on him more rhythmically—and finally she gained the courage to look up into his eyes.

She'd never seen Simon so fraught with emotion as he said, "See, my sugarplum? Perfect. So fucking perfect."

And she hated that she'd made him wait so long for this, and she hated that she'd wasted so much time not enjoying his large, perfect shaft this way herself.

But then, just as she was sinking more fully into her work, eyes shut, sliding her lips sensually up and down his smooth, steely length, he cupped her face in his hands and eased her mouth upward. "Stop, baby."

She was stunned, and her mouth felt pleasantly stretched as she raised her eyes to his.

"It's too good," he told her, voice trembling. "I don't want to come yet. And if you keep it up . . ."

She bit her lower lip. She didn't want that, either. So she simply nodded and began to climb up into his lap as he lifted her toward him from the floor.

She intended to lower herself onto that majestic erection now—if she couldn't have it in her mouth, she wanted it in her cunt. But Simon *kept* lifting her, even after she'd straddled him, propelling her upright on her knees.

She gasped when she realized he was sinking *down* on the couch then, bringing his face level with her cunt. Caressing her outer thigh with one hand as he lifted her short skirt with the other, he studied her there, his eyes so close to her bared mound, then shifted his touch, brushing his fingertips over the smooth flesh between her legs. "I can't believe you shaved your pussy," he murmured, looking drunk on the sight.

She couldn't, either, actually. But seeing Dawn that way had inspired her. She'd figured if she was going to do this, let her inner vixen out, she was going to go all the way. Still, she heard herself asking, "Do you like it?"

A low chuckle erupted from his throat. "Oh yeah, sugarplum. I like it." He cemented the statement by leaning in to place a soft kiss directly on her clit.

"Ohhh . . ." she moaned.

He gazed up at her, eyes ablaze with lust. "Do you want me to lick you, baby? Do you want me to lick your hot little pussy?"

Oh God. Such a dirty suggestion. Yet for the first time, the idea didn't feel too intimate or outrageous. No, it felt just right and was what she wanted more than anything in this moment. "Mmm, yes," she said with a decisive nod. "Lick me."

He groaned at her command, then sliced into her most sensitive flesh with his tongue.

The sensation made her shiver, made her head fall back. "Oh, baby."

"Minty," he said then, on a short laugh. But Emily wasn't even amused. She just wanted more of his tongue.

And—oh yes!—she got it, she got it *so* damn good.

She soon lost track of exactly what he was doing to her—too much pleasure to watch, to take it all in. She felt his tongue dig deep, licking, licking, felt him swirling it around her clit, then sucking intently. Eager fingers thrust up inside her and she moved on them without thinking. The motion thrust her pussy harder against his mouth and he moaned at her enthusiasm.

She soon heard herself crying out, felt her own undulations taking her over. She instinctively lifted her hands to mold her breasts, caress the soft skin there, tease the hard nipples. So much pleasure—everywhere.

But then—oh God—even more. What was *that*? And how was it even possible?

Fresh sensation buffeted her from behind. Her breath began leaving her in harsh, heavy gasps. So good, so very good. That's when she realized, understood—he was stroking the fingers of his free hand over her anus. "Unh . . ." she moaned.

She'd never known something like that could feel so fabulous. She knew about anal sex, but she'd assumed it was just something people did to be extreme—she'd never imagined that area was truly such an erogenous zone.

The pleasure—coming from all sides now—was simply too much. A few seconds longer and Emily could no longer think, reason. All she knew was physical delight, consuming her. She fucked Simon's mouth, his fingers. She licked her lips just to feel something there, missing his cock inside them. She twirled her nipples between her fingertips, pressed her palms harder to her breasts.

"Oh! I'm gonna come," she said, amazed. God, *twice*? This could happen *twice*? But it was—*now*.

"Oh, I'm coming! I'm coming!" she yelled as the orgasm pulled her in completely, pounding through her in hard, rhythmic pulses, shorter but more intense than the first.

The climax left her feeling utterly spent, so as Simon's fingers left her, she sank down into his lap, exhausted. Her arms looped around his neck and his hands rested on her hips, on her little velvet skirt. They smiled lazily at each other—until Simon's expression turned hotter. "Fuck me," he said.

The words didn't even faze her this time. But weariness still gripped her. "I don't know if I can," she said, casting him a well-pleasured grin. "Too tired."

He lowered his chin to scold her. "Oh, you'll *do* it all right, sugarplum. We haven't come this far for you to stop now."

The naughty glimmer in his eye somehow revived her and she lifted her hands to his face to kiss him, realizing she hadn't even done that yet. And she *loved* kissing Simon. As she pressed her mouth to his, their tongues met, and one kiss turned into two, then more. "I love you," she breathed between them, tasting herself on his lips.

"Mmm, I love you, too, Em," Simon growled. "So very much."

And before she knew it, she was rubbing against him, grinding her damp crotch against the hot erection that arced upward across his abdomen. "Fuck me," Simon urged her again, his voice a mere breath now. "Fuck me, baby."

Rising back to her knees, Emily curled her fist around his cock, positioning herself carefully. One more thing she'd never done—been on top. Her heart beat wildly as she eased down, down, warmly sheathing him in her moisture.

"Oh God," she moaned—he felt so much bigger this way, with her weight on him. She had to clench her teeth for a moment as her body adjusted to the nearly overwhelming pressure.

"You okay?" Simon's hands closed on her waist. "We don't have to do it this way if it hurts."

But Emily shook her head. He was right—she'd come too far to stop now. She knew they could have fun in lots of other new positions she'd never tried, too, but this one was so . . . basic, and so intimate, that she intended to *handle* this, to master it, to not let anything she tried tonight fail. "I just need . . . to get used to it. You're *huge*."

He laughed. "See what you've been missing?"

She smiled into his eyes. "Mmm." Her body was beginning to adjust now, to the feel of him pushing up into her, filling her so impossibly full.

She slowly began to move. And to feel. The way her clit met with his body. The way her pelvis eased instinctively into a gyrating rhythm that felt as natural as breathing.

"That's right," he said, caressing her breasts. "Ride my cock."

Her heated sighs came heavier when Simon dipped to take

one breast into his mouth to suckle. The ministrations seemed to connect directly to her pussy and increase the sensation there. Her rhythm on his cock quickened slightly and despite her initial troubles, she already knew why women liked being on top so much.

Simon's hands slid from her fur-outlined breasts downward, up under her little red skirt to knead her ass. "Mmm, that feels nice," she told him, overjoyed at the freedom she felt, with the realization that she was really *doing* this, having fun with Simon, letting her inhibitions run free.

His eyes darkened just slightly as he slid one hand inward, his fingertips brushing over her anus again. She couldn't hold in her moan. "Oh—even better," she purred.

She still couldn't quite get over how that soft little touch in that tiny little spot could spread all through her. It was almost enough to make her weak all over again, yet at the same time, it turned her even more wild, feral, and she found herself kissing Simon feverishly, rubbing her breasts against his chest.

He managed to smile through his heat, though his voice came breathy. "Your fur tickles."

"And what does *this* do?" She rode him harder, amazed she could thrust down so enthusiastically now, feel him so deep inside her cunt without pain.

"*That*, baby, makes me want to fucking explode—so be careful."

Simon continued to stroke across the tiny fissure at her rear, and at moments Emily thought she would lose her mind from the consuming pleasure it sent flashing through her entire being.

Suddenly leaning forward, Simon dipped Emily back over his

knees and took the opportunity to lick one sensitive nipple as he reached around her. When he sat back up, drawing her upright again, she saw he'd retrieved her old friend, the candy cane. "Sticky," he said with a grin, holding it up between them.

"Because it's candy or . . . because of me?" she asked, feeling just a hint of sheepishness as she lowered her chin.

"Both," he said, then put the end of the candy cane in his mouth to suck on it.

Mmm, why was that such a sexy sight?

"I taste you," he said.

Oh yeah, *that* was why. Because it had been in her pussy and was now in his mouth.

Which was when he slowly drew it from between his lips, then held it up to hers.

She parted them slightly, letting him slide the candy cane inside. A burst of peppermint filled her mouth, but she, too, tasted the strangely sweet remnants of her own juices, just as she had on Simon's lips moments ago. Her chest hollowed as she gazed into her lover's eyes. He continued slipping the candy cane in and out of her mouth as they fucked, her clit still connecting with him in front as his fingers kept caressing her in back. A whole new wave of weakness set in. She'd never experienced so much passion or true intimacy in her life and was beginning to wonder how women survived it.

So she nearly collapsed when Simon leaned up near her ear to whisper, "I want to fuck your sweet little ass, baby."

Heat climbed her cheeks instantly—a combination of fiery arousal and abject apprehension, the first *real* apprehension she'd felt all night. "Already, Simon? Don't you think we could . . . save that for next time? Because . . . I'm making great strides here, but that's a whole different . . ."

He grinned lasciviously, their faces still close. "Don't worry, sugarplum. I don't mean with my cock. Not yet. You're right, we'll work up to that." He held the candy cane back up between them. "I meant with this."

Emily blinked, swallowed. "Oh." She hardly knew what to think. She wanted to be aghast at the very notion of Simon putting a candy cane up her ass, but she'd just had it in her pussy, so . . . maybe she should just let the man have his way.

Yet he clearly expected her to protest, so his voice came warm again on her ear. "Let me," he said.

Just those two words. But they hit her so hot that she'd have probably let him do *anything* in that moment. "Okay," she agreed.

Raking another warm, sensual kiss across her mouth, Simon deftly reached behind her until she felt the candy—he dragged the dampened end of it up and down in the valley of her ass, teasing her flesh. She sucked in her breath—it made the whole area tingle coolly, the sensation echoing inward. And to her surprise, she found herself moving against it immediately, even as she continued fucking him.

"Be still, baby," he warned her then, and she complied. She leaned in against him, her palms at his chest, her head nestled against his neck where she could breathe in the smell of him—partly shower fresh, partly scented with their sex.

Behind her, the tip of the candy cane slipped inside her anal opening. "*Oh,*" she said.

"Hurt?"

"No." On the contrary.

And she was just on the verge of realizing that her pleasure was starting to expand—greatly—when the candy cane sank home, sliding deep into her ass. "Oh my God!"

Simon looked worried. "Is it okay?"

She could only nod, her whole body filling with a heady, pulsing sensation that stretched all the way to her fingers and toes, even up the back of her neck into her head. "Ah . . . ah . . ." She couldn't speak, could only make noises that probably sounded as if she were stuck somewhere between pleasure and pain, but she was much closer to pleasure. A strange, searing, *overwhelming* pleasure—that only multiplied when she found the strength to move again, to fuck his cock, and in the same motion fuck the candy cane, too.

From there, Emily could barely think—it was too all-consuming. She only knew movement and heat and pleasure and the intense sense of being so fully intoxicated with sensation that she could barely control her actions. She cried out over and over. She heard Simon yell, too. She'd stopped looking at him because her head had dropped back and her eyes had fallen shut. Every nerve ending of her being was pulsing, pumping. Simon's tremendous cock continued thrusting, thrusting, driving up deep inside her pussy, and her clit rubbed against him over and over.

Oh God, God—was she . . . Could she . . . Was it possible to have three orgasms in one night? She'd just begun to wonder when the hot climax rushed through her with more power than any she'd ever known. The shock waves jolted her body over and over—it was like being electrocuted . . . by pleasure.

"Sweet Jesus," she heard herself murmur as finally it passed and she slumped against Simon, her arms falling comfortably around his neck.

"Oh babe," he said. Then louder, "Oh Jesus, babe—*now!*" Extracting the candy cane and tossing it aside, he used both hands to push her hips down onto his cock hard, harder, as he pounded up into her, rocking her body like never before. They both yelled out . . . until again, she was collapsing on him, and this time his body went limp as well, and they sprawled across the couch together, utterly wiped out.

⁓

Emily lay on the couch, still in her Christmas Girl Gone Wild suit, recovering from the events of the evening while Simon went to open a bottle of wine. She flung her arms up over her head, smiling lazily. She'd done it, really done it. And it had been more spectacular than she'd ever dreamed.

She sat up when Simon returned carrying two stemmed glasses. He'd kicked off his reindeer pants at some point and was now completely and beautifully naked. For the first time in their three years together, she drank in his male beauty without suffering any shyness.

"To fan-*fucking*-tastic sex," Simon said by way of a toast. His grin was almost enough to get Emily excited again as she clinked her glass against his.

"So," he said after taking a sip, "start talking. What the hell happened to you?"

She bit her lip, tilted her head. "I just realized I *had* to get over my hang-ups if we were going to be happy together."

Simon let out a heavy breath and gave his head a short shake.

"I still can't quite believe it, Em. You were . . . astounding. How? How did you get over them?"

She smiled. "That would make a good story for . . . the next time we have sex."

"Like, you mean, tomorrow morning. Or tomorrow night at the latest. Since tomorrow *is* Christmas and we have families to see and turkeys to eat and presents to open, I might give you the morning off," he concluded with a wink.

She leaned in for a quick kiss. "Tomorrow night—it's a date." Then she glanced at the red stockings hanging on the mantel. "And speaking of presents, I actually have a few more for you. Although only little ones, since *this* was your biggie."

"Trust me, sugarplum, I've never gotten a better gift in my life." He put down his wine and moved toward the fireplace to retrieve both their stockings. Bringing them back to the couch, he sat down and started in on his.

He quickly ripped the red foil paper from the first small gift he pulled out, and Emily saw the edible body paints she'd purchased. "Are those silly?" she asked, wondering now about her choice.

Simon laughed. "No way, sugarplum. Anything that allows me to get more of your body sounds fun to *me*."

"I kinda . . . ventured into a sex shop," she admitted. There weren't many such establishments in the area, but a phone call to Dawn had helped her find one where other women shopped and she didn't feel freakishly out of place. Dawn had met her for lunch and they'd gone together.

"Now *that* I would like to have seen," Simon said with a wink as he extracted his next gift. Removing the paper, he found a DVD featuring Kama Sutra techniques. "Nice," he said. "And from the same store, I bet."

She nodded. "I know I'm doing pretty good here, but I figure we might want to find even more ways to experiment."

His dark gaze met hers. "Absolutely, my sweet girl."

Finally, he opened the last little package stuffed in the stocking—a pair of silk boxer shorts, red with white fur trim and the plastic embellishment of a black belt. She knew she was pushing it with that one, and Simon just shook his head. "Reindeer pants are bad enough, Em, but you really want me to wear Santa shorts?"

She simply nodded, flashing her sweetest "pretty please" expression. She thought them adorably cute.

After a moment, he let out a sigh of concession. "Fine. For you, I'll wear the damn things."

And she smiled. "I'll even let you wear this, too," she added, reaching up to remove her red Santa hat—which had amazingly stayed on through their whole encounter—and placed it on his head. Which was when she realized how hot he looked that way, wearing nothing but the hat. She knew she hadn't managed to hide her lascivious reaction, so she said, "Okay, maybe we can forget the boxers."

He quirked a grin. "That's my newly naughty girl. Ready for *your* present now?"

Again, she nodded, and Simon handed over her stocking. It seemed unusually light, but she hardly cared what was inside. This year had been all about *her* gift to *him*.

Reaching inside, her hand closed around something small and velvet, and she pulled out a miniscule red box. "Hey, this matches my outfit," she said.

Then stopped. And gulped.

Because of what it looked like. A . . . ring box.

She shifted her gaze to Simon's, searching his eyes.

He only gave her a warm smile and slowly said, "Open it."

Taking a deep breath, Emily lifted the lid to find a gorgeous marquise-cut diamond ring inside. And then she lost the ability to breathe at all. "Simon, is this . . ."

When she looked up, Simon had dropped to one knee before the couch. "Will you marry me, Emily?"

All the blood drained from her face. Simon wanted to *marry* her? Even before tonight—before she'd shown him the new, improved sexual her?

She couldn't talk—but she threw her arms around his neck, knocking him backward a bit until he managed to get them both back upright. "Is that a yes?"

She found her voice. "Oh God, yes! Yes, I'll marry you, Simon! *Of course* I'll marry you."

He pulled back, releasing a sigh. "Because, to tell you the truth, I wasn't sure. Lately, things have been . . . weird, and I haven't been . . . very nice."

"Well, who can blame you? I was messing up a major part of our relationship."

He looked her in the eye. "In all honesty, Em, that's really been wearing on me lately, making me question our future together. But no matter how I looked at it, I couldn't give up on us. I knew I wanted to be with you forever, no matter what. And what you gave me tonight . . . I can't tell you how much it means to me."

With that, Simon drew the ring from the box and slid it onto Emily's finger. Gazing down at it, she lifted her other hand to cover her mouth, still stunned. "I can't believe I get such a wonderful man—for life."

He smiled. "*I* can't believe you just fucked my brains out."

She lowered her chin, delivering a seductive look. "There's more where that came from, baby. And you may not even have to wait until tomorrow night. I might just have to have my way with you again right now."

She watched the heat of desire reinvade her lover's eyes and realized, more fully than ever before, how much she'd been missing by letting so much sex with Simon pass her by.

"You know," she said, holding up the hand bearing her new engagement ring, "sometimes the best gifts come in *small* packages. And then, other times," she went on, perusing his whole body, top to bottom, still naked but for the Santa hat, "the best gifts definitely come . . . unwrapped."

WHEN I CLOSE MY EYES

MELANI BLAZER

Every morning I have breakfast with some wonderful women who offer laughter, support, encouragement and friendship. This book is to them, as a tribute to how much I appreciate them.

I can't fail to mention my dear husband, who continues to make me believe in destiny—the belief that two people are meant to be together. Love you, hon!

One

Outclassed, that's what she was. Flat out, out of her league on this one. And perhaps a little out of her mind as well.

Kenna McGurly stood in front of the enormous white house she thought had existed only in her dreams.

It was real. That left her more off balance than if she had driven all the way to Lake Tahoe and found nothing. In fact, she had expected to drive for more hours than she cared to remember, only to face the truth—it was all just some fantasy she'd concocted as a young teenager, not only the house but the whim that there was another human with whom she had some extraordinary connection.

She was awestruck but knew it was more than déjà vu that had her stomach tied in knots. No way could someone have accidentally created this enormous home, with its ethereal grandeur and breathtaking beauty that matched her dreams exactly. Even in the weak light from decorative lamps and landscaping lights, she could make out the lines of the home. Modern architecture made to look as if it had been carved out of the side of the mountain centuries ago.

It was real. By whatever miracle, the house was real. *Now what?*

Her bravado had seemed to desert her the moment she'd gotten out of the car. Oh, she knew why she came—the house was only part of it. There was a man tied to this place somehow. His presence had resounded in so many of her dreams. She knew his voice, felt his touch so often she often wondered if they were truly two separate people.

She sighed and closed her eyes, feeling the emotion roll over her like the fog that coated the lake. No way could she describe out loud the pull, almost like she only had half of a heart and somewhere, this man possessed the rest of it. She dreamed of him, and when she woke, she could almost swear she'd touched him, kissed him, heard his voice, felt his breath against her cheek.

She shivered and opened her eyes to look again at the house, to convince herself this was real. She was here.

Right now he—whoever he was—was the one last thing she treasured. On a level she didn't quite understand, he belonged to her. And only her. No one could take that away.

Kenna swiped her hand across her eyes and sighed.

She'd come here on a whim, taking vacation from work for the entire week, draining her savings and hopping in her car. If nothing else, it was a good break from the gray existence her life had become since her boyfriend Paul had announced he was going to be a father—and she knew *she* wasn't pregnant.

That bit of news had spoiled any chance of her having a merry Christmas. So in all honesty, she had taken the opportunity to avoid all the questions about her newly single status and do something she had wanted to do for a long, long time—find out if there really was anything to these dreams, these visions. They had led her here, and by God, the house, at least, was real.

But was *he* really real? Or was the man she imagined nothing more than an adult extension of those invisible childhood friends her parents always said she chose to play with? How many times had she asked herself that? But now, with the steam of her breath the only thing between her and the unusual mansion, did she want to know?

She shivered, once again facing the truth. Christmas miracles were for Norman Rockwell paintings and classic television movies. They were the things kids believed in and adults, well, adults didn't believe in much, did they? Yet she'd just placed the biggest gamble of her life on a simple feeling. If she did learn it was nothing more than a figment of her imagination, wouldn't the magic be gone?

Magic or no magic, she couldn't overcome the aura of old money and class that radiated from this part of Lake Tahoe. The house was huge—probably bigger than her entire apartment complex. The yellow glow of light from the giant windows fell on the neatly manicured shrubs and flower beds.

The gap in social status was already so apparent, Kenna couldn't bring herself to knock on that door and face being looked down upon by an aristocrat. Her lower middle class existence would hardly make her welcome in places like this. Besides, who would she ask for? The man she felt she knew so well had never shared his name with her.

"Merry Christmas, Kenna," she whispered, blinking back a tear. Her heart was torn, half wanting—needing to believe he was there—the other half already convinced the whole idea was the biggest mistake she'd ever made.

Tomorrow, she'd come back. She hadn't come all this way to simply give up.

—☙☙—

He turned from the birthday celebration taking place at the other end of the dining room table and stared at the long windows lining the wall. The glass reflected the colorful festivity of his younger sister's party, hiding the dark, lonely waters of the lake. And so much more.

"Seth?" His mother's voice pulled him back to the table. Her eyes asked much more than her voice did. "Piece of cake?"

He nodded and held her gaze a moment longer. Had she sensed what he had? She *had* asked him several times if he felt different today. Her sixth sense or whatever she called it was so much stronger than his. Was this what she was talking about? This feeling hadn't been something he heard or felt. He supposed if he asked, she could describe it. But now wasn't the time. He'd just remain content in knowing, however it was he came to know. It would simply remain one of those unexplainable phenomena that couldn't be proved or disproved.

Taking the colorful plate from his nine-year-old foster sister, he winked and got up from the table. "I'm getting out of here before someone cries food fight!" he teased her.

"Don't *even* give Gina any ideas," his mother gasped, then addressed the other fourteen guests. "Pretend none of you heard what evil Seth just said."

He winked at his mom. The smile she returned didn't reach her clear blue eyes. He saw a longing there. A sadness. An emptiness that told him it was useless to walk over to the three-story floor-to-ceiling windows and look out onto the rocky beach below.

Because she knew what he'd find, and so did he. Nothing. The heart-wrenching sensation was already fading.

He searched the barrenness of the dark December night anyway.

"You staying tonight?"

"Are you nuts?" Seth turned and laughed at his stepfather, a distinguished businessman fresh from the office who looked ridiculous eating white cake with pink frosting from a cartoon character plate.

"I was hoping you were. I was going to ask for your keys."

Seth reached in his pocket. His condo was a stone's throw from the huge beach house he'd grown up in. "Here, take them. I've got a pull-out sofa."

"I'm just joking. Besides, your mother would shoot me between the eyes if I deserted her tonight. Why don't you get out of here while you have a chance?"

Despite the conversation, Seth's mind was on other things. His heart rate hadn't slowed even after visual confirmation of an empty beach. The feeling wouldn't go away. "I might have to. Hey, um, any truth to that heavy snow forecast for tonight?"

Richard Nelson took another bite and then shook his head. "That's a question for your mother. She's the one with the knack for those kind of things."

Indeed. A knack she didn't talk about, except when she coyly hinted he'd inherited some of her sixth sensing abilities. He'd have dismissed those claims too if there hadn't been those recurring, mysterious dreams. They made him feel exactly the way he felt now.

Seth's cell phone rang. Both men looked at it then smiled. The elder shook his head. "Shall I take your plate?"

Seth nodded and flipped open his phone as he jogged down the much narrower stairway leading to the lowest levels of the house. "'Lo," he called into the static greeting his ear.

"Excuse me, where the hell are you?"

He grinned. Samantha, bless her heart. "Sweetie, I told you today was Gina's birthday."

"Little girls have parties on Sunday afternoons, not Saturday nights."

"Since when did this family do anything normal?" he teased. "Besides, they're having a sleepover." Sam really was a beautiful girl, when she got her way. But that wasn't going to happen tonight. He really didn't care if she got riled up. He had no intention of letting her talk him into taking her out. There was something else he needed to figure out, something—someone much more important.

She huffed and likely pouted. This stunt was as old as time itself. It was a weekly ritual to remind her they were *not* together—they'd met when she dated his best friend, for God's sake—only to have her call and need a favor and end up touting herself as his girlfriend. He felt sorry for her, often went just to rescue her from herself. He did what he needed, and no one on this side of Carson City could blame him for taking from the woman who seemed to never learn how to give.

Seth glanced at the sky as he exited the house at the lowest level and started the trek up the outdoor stairs. "What was it you had in mind for tonight?" he asked, even as he thought of ways to weasel out of it. Sure, he could use a good fuck to get rid of the pre-holiday stress, but it wasn't Sam's perfect body he was thinking of.

He shivered and turned, only half listening to Sam's prattling about the clubs she wanted to visit. While different from earlier, he still felt . . . something. It was in the very air around him, as if it were charged with electricity. He wanted—felt the empty need inside him so profoundly he could scarcely keep his mind on the conversation.

"I d-d-don't think I'm up for that tonight," he stuttered as he scanned the shadows around him. "I'll call you tomorrow."

He closed the phone and slipped it back onto his belt and waited.

The feeling washed over him, coating him along with the cold mist. The emotion it carried burrowed into his flesh and warmed him. He hadn't felt anything this intense since he'd fallen down these very steps and broken his leg. When he'd woken from surgery, he'd felt the pull. He'd sworn he was being tugged from his lover's arms. There'd never been a memory more clear than those hours he'd been unconscious but so very aware of the woman who shared that time with him—and shared herself so fully.

"Where are you?" he whispered into the night. It'd been so long since he'd felt her touch, heard her voice. She'd haunted him so often as a teenager and even through his wild college years. Hell, she was probably the one thing that'd kept him alive.

Just the memory of those wild parties and willing girls made him shudder. At the time, there was nothing better, nothing more he could have asked for—except to find the girl he dreamed about.

He'd searched for her everywhere, every vacation he'd gone on with his parents, all the traveling he did while playing college baseball and even now with the league. She was the one goal he held above all else and the one thing that had kept him going when he'd sprained his shoulder and sat out half his junior year. She kept him from drinking himself to death. When he broke his leg and he was sure his career was over, she had been there. God, she held him! Stroked his hair when he cried in his sleep, pressed her lips to his to quiet his insistence that he'd never be able to run. He'd chase the belief she was real, and out there looking for him, until he died.

Shaking off the chill of those memories, he opened his eyes and looked around, knowing he'd never see her. The storm he expected still lumbered to the west, preceded by the icy rain that was just starting to fall. The house was well lit, but where the shadows began, an opaque fog blurred the landscape and made him feel so incredibly alone.

Yet she was here. Part of him. Part of every breath he took, every beat of his heart, he felt her. He couldn't ever remember experiencing these feelings with such clarity, at least while he was awake. This pull, this recognition is what he'd expected if he ever found her. He'd instantly feel the connection as soon as he saw her. His chest tightened, his skin went cold, his palms damp as he clenched and unclenched his fists.

His breath shuddered as he breathed out. "Where are you? I know you," he said, lifting his hand. "Who are you?"

A brush of something warm touched his fingertips. He closed his eyes, memorizing the moment. Then he closed his fist, shook off the layer of dampness that had settled on his clothes and got into his truck. He didn't know what he was chasing, but he wasn't going to question it.

His heart pounded rhythmically, *she's here*.

Halfway to the main road, he nearly hit Samantha's Mercedes.

"Shit," he muttered. All he wanted to do was try to figure out what the hell he could do to find this woman who touched his mind so easily. He had no time for his ex-girlfriend's shallow prattling.

The mirror of her low-slung sedan was dangerously close to pinstriping the bed of his truck as Samantha backed up so their windows were even. "You hung up on me!" she accused, arranging her features into just the perfect pout.

Not tonight, sunshine. There wasn't anything that could convince him to take Samantha instead of the woman who occupied his thoughts—no—occupied his very soul. "I never promised I'd take you out."

"But we always go out on Saturday night."

"We don't always do anything. I've made it clear many, many times. I will make no commitment to you—on any level. Get it out of your head. That includes standing Saturday night dates. Hell, last week you left with another man anyway."

She fluffed her hair and laughed at him, finding his cruelty amusing. "That's because you said you were going home and I still hadn't been to The Peak."

Seth rolled his eyes and refused to argue his point on visiting the area's newest club on opening night. He was a local, not a tourist. He didn't thrive on neon lights and watered-down beer. "Then perhaps you should have called that guy instead of driving all the way over here to practice your guilt trips."

She didn't seem fazed. Usually he found her attitude entertaining in an arrogant sort of way. Right now it was damn irritating. "Speaking of driving out here, my bad, bad Seth, who was the girl in the silver car I passed on the ridge?"

"There's been no one else down here." Surely he'd have known if there was another vehicle near the house. Wouldn't he have heard it? Seen the lights curling around the slippery roads?

"Well, I sure as hell wasn't imagining it. Oh, well, probably a tourist got lost or something. Come to think of it, she did have out of town plates."

He shrugged even as the knot in his gut twisted painfully. No. Not possible. *Was it?* Or were his mother's comments and the earlier sensations making him look for clues that weren't really there? "I'm going home," he lied. He was going to drive around until he was sure it was all a figment of his imagination.

"Need company?"

"No." He floored the truck and took the corners as quickly as he dared.

$$\sim \!\! \infty \!\! \sim$$

Kenna sat at the four-way stop and struggled to remember which road in this maze of hills and cliffs would take her back to the outrageously priced resort cabin she'd rented for the week.

She flexed her fingers, still awed at the sensation she'd felt there—the warm touch of his hand. It was the first time she'd ever experienced such intensity outside of her dreams. No one would believe it if she tried to explain it. They'd say it was just her mind making it up or nothing more than the air current blowing by. But nothing could replace the warm, electric feel of skin on skin, even if it was for a brief, fingertip-grazing moment.

She sighed as the voltage of his touch circulated through her body. Every time she'd felt their physical connection, there'd been a rush of emotion. She could recall the empty loneliness, a starving sadness. But this time—maybe that's why she'd felt it without the aid of her dreams—this time she'd felt a hungry passion.

Her body tingled with excitement. It scared her—frightened her terribly. If she thought too long about the fact she'd driven hundreds of miles, following nothing more than a mental notion and some strange dreams, and now sat at a stop sign, lusting over a man who very possibly didn't even exist, well, it was almost too much to fathom.

A horn sounded behind her.

With a half laugh at herself, she proceeded forward. She was more than lost in these rambling roads. If anything, however, the trip was worth it. To say she'd been to Lake Tahoe—and now, the week before Christmas with all these fabulous houses pristinely decorated with twinkling white lights . . . it was a sight she'd never forget.

The bright lights of the truck behind her flashed in her rearview mirror, blinding her. She shielded her eyes and pulled as far to the right as she could. Asshole. If he was so damn impatient, he could go around.

Instead, he stopped behind her.

Shit. She punched the button to automatically lock the doors and debated if she should just take off again. When she saw the interior light flicker behind her, she knew he was getting out.

Kenna's hand still tingled from that . . . connection? Had she really felt his touch? She closed her fist over that grasp of hope and held on tight. Maybe she was close. Maybe he was here.

She shut her eyes, took a deep breath. But the decision was easy. She wasn't going to stick around and have God-knows-what happen to her before she had gathered up enough courage to knock on the ornate door and . . . and what?

Precisely. She hadn't figured that out. She needed to create a plan. And she definitely needed to be alive to do it.

She hit the gas just as the shape of a man reached the rear bumper of her car. Eying the rear mirror as she pulled away, she saw him throw his arms up, as if amazed she'd bolted.

Phew!

For the first time since she'd driven out of her driveway—with the exception of that much-too-brief touch—she laughed. A bit of a frantic, panicked laugh but a laugh nonetheless.

It turned into a whimper when those headlights bobbed in her rearview mirror just moments later. She refused to pull over again. While she could call 911, she'd first have to get to her phone, which was in the bottom of her purse on the passenger side floor-board. Then there was the minor problem—she didn't even know what *road* she was on.

No, she'd continue driving until she came to something public—bar, restaurant, gas station. There had to be something nearby.

By some stroke of luck, she turned a corner and found a strip of brightly lit shopping plaza and several fast-food restaurants. It was at one of these she pulled into a parking place right near the front windows and grabbed her purse.

Swallowing her fear, she willed her fingers to open her car

door and then made a beeline for the entrance without looking at the giant black truck pulling into the parking place beside her.

"Wait!" he called out just as her hand connected with the door.

Kenna froze, every nerve in her body unable to respond as her mind processed his voice.

"—mean to scare you," he was saying as her vision came into focus again. Her skin felt on fire as he reached around her and pushed the door open. "Get inside, it's freezing out here."

She complied, glad to be out of the cold and in a place with lots of witnesses.

He wore no coat—only a thick hooded sweatshirt. Breathing became a voluntary activity as she looked at him—really stopped and looked at him. People pushed past them and got into line as they stood there, the busy activities of the busy restaurant around her were only barely registering.

Was it him? It was. Her body screamed its acknowledgment. She couldn't help but stare at him. She memorized his features, from his sparkling green eyes and sinfully thick eyelashes to his beautiful mouth with its full lower lip. His jaw was strong, the lines of his face classically masculine. And she thought she'd made up the idea that he was utterly gorgeous.

But it wasn't his physical familiarity, because she couldn't have picked him out of a crowd based on looks alone. There was his voice, his . . . aura, his essence. She couldn't define it—never expected to have to. She just knew.

"Are you okay?" he said.

She sucked in oxygen then exhaled slowly. "You—uh . . . I . . ." Words wouldn't come. God, she felt so thunderstruck.

"I really am sorry for scaring you like this."

She fixated on his hands as he rubbed them together and then wiped them on his jeans. Oh God. His jeans. Snug, faded denim hugged his muscular thighs. His right pocket was frayed from shoving his hand into his pocket, as he did now. Damn shame the rest was hidden by the sweatshirt.

"Please say something because you're starting to worry me."

She jerked her eyes upward and met his laughing green eyes. So much heat radiated from their depths she broke into a sweat. It was a damn sin to look so cute and sexy all at once, yet he pulled it off.

"Sorry," she managed and bit her lip.

He grinned, creasing his cheeks with deep furrows that couldn't be called dimples and were devastatingly more delicious. But at the same time she realized it couldn't be him.

She'd always imagined when they met, they'd know. Their eyes would connect and there would be no question, no doubt. The entire world should have melted away, leaving just the two of them and their magical connection.

Wake up, Kenna—that hadn't happened, at least on his part. Which made her wonder if lack of sleep and the shock of finding the house had shorted out her senses.

"I-I . . . was lost. Sorry. I don't know this town and, well, one can't be too careful. You never know who you might meet." She tried to smile. The man before her was nothing more than a handsome stranger. The rush she'd felt was nothing more than a side effect of her whole purpose of coming here, coupled with being followed. Adrenaline rush. Nothing more.

"It happens. I would have helped you find your way out."

"I managed." She said it quickly and fisted her purse then looked back at the line. Last thing she wanted was food, but it'd seem foolish to walk back out.

"I see that."

She shuffled her feet and stared at the university insignia on his chest. "Well, sorry I made you run all the way over here. I'll just be—"

"What's your name?" he asked, sticking out his hand.

She took a deep breath and steeled herself against the disappointment she knew she'd feel when it was once again proven he wasn't *the one*. "Kenna. Kenna McGurly."

"I'm Seth Parker. Nice to meet you."

She placed her hand in his.

Two

Seth watched as her small hand slid into his. She trembled like a frightened rabbit. And the smile that should have made her beautiful left her eyes tragically empty.

What an ass he was, following her like that. Poor girl. He'd followed her as if—as if what? She'd been the woman of his dreams?

The sadness in her features echoed in his soul. While she was dainty, almost fragile in size, those giant brown eyes gazed up at him with carefully guided interest, and something else. Hell, he should be counting his blessings she actually accepted his apology for such behavior. Men were arrested for less.

"Can you get to your place from here?" he asked, finding himself wanting to pull her into his arms and protect her from the others out there who would dare to endanger her. It broke his heart to think of her getting lost, alone in those spiraling, empty roads. The rain was already turning to ice and soon it'd be covered under a layer of snow—making it extra dangerous, especially to those who didn't know the terrain.

Not to mention his emotions were crashing quickly from the

letdown of feeling—and sensing no recognition from her. The hum of electricity had nearly ebbed from his body in disappointment.

"I think so. I have a map in the car."

"Let me buy you a coffee. Do you want to grab your map and I'll show you the best way in?"

After he said it, he realized he was giving her an out, an escape. Probably not a bad idea, considering the way he felt right now. Despite his best efforts to ignore it, the subtle floral scent of her perfume and the way her slight curves filled out her jeans were etched in his mind.

He let his gaze follow her as she rounded the front of the building to where her car was parked. Kenna seemed nice, was attractive enough and there seemed to definitely be chemistry there, but it wasn't the . . . the what? She wasn't *the one*. Shaking her hand had been no different than touching anyone else. And it should have been different. Like that graze against his fingertips that sent his blood racing and heart pounding.

Still, he'd frightened the shit out of her, based on the way her hands still shook and her eyes darted to him and the door several times. It'd be a miracle if she came back in.

Seth pushed back his damp hair and noted it was now snow, not just rain falling. Perfect. He got in line and figured he deserved a coffee before pointing the nose of his truck toward his condo and putting an end to this very much fucked-up day.

"Seth!"

He caught her as she rushed in, dripping wet with remnants of snowflakes in her hair. Her eyes were red. Tears? Oh, shit. He couldn't, didn't want to, handle tears. Too late—his heart had seen them. "What is it?"

She stepped into his arms and dropped her forehead against his chest. So much defeat in her gesture. He pulled her back, needing the story before his body got the wrong idea. "What happened?"

"I—oh I'm such a dunce. I locked my keys in my car." She backed away and looked at him like Gina did when she'd gotten caught snooping through his room. Apologetic, meek. He didn't want to see those things on Kenna's face.

Then she smiled. God, that twisted something inside him.

"I'm sorry. I'm just so tired. I don't normally just fall apart like this. In fact, I don't think I ever—"

"It's easily fixed. Sit right here." He gripped her shoulders and pushed until she sat in the chair behind her. "I'll get us some coffee and call in a favor. Can't have you paying tourist rates for a lockout when it was all my fault."

She tried to object, her face red with her obvious embarrassment, but he shook his head and touched his finger to her lips.

That innocent touch sent the air rushing from his lungs. Wow. Her eyes were wide, as if she'd felt the connection. But no, duh, how stupid of him. *Just scare her some more, moron. Normal people don't go around touching strangers on the mouth like that.*

He sat down across from her after procuring a pair of small coffees. In line, he'd needed to pull his mind from the enigma of Kenna and how he now couldn't tell the difference between the way she affected him and the weird feelings he'd had earlier, so he made the phone call and was promised help was on its way to take her back out of his life.

"So, you're uh, meeting someone here, for vacation, I mean?"

Kenna studied her cup and twisted the sugar packet. "Nuh uh."

"Really? You're here alone?"

Goddammit. He'd done it again—gone and scared the light right out of those beautiful eyes. "I just can't imagine," he stammered to explain. "You're not up here on a romantic getaway or honeymoon or something. This side of the lake is so beautiful. And secluded."

What was *wrong* with him?

She silently twisted her cup.

"I'm just gonna shut up now, because clearly I can't seem to keep from upsetting you." He took a swig of the coffee and wished he'd had something to strengthen it. Best thing he could do, despite wanting to know this mysterious woman who vacationed alone—in an expensive resort town like this, right at Christmastime. There was definitely a story behind those haunted eyes, one that called to his soul. Still, he couldn't help but believe he was personifying the woman in his mind more than he should. Good thing he hadn't blurted *that* out. She'd surely believe him to be some psycho head case then.

"I-I came here . . ." she started, looking at him with such intensity he wondered if she were looking through him. "I needed to come here."

Kenna swallowed. Did she want to tell him? Did she need someone to talk to? Who else was going to listen? The idea of another man picking her up or even talking to her had the hair standing up on the back of his neck. No. If she wanted to talk, he'd listen.

"Needed to get away, then?"

Kenna nodded then tilted her head and chewed her lip. He stared, wondering why that gesture seemed so inviting and almost . . . familiar. He took in the rest of her. Her hair was brown. No sign of highlights or all the other fancy stuff the women seemed to love adding to their hair. She wore little makeup, just a bit at the corners of her eyes—enough to make them seem to dominate her entire face. If she'd put on lipstick, she'd chewed it off long ago. But her lips looked soft, a pale pink reminding him of the inside of seashells he'd loved to pick up on vacations in Mexico.

"Why are you smiling?" she asked.

"Something—you just reminded me of something from my childhood. A good memory. Thanks."

"Care to share?"

"Only if you're willing to tell me what you're running from."

She stood up and pulled her purse back up on her shoulder. "I didn't say I was running away. I'm actually looking for something here. Oh, and the locksmith pulled up."

Seth turned in his seat and watched her walk to the door with amazing poise.

His mom could have her sixth sense mumbo jumbo. Right now the hum in his body wasn't caused by some invisible force that seemed to play havoc on his senses. No, the reason he'd started stuttering and staring had everything to do with the new girl in town. And he wasn't done with her yet. He kept one eye on the locksmith's progress as he sipped his coffee and tried to get his jumbled brain to work.

—◦◦◦—

Kenna glanced up at the knock on her window. Seth. Half of her was giddy he'd followed her out, the other half disappointed because she knew it wasn't for the reason she wanted. She'd even begun to wonder if she was wrong.

"Thanks for helping me out tonight. And for the coffee. It was great meeting you."

"My fault, remember? And listen, it's dark and the roads are icy. Why don't you let me get you where you're going? I'll feel much better if I know you're not lost again."

Her first response was something like "Hell, no." But she wavered a little at the thought of negotiating the roads in this weather. The snow was getting thicker and the wind was picking up. "I suppose," she started, studying his features in case she never got this close to him again. "If you were a bad guy I'd be dead already. Can you get me here?" She passed over the notebook paper with the address of her cabin sprawled sideways on it.

"Hey, that's pretty close to my house anyway. You weren't far off track."

He smiled. God, he had a nice smile. Made her all warm inside. It'd do more than that if she allowed herself to think about it. *Maybe tonight,* she came just short of whispering as she rolled the window up and waited for him to back out of the parking place. *A hot bath, a hot fantasy . . .*

For once she'd made the right decision. The weather disintegrated quickly, forcing her to lean forward and squint just to see the road in front of her. Seth's truck was nothing more than a pair of faint red lights in front of her. She'd never have made it alone.

She didn't even argue when he took the key from her hand and opened the small cabin. She followed behind slowly as he walked through and turned on lights and cranked up the furnace.

The house was amazing. She'd dreaded she'd gotten suckered

into renting a shack with a dirt floor—but just the opposite, this place was worth what she was paying—and more. Way more. The man she rented it from hadn't said anything about it being decorated for the holidays, yet it was, from a gorgeous, rustic-style decorated tree in the corner to the quilted and patched stockings above the mantel—and a wonderfully scented pine wreath above that.

The fireplace caught her eye and held her attention. "Did you see any wood outside?"

He didn't answer, so she turned to go look for herself, but he was there. Right there.

A step back and a few long seconds later she inhaled again. His scent surrounded her, coating the air around her like a comforting blanket. Without even touching her, he held her—mesmerized in his presence. Their breaths, puffs of silver mist, merged and then faded. It was a perfect moment—to her at least.

"Excellent," he said, clearly unaffected and probably thinking she was losing her mind staring at him all starry-eyed. "I was hoping you got a place with a fireplace. You'll be wanting a fire to keep you warm tonight." He knelt on the bricks in front of it and opened the glass doors.

Considering she had no warm body to hold on to . . . The emotion poured out of her. She closed her eyes at the overwhelming emptiness she felt, just in that moment. The memory of why she was here, what she'd left behind and what she'd hoped to find all tangled together in one big sigh of despair.

She jerked as an iron prod clanged against the brick. Seth jumped to his feet and backed away from the hearth.

"Something wrong?" she asked, frowning at the fireplace.

He shook his head. "I'll get you some wood. Then I'll help you unload your luggage."

She noticed the tiny ceramic Christmas tree near the window and the golden star above it just as he opened the front door and let in the icy blast. It made her shiver, both from the cold and from the reminder why she was here. It had been her Christmas wish to find Seth, and here he was. But he was a damn riddle. One minute she swore there was something there in his eyes or the way he spoke, but then he seemed to draw back and looked at her as if she was nothing more than the stupid tourist girl he rescued from herself.

Last thing she wanted was to be a charity case. He made a damn fine knight in shining armor, but if the reasons were wrong, she could do without his help. Kenna made her way to the kitchen and checked the cabinets. Not exactly stocked, but there were some basic staples that would suffice until she could get to the store tomorrow. If she could find the store—she hadn't even attempted to pay attention to which way they'd come. She had just wanted to get here in one piece.

Still, it was something more than curiosity that pulled her back into the living room and made her lean against the doorway while watching him build a fire. His hands moved deftly, the tendons of his forearms flexing beneath pushed-up sleeves as he lifted chunks of wood and arranged them on the cradle. Capable, hardworking hands that defied the aura of money that seemed attached to him. Judging from the label of his jeans and the brand-new truck he drove—not to mention the house she assumed he lived in—well, her guess couldn't be far off.

It just made him a little more real—a little more like her when she saw him barely flinch as he jerked a sliver out of his thumb and continue arranging what would soon be a blazing fire.

"What?" he asked, catching her staring.

"Nothing," she said honestly. There was nothing she could, or was willing, to explain. She enjoyed watching him. It fed some deep need to feel his companionship. It felt natural. Right. It filled the void she'd been way too conscious of on the long drive here.

Even if she left without it, these moments, these fractured bits of dreams come true, made it all worthwhile.

"There's a ton of wood out there, but most of it's wet. And the snow has no intention of slowing down. The fun part about being up in the higher elevations." There was nothing fun about the grimace he gave her as he got up and walked toward the door. "See if you can find a large trash bag or two . . . or four. I'll help you get some wood in here to start drying."

"Hey, Seth," she said, amazed at his generosity. "Thanks."

His smile was warmer than any fire he could have built.

With her bag stowed away in the bedroom and enough wood for her entire stay, she realized there was no more reason for Seth to stick around. He even brushed his hands repeatedly on his jeans and glanced around.

"You should get going. Used to it or not, that's a helluva storm out there."

"You got a phone, right?"

"Yeah, I was prepared for a few days of roughing it alone. I'm set. But I do thank you for saving me the struggle of hauling in the wood."

"Sure."

Silence.

Go, Kenna screamed silently, *go before I read more than just some Boy Scout honor thing into your hesitance to leave.*

"Take down my number then. In case there's a problem. If I can't help, I can find someone who can."

"I—"

"Just humor me, I'll sleep better tonight."

At least you'll sleep. She just knew she'd be up all night imagining a million different ways this meeting could have happened. And then she'd think of a million more scenarios about how this night could have ended. "Let me dig out a pen."

Fate was laughing at her, she thought as she walked in the kitchen.

Two steps later and she realized just how badly she'd jinxed herself with that mental statement. The room was plunged into darkness. As if she knew where to even start looking for a spare lightbulb in this house.

"Kenna?" Seth's voice seemed to surround her—filling all the spaces she couldn't see. Just the soft, inquiring way he said her name left her shivering.

"It's just my luck. You wouldn't happen to know where they keep the spare lightbulbs in this—"

"The power's out. Storm knocked it out."

She swallowed. "Oh." What was she going to do now? Sit in front of the fire until the lights came on?

"Which means I'm staying here tonight."

Three

You can't—" Kenna stopped short, realizing she was suggesting he head out into the blizzard. "Never mind."

She felt him step closer. His warmth permeated the room, his presence like a blanket around her. She knew his relief as if it were her own. Stranger or not, she couldn't live with herself if something happened on his way home. And it seemed hard to regard him as a stranger even though she'd known him less than an hour. It became more and more apparent there was some link—some unexplainable connection between them had been present for as long as she could remember.

Despite the concern she should have over the weather outside, it was the storm inside her that kept her attention. The room suddenly seemed thick and hot. Every sense strained to learn where he was in the room. The very slight rasp of his breath put him near the edge of the room. A brush of clothing made her think he had moved closer. Her imagination had him stepping behind her. His hands slid around her waist and pulled her against him. Unbelieving, she reached down and grazed the fingers resting on her hips.

"Hey!" he said from at least five feet away.

"What?"

"Nothing. I just must have hit something that shocked me."

Her knees locked. She grabbed for the counter she knew was just behind her to steady herself as she digested the news. Was it true? Or were his fingers tingling from the brush with hers—*the one that happened in her mind?*

But he said nothing more. Her heartbeat slowly slowed to a reasonable pace as he cleared his throat and said, "I, uh, know I've not exactly given you reason to trust me so far. But answer honestly. Are you afraid of me?"

"No."

It was the truth. Afraid of herself, maybe. Afraid of how she might react if he gave her any more signs he sensed their amazing connection. But she didn't fear him, despite the fact he was a stranger who had just announced he was staying the night with her.

"You're sure? Because I've got another bombshell to drop on you."

Her heart threatened to leap out of her chest. She gasped— she heard it echo in the room. Her fingers ached from the death grip she had on the edge of the counter. Never had she felt such anticipation. She absolutely shook while she waited for him to say it—say anything to acknowledge her.

"Two bits of news, actually. First—I'm not getting any signal on my cell phone and likely you won't either. We're rather remote and the thick cover isn't helping. However I can try to get a message through using the CB I have in my truck. I'll go out in a minute and get it and the emergency kit I keep in there. I don't know how long we might be stuck here. And that, actually, is the second part of my news. We need to get settled in for the long haul."

"How *long?*" she repeated.

"Where are you from?"

She nearly laughed at his question—and the way he delivered it. He must think she'd never seen so much snow or never known the power of a blizzard. The opposite was true. But perhaps living in a place where snowstorms were the norm in late December made one take things like snowplows for granted. "Just north of Lansing, Michigan."

"Oh."

"And yes, we have a lot of snow there," she answered his unspoken question. "But I've never been snowed in. Not in the true literal sense."

"You're snowed in now. You have no electricity and the only source of heat is the fireplace." She smiled as she imagined him ticking these things off on his fingers. "We'll try to find candles and set out some bowls to collect fresh snow for water. And we'll both be sleeping on the floor in the living room."

That was supposed to shock her. Not only was this stranger staying the night, but they were going to be sleeping in very close proximity. It hadn't crossed her mind—there hadn't been time to think that far ahead. But he was right. The furnace hadn't been on long enough to even start chasing the chill out of the cabin. It would only get colder as the arctic wind buffeted the outside walls. However, the prospect of curling up to Seth's body heat had her skin burning in anticipation. A mental picture popped into her head—a vision of the two of them with their arms wrapped around each other.

Her nipples tightened and stomach clenched. A tingle of awareness shot between her legs as the fantasy picture added the thought of a hard cock pressed against her backside, hot breath on the back of her neck.

"Kenna," he breathed. He was there.

Right there. Standing behind her.

Her body swayed, pulled toward his like a magnet. The connection was every bit as electrical as she'd expected, the hard planes of his chest against her shoulder blades, his thick muscular arms curling around her. And the pressure of his groin against her ass left nothing to the imagination. Nothing.

She breathed out but intentionally kept her eyes closed as she savored and memorized each of the sensations he created within her.

But as quickly as he caught her, he righted her and stepped away. Clearing his throat, he muttered, "I've got a flashlight with my stuff in the truck. I'm going to get it before I can't get *to* my truck."

This really was happening.

Kenna wrapped her arms around herself and refused to move from the support of the counter. Fearing the magic would disappear haunted her, yet she knew there was more—so much more left to experience with him. No one had ever affected her so deeply. How could she doubt his identity when the slightest things—his voice, the proximity of his body, the depth of his eyes all set her world on its axis. Of course, there was only one man she dreamed about—and in her dreams he'd never been more than a silhouette, a figure in the mist and, if she were lucky, the amazing sensation of touch.

This was what she came for—the culmination of all those fantasies, wishes and unexplainable dreams.

Yet there was a certain amount of melancholy that hung with her, the sadness of knowing it was all one-sided.

The cold air was a welcome blast. Had it been just a few hours before he'd asked Richard about an impending storm? He'd expected cold rain, perhaps sleet—even anticipated a thunderstorm—not this uncharacteristic blizzard. He glanced skyward, the empty grayness all around him dotted with giant white flakes—and little else. It was as if the rest of the world had been obliterated and it was only him—and Kenna—left.

And *her*.

He'd felt her. Heard her whisper something provocative in his ear, though he couldn't remember the precise words. He'd closed his eyes to relish the sound, to absorb as much as he could there in the darkness. But then she'd wrapped around him like a warm blanket, teasing, calling to his most primitive instincts. His body had immediately responded with a gnawing hunger for her.

She'd touched him. He'd felt her graze his face, her fingers traced his jaw before she was gone.

When he reached for her, his hand had connected to warm, feminine flesh.

Kenna.

That had scared the shit out of him.

He certainly hadn't been able to ignore the fact they'd be sharing blankets in front of the fire to stay warm, but he had every intention of remaining a perfect gentleman. There was definitely something between them, a chemistry of sorts, but she'd given him no invitation to come up from behind her in the dark room and touch her that way. Come to think of it, he was damn lucky he'd gotten away without a good blow to the head. Or groin.

He closed his eyes and let the snow melt on the fevered bare flesh of his hands and face. But even dispensing with all his clothes wouldn't be able to cool him down. Not tonight—maybe not ever.

Because even if he did let the attraction between himself and Kenna lead to sex, he had a feeling it would only remind him how much he needed to find the woman who haunted him—and taunted him.

"Any clue what time it is?" Kenna asked him as he piled his extra sweatshirt, spare blanket, first aid and emergency roadside kits beside the hearth. The dim light of the fire glanced off her silhouette and made her seem nothing more than a ghost in the middle of the room.

"Little before seven."

"Too early for bed then." Even from several feet away, he heard her sharp intake of breath then watched her turn so her profile studied the fire. Her throat undulated gently as she swallowed, her words clearly embarrassing her. "I mean—"

"I know what you mean. But why don't we get everything set up anyway. Do you want to go strip all the blankets off the beds and bring them in here?"

"I would. But I don't think I can find the bedrooms."

He laughed then, the amusement in her voice cracking through the awkwardness that had settled between them. They were taking this way too seriously. Both of them. "You didn't happen to find any candles, did you?"

Her hands lifted to her hips. He bet her eyes were sparkling with some sarcastic comment she had the willpower to hold back. Maybe there was hope for them yet.

He had to say it. "You mean you can't see in the dark?"

"Uh, no. That particular skill isn't in my repertoire."

Shit. The throaty way she'd formed those words had his mind suggesting he'd want to explore what her other skills *were*. He shifted away from her and dug into his bag to find the flashlight he'd tossed in there. His hardened cock stretched against his jeans painfully. His problem. No sense scaring her off yet again.

"Damn. Mine either. Hold on, I'm looking for the flashlight." His eyes were adjusting to the low light, but that didn't help him as he searched through his bag by sense of touch. He couldn't take his eyes off her.

"You don't happen to have a whirlpool tub in there, do you?"

"What?" She'd moved closer to the fire and he could see the way her eyes crinkled just slightly at the corners when she laughed. Her lips were pulled tight into a smile. With the fire-light's reflection, what he'd considered plain brown hair had come to life with its own flames of red and gold. She really was beautiful. Maybe not classically pretty like Samantha, but there was a life that shone through, lighting up her features. He couldn't tear his gaze from her.

"I said," she repeated as she knelt down beside him and peered into his bag, "I wondered if you had a tub in there. You know, Jacuzzi? All I wanted all day was to get here and soak in a nice hot tub."

His mouth went dry. How could this woman be disarming his ability to think, piece by piece? There was nothing... wrong with what she had said, but in his mind, he'd watched her slide her shirt over her head, letting her fingers trace over the smooth skin over her stomach as she then loosened the button of her jeans. The wicked way she shook her hips to pull the stubborn denim over those gently swelling curves...

"The flashlight. Can I have it?"

He passed it over, unable to speak or even blink.

"Thanks," she said, leaning so close he could smell her shampoo. Clean. None of the fancy floral or fruity scents the women of his past had used. The scent of a woman. He breathed her in, catching a whiff of the coffee she'd recently sipped and a light hint of subtle perfume she'd probably dotted to her wrists and neck. Nothing overpowering. Sexy as hell.

And just as quickly, she straightened, flipped on the beam and illuminated the far wall. "Perfect," she said. "I'll be right back."

He exhaled. So much for him staying to make sure she'd survive this storm. It was he who needed rescuing right now.

"Here." Kenna handed Seth a pair of long, thin candles. "I think they were intended as decoration but..."

"They'll work."

Together they'd pulled every sheet, blanket, bedspread and even the afghan off the couch and spread them out on the floor in front of the fireplace. The wind howled through unseen cracks in the frame structure without pausing for breath. There were times she wondered if it were possible for the entire building to be lifted from the side of the mountain.

Their fingers brushed as he took the tapers from her.

"You're cold."

Freezing. So was he. He'd rubbed his hands up and down his arms several times in the last few minutes. "Are we going to have enough wood?"

"We should. Or else we start burning the dining room furniture."

"Oh God. There goes my damage deposit."

"I don't think it'll come to that. Besides, we've got each other to keep warm."

Damn the weak light. And the angle she'd chosen to sit, which prevented her from seeing his true expression. She silently cursed her heart *and* her body for reading way too much into his statement.

Damn him for leaning forward and grabbing her hand, forcing her to slide up beside him.

Damn her for even questioning the purpose. At least she didn't let it stop her. Seth tugged a blanket up over their shoulders and stretched another over their laps. It wasn't so different than sitting in the stands for a football game or even gathered around a campfire—though she'd never been camping where one had to snuggle close to another person for the sake of staying warm. There was usually a different reason.

Oh, there went her mind again.

She pulled her lip between her teeth and bit down, hoping the pain would keep her thoughts above the waistline. Glancing over, she smiled.

"You shouldn't do that." His eyes strayed down until he focused on her mouth. She couldn't help it, she licked her lips. "You shouldn't do that either," he said, his voice much lower and softer.

Kenna swallowed. And waited. He was going to kiss her. She was about ready to explode with a rush of adrenaline that coursed through her veins at the thought. Him. Seth. The man who she connected with mentally on so many deep, deep levels was here, in her place, literally—in her bed and now he was going to kiss her.

"Kenna?" he whispered.

She barely heard him above the sound of blood thundering through her veins. "Hmm?" she said, her eyes flitting from his mouth to his very intense gaze.

He didn't answer. His eyes captured her gaze and held it until he was too close to focus. His breath hit her first. It seared through her flesh and went straight for her heart. Then his lips grazed hers, a touch so soft and tender it made her ache with the purity of it. It was all she could do to stifle a sob. The flesh along her lower back ignited as his arm snaked around and rested on her hip. From the point of contact, thousands of firework-type sparks burst throughout her body and all seemed to land at the juncture of her thighs. My God, she was going to spontaneously combust—from just one kiss.

She lost it when he touched her chin, lifting and angling her mouth, and then brushed his lips across hers again. She gasped, giving him an opening to deepen the kiss.

Fire leapt from his fingertips as he slid them along her jaw. Kenna fisted her hands, digging her fingernails into the blankets as she sought something to ground her, to remind her this wasn't a dream, some special, all-too-real dream that would end with her back in her lonely, cold bed.

This was real.

Seth's fingers tightened on her waist as he took her lower lip between his and lightly suckled, then closed his teeth over it.

Lightning bolts shot through her body. She jerked at the jolt she felt directly in her womb.

"Okay," he breathed out after releasing her mouth and resting his forehead against hers. "I can see why you bite your lip. It's rather a pleasurable experience."

Dead. History. How would she *ever* survive a night with him?

Her panties were drenched, though they'd been damp since she'd first laid eyes on him. Her sex was swollen. Her pulse beat there, where her jeans pressed against her sensitive pussy lips. But that wasn't the pressure she wanted—what she craved.

She had a feeling all she had to do was say yes.

Yes! Yes! Yes! Her mind screamed it for her. "I agree," she said. All she had to do was lift her chin and she could do the same to him. Need coursed through her body as she lowered her eyes to his mouth.

Sweet Lord, the things she imagined his mouth doing to her body. Never had she imagined simply looking at a man's lips to be such a turn-on, but now she couldn't find the self-control to tear her eyes away.

Seth settled the dilemma for her by tasting her again. He turned her into putty. Her body felt languid, some strange mix between totally relaxed and stretched to the edge with desire. Emotions, sensations, need, want, all swirled inside her, fueled by the intangible, unnamable drive that had brought her to this place so she could be in his arms.

She could kiss him forever. The more his soft lips slid over hers, the sharp edges of his teeth enhancing the pleasure, the hot, sweet texture of his tongue as it tangled with hers. It'd be so easy to lose herself. Oh hell, she was already lost to him. The crackling sound of the fire, the soft blankets, the snowstorm raging outside, forcing him to stay with her. She couldn't have staged it any better herself.

A whimper escaped her, an overflow of the emotion she couldn't hold in. And he took it, devouring the sound with his mouth. The slight stubble of a day's beard scraped her cheek as he angled his lips over hers. She felt it all the way to her pussy, the muscles there tensed and shuddered. She wanted to feel that sensation there, the gravelly hint of sandpaper against her inner thighs as he rose between them to taste her. Even now, the way his tongue lapped between her parted lips mimicked the intimate kiss she craved.

The room vibrated with the growl he emitted as he pulled away from her and stared into the fire.

She feared empty coldness would replace the heat that had built up in her body. She waited for it, waited for his words to turn her blood from molten lava to pure ice.

It didn't come.

"Before we regret this—before I question what the fuck I'm thinking by even doing this—Kenna, tell me. Do you want to stop?"

Incredible. Half his face was bathed in the yellow firelight, defining the sharp edges to his cheekbones and chin and giving him almost an ethereal look. The other half was shadowed, not quite sinister but certainly mysteriously sensual. A barely-there smile played at his lips. His eyes were dark, heavy lidded with the desire she felt radiating off of him. That moment was the one she wanted imbedded into her mind forever. Those words. *Do you want me to stop?* Never.

She blinked then let her eyes trace his contradiction in features one more time before parting her lips, but then shaking her head as no voice would come forth. He rose to his hands and knees and advanced on her. This was wild, untamed. She felt no fear, only pure amazement that he looked at *her* with such dark hunger. Her.

Her heart slammed into her chest when she understood the depth of her love for him. It encompassed all she was—to the point of totally surrendering herself, heart, soul and body to the man of her dreams.

Four

Okay, she was hot. Between the fire he'd built with matches and wood and the one he'd stoked inside her, she was doomed to combust. Kenna tried to breathe as she pushed at the covers, unable to see her awkward movements because her focus was so locked on Seth's face.

One side of his smile tipped upward, emphasizing the devilish glint in his eyes. He grabbed her ankles and swung them around, then tugged. The blankets bunched. She fell back. And died. No other way to describe the heat of hell and the taste of heaven she experienced as Seth loomed over her.

He would take her. Oh God, just the formation of that thought in her head made her pussy swell and create more fluid, preparing for his invasion. His welcome invasion. She licked her lips, anticipating. The moment lasted forever but was hours too long. She could read nothing in his eyes, nothing except the mirror of her own lust—there was no denying this volatile chemistry.

A charm slid from his sweatshirt and swayed between them. A sterling symbol on a black rope. She reached for it, needing to touch him, something of his. It called to her, she didn't question it, just acted.

Seth lifted his hand and covered hers. She gasped and met his eyes. Something passed over his face, a moment of closure, of opaque doubt.

"Seth," she whispered, unable to release her grip. Afraid he'd pull away, end this magic, she tugged downward, forcing him toward her body.

The twinge of fear melted when the heat in his eyes reignited the fire. Their hands dropped away from the token between them. He lowered his head and pressed a kiss to her stomach.

The skin there burned as if the layers of clothes didn't exist. The innocence of the act tore at her heart. Hope lingered. Maybe it wasn't all about blistering lust. Maybe there was some affection, a return of one iota of the feelings she recognized between them.

Thought of such things disappeared as Seth pulled himself up and lowered himself to one elbow. She bore the weight of him along her body—the blessed weight a woman aches to feel. It was all she could do not to arch up into the erection pressed against her groin. He was tall, lean—an athlete's body of hard muscle and taut flesh. Clothes mattered little, her body already knew.

The more she touched him, sliding her hand through his dark hair, the more confident she felt. She cupped his jaw and led him down to her for a kiss. As her finger grazed the velvety lobe of his ear, he shivered. His reaction fed the fire. She felt bolder and reached out to swipe her tongue over his lips before pressing inside for another of his intoxicating kisses.

His free hand stroked the length of her body—from the sensitive skin over her ribs that made her squirm with a new sense of erotic awareness to the way his fingers dug in and lingered right at her hip. *Touch me,* she wanted to plead. The anticipation was preparation enough. She was ready to push the slow, torturous foreplay aside and dispose of their clothes so she could feel his hand on her bare flesh.

A moan slipped from her at the thought. She arched her head back, offering up her body. It wasn't about planned moves or taking certain steps. Fire had no roadmap, and neither did the equally destructive flames Seth conjured from his fingers.

He pressed his hips in accordance. She was breathless with need, wriggling beneath him so she could feel his hard length pressing against her pussy. Something had to stop this frantic feeling.

Oh God.

She wanted. Needed. The feelings were too new to analyze, too strong to ignore. There was no going back, even if she could think of stopping. She'd die first. There was no time to even commit to memory every detail, like he'd removed his hand from her and was untucking his shirt with frustrating slowness. Or that in doing so she bore even more of his full weight as he did so. Could one orgasm from such sensations alone? At this moment she'd believe anything was possible.

"Don't move," he whispered. She doubted she could, even if she had the notion. Her eyes were locked on the smooth, tight skin of his abs as he sat up and pulled the sweatshirt, then T-shirt over his head.

Her mouth watered at the ripple of muscles across his chest.

Oh my God. Those arms. The urge to feel, taste, *know* every inch of him overwhelmed her. And he was just out of her reach.

She gasped when his hands went to the waist of his jeans and those deft fingers loosened the button. He paused. Refusing to be embarrassed, she lifted her eyes to his. Amusement danced amid the dark desire there.

Seth nearly lost control when Kenna's tongue circled over her lips, leaving them glistening with moisture. Her hair was tousled around her, the dark strands shot through with pure gold that reflected the flames. Her cheeks were pink from the fire—and desire. Her eyelids flickered half closed, despite the intense way she watched his every move. The whole picture left him aching for more. Just imagining the way she'd arch up, her mouth open with cries of passion when he entered her, had him desperate to get rid of the damn clothes that delayed everything.

He needed skin. "Sit up," he commanded, pulling her up even as he spoke. His body echoed the shivers he felt ricocheting through her form. Her eyes stayed clear as he pulled her shirt over her head and then leaned back to drink in her beauty.

Damn. He'd seen plenty of shirtless women in his life, but never had a vision like this sent his blood pressure into space. Her white lace bra was more practical than sexy, yet it tore at something inside him to follow the lines of the material as it hugged her curves. Her nipples were tight, pressing against the fabric.

When she reached behind her to release it, he stopped her. "I'll do it," he whispered, his hands smoothing over her long, thin arms as he pulled them back to her sides. "God, you're beautiful."

The firelight highlighted the blush that colored her cheeks and stained her neck and chest. He put his hand there, between her breasts, and absorbed the heat radiating from her. "Look at me," he said, barely able to keep his breathing regulated as he felt her pulse beneath his hand.

Her eyelashes nearly skimmed her cheeks as she blinked then lifted her eyes. She'd caught her lower lip between her teeth again, a gesture that continued to drive him crazy. He pressed a kiss to her mouth, making her release her swollen lip so he could taste it.

His cock throbbed against the tight denim that still imprisoned it. He'd never survive letting her press it between her wet, swollen lips and swirl her tongue over him. If she dared to tease him with her teeth, he'd die. And die happy.

Biting back a groan, he pulled back and focused on her again. "You . . ." He looked deep into her eyes, deeper than he'd ever done with anyone. The emotions that rolled on the storms there found its way to his soul. Hope. Fear. Desire. Need. Something deeper and darker—stronger than he'd ever known. He knew it because he'd felt it before himself but never seen in another person.

She smiled.

He shattered.

"What?" he croaked, closing his fingers into a fist but keeping it firmly against the warm, pulsating skin just above her heart.

"You're not finishing your sentences."

He couldn't. That thought had come and gone. He shook his head and smiled back at her. Enough playing. Enough games. Somehow he'd still expected her to stop him and had given her ample opportunity. He nudged her knees apart, lifting himself between them as he bent in to taste her flesh just above the rise of her breast. He could smell her, the sweetness of faded perfume and the musky scent of aroused woman. The saltiness of her skin sent his senses into a whirlwind. He wanted to taste all of her—to revel in her mouth and later, to learn the taste of her cream as she came on his tongue.

He arched into her, grinding his erection against the juncture of her thighs, wishing like hell he'd had the insight to get those damn clothes out of the way.

Beneath his tongue, her skin tightened into goose bumps. She shivered, her entire body rocking against his. Sweet Jesus. This woman was poison to him.

Enough, he had said. Yet here he was, torturing the both of them even further.

There was time for that later. He fisted a hand in her hair as he pressed forward, forcing her to lie back. Once reclined, he braced his hand on either side of her head and held his body just above her.

Her breasts rose and fell, still encompassed in tantalizing white lace. Her lips were parted. So inviting.

"You're killing me here," he said right before he lowered his lips and vowed not to stop for anything, even if this damn blizzard lifted the house right off the mountain.

She pulled him down. He couldn't kiss her deep enough. She held him to her when he thought he must be crushing her and barely let his lips leave hers, even for a breath. Tendrils of her hair wrapped themselves around his fingers, as if trapping him there. Flitting thoughts of her being a temptress barely registered. He'd be anything to her, as long as she didn't make him stop.

Kenna's hands were pure fire as they roamed over his arms and the sides of his chest. Their teeth clashed when her fingers snaked under the edge of his loosened jeans, dipping so close. He growled and forced himself to ease up. At the rate he was going, he'd bruise her mouth in his desire to consume her.

Seemed as if she fought similar demons. She tore her mouth from his and fisted either side of his jeans, then pushed. He lifted, then closed his eyes to fight the nerve endings that stole his sanity. The light touch of her fingers against the tight denim as she felt for his zipper and slowly lowered it.

Each tooth releasing vibrated against him. Awww, damn. He ground his teeth together as she teased his fly open. Breath left him when she reached in and cupped his cock through the thin material of his briefs. What would happen to him when she touched bare flesh?

He shuddered to think.

"Enough." He voiced the mantra echoing in his head. He sat back on his knees, brushed her hands away and quickly got rid of his clothes. He didn't look up at her, afraid her face would mesmerize him again into delaying the inevitable. He was normally a patient man. Not today.

"Lift," he instructed after unsnapping her jeans. He fought dwelling on the idea of slowly teasing the material over her hips, kissing the flesh as it was revealed, inch by inch.

No! He'd rip the clothing from her body if he had to.

But he stopped once their clothes were discarded and watched the light from the flames flicker over her body like lovers' hands. The color rose in her cheeks again, a hint of innocent humility of being appraised so intimately. It hit his chest soundly, meaning something. He didn't know what, didn't want to know. The passion was too great to analyze emotions. The need was physical, the chemistry deadly dangerous.

"You're beautiful," he said, holding his hand just above her quivering stomach. She arched into him, closing her eyes and sighing as his flesh connected.

Enough, indeed. His cock twitched, pre-cum pooling at its tip as he crawled up over her. He waited, painfully, until she opened her eyes. He wanted to watch her as he claimed her. His. He wanted her to know, clearly, she was his.

"Kenna," he breathed, using one hand to stroke over the soft curls of her sex. His fingers spread the lips of her pussy and pressed just inside her velvety wetness.

She moaned and dug her fingers into his biceps. Oh yes. His. With his thumb, he found that sensitive nub and brushed it in time with the strokes of his two fingers. She writhed under him, arching and begging wordlessly. So hot. So wet. So ready for him.

He cursed himself now for not releasing her bra, as he'd have loved to wipe his cream-covered fingers over those peaks and then suckle them, tasting the flavors of his woman all at once. He pressed his fingers to her lips instead, nearly laughing when she tried to turn away.

That excited him. He wanted to teach her, show her all

the pleasures of sex—which wasn't simply the feel of his cock buried deep within her cunt.

Seth didn't give up, reaching down to her pussy and coating his fingers in her fluid once again before bringing them up to her lips. When she refused, he simply glossed her lips with her own arousal then took her mouth in a demanding kiss.

Oh shit. The flavor of her pussy exploded against his lips. Her murmur vibrated against him, and he took the opportunity to thrust his tongue inside and share the tang of such an intimate kiss.

She tensed, if only for a moment. He didn't care. Again and again he ran his tongue over her lips before sliding between them and teasing her with her flavor. He wanted her to know that to him, there was nothing better. Save maybe for the flavor of their juices mixing together.

"Do you have any clue how hot that is?" he whispered, gasping for breath as he dropped kisses along her cheek and to her hairline. He fumbled to pull his wallet out of his jeans and withdraw the little foil packet. It seemed like an eternity before he could get it open and on.

She shook her head slightly.

"I want you. Now."

Her eyes widened, so dark in the dim light of the room, yet so expressive. He shifted, bringing the head of his cock to nestle between her damp curls.

Kenna lifted her hips, tilting her head back as she pushed up into him. He nuzzled her neck as he slowly pressed into her tight pussy, concentrating on dropping little bites on the skin beneath her jaw rather than the sensation of his cock head being squeezed.

He nearly shouted with the tidal wave of sensations that hit when she gripped his hips, wrapped her legs around him and pulled him mercilessly deep inside of her. She gasped and moaned as he held there, willing himself not to simply explode. He'd never lost control during sex before. Never doubted he was going to outlast the woman he was with.

Until now.

He felt her muscles convulsing around his cock and from the abandonment on her face, she felt the same. He tried to focus on her features for a moment before moving.

"Seth," she gasped. The way she lifted her hips made his cock press deeper into her. He had to pull back—but as soon as he slid out just slightly, she pulled him back. He let her only to pull back again and use his strength to prevent her from completely taking control.

He waited until her legs relaxed their tight hold on his back and then pushed into her, one slow inch at a time. Then he withdrew quickly, her cunt tightening on his cock with the same desperation he watched wash over her face. Her eyes were squeezed shut, her bottom lip once again caught between her teeth. She'd fisted the blankets beneath them and tried to arch up. He held her down, gave her no opportunity to steal away his control.

It still slipped away. His entire being was pulled into the friction of her cunt closing over his cock. Her pussy was wet and aroused for him, pouring juices that ran down his balls. She began to whimper at each stroke. His fingers tangled in the strands of her hair that were spread out beneath her as he increased his tempo. She encouraged him, lifting herself so he could impale deeper and faster. She cried out and dug her nails into his back.

Sweat rolled down his forehead as he held his orgasm at bay until he was sure she was at the brink of coming. Sobs escaped at each thrust. Her face was flushed, her eyes now open and locked onto his as their bodies erupted into a blistering flame.

He felt it, her muscles clenching him so tight he nearly cried out with the pleasure of it. She tensed beneath him as he drove in, faster, deeper until their flesh slapped against one another in the race to the peak.

She screamed. He was already in his own pinnacle, the pressure of her cunt closing on him, milking the come out of him simply too much to bear. His strength emptied from him as he thrust into her, emptying every last drop of desire into her as she shuddered around him.

Unable, and honestly, unwilling to do anything more, Seth lowered himself beside Kenna. He kept his leg thrown over hers and tucked another arm over her chest and against her neck as he lay there, waiting for his blood pressure to return to normal and his breathing to regulate.

Damn.

Even that word didn't express the intensity of their actions.

And he was at a complete loss for words. Kenna, thank God, seemed content to lie there, eyes closed, with their sweaty bodies still entwined. But then what?

What was he? Seventeen again and completely clueless? Despite all he wanted to read into the tug of emotions, this really wasn't more than a culmination of the external events that had thrown them together. Mother Nature had helped by making them sexually compatible. They had chemistry.

Kenna shifted.

The spell was broken. He rolled over and gathered his clothes. She looked up at him, smiled and pulled her sweatshirt over her head and tugged on her jeans. Then she pulled her bottom lip between her teeth and turned away.

The tightness in his chest, he told himself, was just the uncertainty of knowing literally *nothing* about this woman. He'd never been a fan of one-night stands or no-strings sex. Truth is, he hadn't even thought about it here.

Dammit. He hated awkward and this whole thing smacked of awkward. Another reason to be completely convinced his heart, mind, soul, imagination, whatever it was—got Kenna confused with the voices in his head, the woman in his dreams. Hell, maybe he wanted her to be. Seth studied her profile for a bit before climbing to his feet and shrugging his jeans on. He busied himself adding fuel to the fire.

Kenna was outclassed. Not only did Seth have a huge home and a kick-ass truck but also the sexual ability of Don Juan. Not that she regretted a moment of sex. Oh hell no. That ranked up there as the best moments of her sex life. In second place ranked some risqué things she'd done with her vibrators. She fanned her face and snuck a look at Seth, who was stoking up the fire as if what had happened between them had been, well . . . ordinary.

"Hot?" he asked.

Oh, if you only knew. "Can't believe you're not. I need a drink." Before she said something stupid or read too much into what should have been an intimate act between soul mates, she got up and walked to the kitchen.

Once there, however, she realized just how off balance he had made her. She'd forgotten even the flashlight.

"What were you going to get to drink?" he asked, lifting an eyebrow when she came back and pointed at the light on the mantel.

She could look at him forever. He came straight out of her dreams and fantasies to sit there before the fire, the flames casting dancing shadows on his face, his eyes alight, his smile warm and aimed right at her.

"Water," she said, accepting the light. "You want some?"

"I'm doubting water works. Electric pump."

"You're kidding."

He shook his head. "There's . . . snow?"

Oh God. Snow. Her body was so overheated she was tempted to walk out like she stood, in one layer of clothes and sans her shoes. Perhaps lying facedown in the white stuff would clear her mind enough to think about what was supposed to happen next.

"Snow. Right."

"I'll get some." He reached for his boots.

"I can handle this." She put her hand on his shoulder and stopped him from getting up.

He reached up and covered her hand, squeezing.

She stared into the flames, wondering what his gesture

meant. She'd never slept with a man she didn't know. And while her heart argued the truth of that statement, her mind knew—she may know his heart, his soul, but she knew nothing about his life, his past, his job . . .

So she let her fingers slide away and went back into the kitchen to find a large bowl to gather snow.

"I'll go with you."

She whirled, amazed he could sneak up right behind her without her knowing. Obviously she wasn't as in tune with him as she thought.

"I think I can gather snow. I promise to avoid any that looks yellow."

She expected—hoped for a laugh, something to break the ice and let her know a shred of respect still remained—that she wasn't just a piece of meat he'd boned because she was handy.

"I want to go with you. Fresh air will do us both good. Besides, I want to see your face when you look around out there."

He must have expected her to be in awe of the white stuff. "I've seen snow before. Lots of it."

Instead of answering, he nudged her back around, facing away from him. He touched her shoulders—only her shoulders at first. But then his hands tickled the sides of her neck, then encircled her hair and lifted it up, exposing the back of her neck to the cool air of the room.

God, that felt good.

The icy blast was replaced with hot breath. Then featherlight lips nipped at the base of her shoulder. She shuddered, half with shooting nerve endings, half with the unspoken message his tenderness implied.

"You have great hair," he said. "So thick and soft."

"Ugh. It's mousy."

"Excuse me," he said, dropping it. Her body temperature skyrocketed once more. "But my taste is exquisite and is definitely not interested in mousy. Therefore neither you nor your hair are even close to mousy."

"Oh please. I don't think you need to use any pick-up lines. Kinda late for that." She hated the words the moment they slipped out. She gnawed her bottom lip and waited.

He turned her around and lifted the flashlight out of her hand. "Oh, really? But then again, you were the one to pick me up."

She tried to step back, but she was trapped between the door and his hard body. It was amazing how he could steal her breath so quickly. "I-I-I did nothing," she gasped, only half able to think as his thighs brushed the front of hers. "I got lost. You followed me."

"Likely story," he teased, lowering his head to her.

Her eyes fluttered closed as his lips grazed her temple. He kissed her eye, trailed tiny kisses down her nose and then pressed his lips to hers.

Those were the actions that slid right through any sort of protection she had around her heart. Not that her body bothered to listen. Her breasts felt heavy, her nipples almost sore against the lace holding them captive. She wanted to feel them against his chest—against his bare chest.

Tingling awareness coursed through her and settled right between her thighs. Her pussy, still wet and swollen from earlier, throbbed with need. "About that snow," she choked out when his lips left hers to travel down her neck.

"Hmmm, yeah. Snow."

It wasn't fair. She was helpless, able to do little more than lean against the door for balance as he kissed the exposed flesh of her throat, following the line of her pulse to where it disappeared beneath the fabric of her shirt.

He paused. "Snow?"

"We should," she agreed, reluctant to end the blissful pleasure of his tender kisses. But she knew it wasn't over for them. Not for tonight. She could feel the tension in the air, the need that still coursed between them. He may not have acknowledged any mental connection, but there was no way either of them could deny their physical attraction. And now that they'd acted on it, there was no reason not to take advantage.

"We'll get back to this."

Music to her ears.

She may have been feverish, but after just a few minutes out in the blistering wind and driving snow, she felt like a human Popsicle. Seth insisted on digging out as much wood as they could and bringing it in. Gloves would have been nice. And a hat, a parka and the promise of hot cocoa when they were done. She wouldn't complain one iota, however, because Seth was outside in nothing more than his sweatshirt and jeans, using his body to make a path to their vehicles and his arm to swipe the snow from the top of her car. He thought it was a good idea to wipe them off. She could see why, with the way things were drifting, the landscape had a way of grasping everything and turning it into a huge ocean of white waves.

"C'mon!" she yelled. Her clothes were soaked, her nose and fingers and toes were numb. They'd packed snow in everything watertight they could find and she'd lined them up near the hearth to melt. Hopefully they wouldn't have to do this again. They could just get these wet clothes off and . . . keep warm.

Her cheeks burned with the images her mind painted for her regarding methods guaranteed to chase the chill from her bones.

"Seth?" He hadn't answered her. Where it wasn't the inky black of night, it was thick and gray with the falling and blowing snow. She dared not venture far. With her lousy sense of direction she'd end up lost. Wandering.

She shoved her hands in her jeans pockets and shivered. Ironic her real life seemed to mirror that thought.

The wind whipped up around her, hitting the door of the cabin and spinning, encircling her like an icy fist. She feared it would pick her up and take her away—away from any chance of warmth and fling her cold and useless into the white abyss.

Five

"You act like you're enjoying this," Kenna accused when Seth finally came around the front of his truck. Snow clung to every inch of him. As he got closer, she couldn't imagine he'd done anything short of roll around in the snow. "You out there bear-hugging the abominable snowman?"

He looked down and laughed. "Your car's fault. Wind gust hit it as I was wiping and . . ."

"And whoosh, huh?" She shook her head. Despite the cold, the playful grin on Seth's face made her wish they could remain outside, here on the edge of the earth, hidden behind the curtain of thick snow. It felt magical. Of course, that could be the residual of great sex and the promise of more. But there was something in the way his eyes focused on something far beyond the visible horizon when he looked away from the vehicles.

His fingers slid into hers. Instant warmth hit her bloodstream and circulated within her. She hated that it renewed the hope she tried so desperately to damper.

"C'mon," he said, glancing back over his shoulder one last time. "We need to get inside."

She nodded but knew she'd never look at a snowstorm the same way again.

"I'm going to change." Then she looked at him and frowned. "Get out of those clothes and wrap up in a blanket. I promise I won't take advantage of you."

"Damn."

Kenna laughed and aimed the flashlight down the hall.

Her fingers were numb from the cold as she fought with the zipper of her suitcase. She shivered, the dampness of her clothes against her skin seemed so much more pronounced now than when she was outside. Probably psychological. Hell, her reaction to this whole . . . escapade was triggered by her mind.

She held the flashlight between her thighs, pointed at the suitcase as she ripped at the zipper. "Oh, you bastard. Open already."

Seth chuckled behind her. She straightened, the flashlight falling to the floor and rolling half under the bed. She was doing everything wrong.

He seemed much less frustrated despite his decidedly wetter clothes.

"I thought you were getting undressed." She retrieved the flashlight and aimed it at his chest.

"I had to come in here to make sure you hadn't um . . . turned into an ice cube or anything."

She laughed but read deeper into his words, perhaps even deeper than he intended. She doubted he was worried about her, but it was a nice gesture, one that kept her body warm enough on the inside to ward off any sub-polar conditions. "I'm okay, just had to sweet-talk my zipper into cooperation." She gritted her teeth and pasted on a smile as she flipped up the lid to her suitcase in triumph.

Immediately she wished she could melt into an icy puddle. There, tucked beside her "just in case" heels lay her neon orange vibrator.

She was speechless. What could she say? And by no means was she going to look up and see Seth's reaction.

Her heart pounded. Her cheeks were on fire. Her mind whirred with options—all of which took the cowardly, denial way out. As if. There was no disguising or explaining away the plain truth. She wasn't ashamed she owned the sex toy. Buying it had made her blush furiously, but there was just something about exposing that vision to a man she'd just met. Hell, it'd only be worse if he'd caught her using it!

"Kenna, get your clothes."

Just like that. She sucked in a deep breath. At this point, there was no sense trying to hide her mortification. "Right."

She pushed the shoes over, pulled out a pair of jeans and a turtleneck, then dug for socks.

"I'll carry this."

It was like slow motion. Seth reached down, wrapped his hand around the base and lifted the orange cock.

His smile didn't make sense until she realized how unguarded she'd left her expression. She had to look as shell-shocked as she felt.

"What? You brought it, let's use it."

Let's use it.

Dear God.

Seth's cock hardened the minute he realized what Kenna had

tucked away in her suitcase. The images that popped into his head were hotter than anything he'd seen on cable or in magazines. The visualization of Kenna lying naked on her bed, eyes closed, mouth open, gasping as she pushed the rubbery cock between her wet pussy lips.

There was something darkly arousing about the way she kept her eyes lowered now. He doubted the pinkness on her cheeks and neck was there because of the coldness in the room. Clearly this was a woman who enjoyed sex but didn't advertise it. Damn, that was hot.

He stayed silent as he followed her out of the room. He'd give her a couple of minutes to get used to the fact he had her vibrator—and intended on using it on her.

Sex games weren't new to him. There were places he could go—both because of his family's money and his own sports status—that took the extreme one step further. The whole bondage thing had never done anything for him. Nor had spanking. He didn't want a submissive female. He had always wondered what kind of power trip the guys were getting off on. The women playing domme scared him even more. No, he knew what he liked—a woman with sexual confidence, one who could give as good as she got.

His eyes strayed to Kenna. So far, she'd met those expectations. He sensed her strength from the beginning. Hell, admired her for driving so far and spending the holiday alone, even though he might have seen it as cowardice had it been anyone else. Maybe it was her eyes, the inner power and knowledge that bubbled to the surface when he looked at her.

"Can I have that back?"

Her face darkened to a deeper red as she pointed at her vibrator.

"Why?"

"Because it looks funny as hell to see you holding a cock. And because it's mine."

He looked down and groaned. Thank God the guys didn't get a picture of—oh hell, why was he thinking like that anyway? The guys had nothing to do with his night with Kenna.

"Actually, I think I'll keep it here for a while." He tucked it under a pillow with his spare condoms and then gestured her to come over and sit by him.

"I really would rather—"

He grabbed her outstretched hand and pulled her down on his lap. "Shh," he teased her. The sparkle in her eyes defied the stern look she tried to portray.

She stilled for a moment, even adjusted herself. But not to get comfortable, he realized after hearing her fingers ruffle against the cotton of the pillowcase. "Oh no you don't," he said. He shifted quickly, dumping her off his lap and easily pinning her to the floor.

Ah, shit. Here we go again.

"Rushing things, aren't you?" he teased to break the overwhelming tension that seemed to fill the room.

"I've no idea what you're talking about. You're the one who just wrestled me to the floor like we were a couple of twelve-year-olds."

"Um, I'm nowhere near thinking like a twelve-year-old right now, sweetheart, and neither are you." Not that he didn't enjoy the teasing sparkle to her eye and playful smile to her lips. But those lips were just too damn tempting for him to keep up the joking. His cock had been hard since he started thinking about her and her . . . toy. Now with her under him—squirming, he couldn't think at all.

Seth lowered his lips to hers, noting triumphantly her eyelashes fluttered against her rosy cheeks. While he didn't want surrender—the battle for control was way too much fun—it was nice to see her concede to his way of thinking.

It'd felt like days had passed since he tasted her last, the sweetness of her against his tongue energizing his body. Despite the wet clothes they both wore, it was unbearably hot. While still entwining his tongue in hers, he started pulling at the button of his jeans.

"Easy, mister," Kenna laughed and pushed him back. "We can be a little civilized about this."

Civilized? Hell, all he could think about was feeling her cunt wrapped around his cock. He didn't question the power of his desire—didn't care why the need drove him to damn near recklessness. It was as if what they'd shared earlier had been just an appetizer.

She toyed with him, grinning shyly up at him as she plucked at the hem of her wet sweatshirt. "This isn't coming off until you get up. And not only the sweatshirt, but the jeans. And you do realize we're getting our bedding all wet."

Who cares? Though he did see her point about the blankets. He bit his tongue and stood, immediately stripping off his shirt and dropping his jeans to his ankles. He was about to kick them aside.

"Give me. I'll lay them out so they'll dry."

Damn woman was about to kill him. He stood there, naked, before the fire. He'd grown up in locker rooms and had gotten used to nudity. He'd never thought twice about walking— no, strutting his stuff naked—with the other women in his life. He wasn't ashamed of his body or his cock. But even though Kenna removed her clothes without hesitation, he felt . . . self-conscious.

It was then a cool breeze threaded itself around his neck and seemed to perch on his shoulder. He looked but of course saw nothing.

Was that it? Was he subconsciously thinking about . . . *her* while he was enjoying Kenna's company? Was it guilt that kept him second-guessing?

"Okay," she said, snagging him out of dangerous thought trails. "This is really weird because I'm suddenly realizing we're standing here naked, knowing what's going to happen next, and we just met a few hours ago."

I've known you my whole life. Shit. Where had that come from? He was really losing it—just as he thought, mixing up the woman he dreamt about with Kenna. Because he wanted to be in this place with his life mate. God, that even sounded corny. If he so much as suggested it to Kenna she'd run naked through the snow to get away from his lunacy.

She lifted an eyebrow and bit her lower lip.

He groaned.

"You're not going to comment on that? Do you do this often?"

"Do what?" His eyes were trained to the plump, pink flesh peeking out from beneath her teeth.

"Seduce lost women in desolate cabins during blizzards. After the electricity goes out, of course."

"Well, usually I can't get the weather to cooperate with me."

She sucked the whole of her bottom lip into her mouth and closed the top lip over her teeth. She looked so innocent, so . . . fragile. That had to be the reason his heart was aching. At the same time, he wanted to laugh out loud at the gleam in her eyes.

"Pull the chairs closer then get over here before you get chilled again."

"Why? You'll just warm me up."

"You bet I will," he promised and held out a hand.

Kenna liked this side of him. It was a side she hadn't even witnessed in dreams. There he was a quiet, mysterious, shadowy figure. But the way his eyes now danced with the reflection of the firelight and the gentle curve of his lips upward made her even more convinced he was *the one*.

As he pulled her into his embrace, she realized she'd never stood naked next to a man before. The idea of dancing nude shot into her head. And it stayed there, visions of her and her secret lover turning round and round, nothing but a silhouette circling on an empty dance floor.

"You're humming."

Kenna cleared her throat and looked up at him, scared he could see her very thoughts. But of course he couldn't. "I was?"

"Yep."

"Um . . ."

She didn't get to finish creating an excuse because his mouth was on her, nudging her teeth away from her lip. Her nipples hardened as they brushed the warm, smooth skin of his chest.

While her breasts had already felt swollen with arousal, they ached for attention now that they knew the heat of his body. Her pussy swelled and opened and she felt the juices run down her thigh. Oh that definitely had never happened. She never knew it could happen like that.

He suckled her lip, tugging and nipping. The intensity shook through her. If it were this bad, how could she survive if he did that to her clit?

Seth moaned and smoothed his palm over her back, reaching down and cupping her ass, pulling her body against his. His cock slid between her thighs, the sweet pressure just enough to make her squirm. She needed to feel him there, needed the intensity of him stretching her, filling her. Damn, she even wanted to feel him pounding in her with all the force he dared.

She wanted it a little rough.

A little laugh escaped from her lips. She dug her nails into his lower back and tried to urge him to press harder against her. Damn him, he held back, teasing, enticing, using just his mouth to promise her the magic he had in mind.

By the time his lips left hers and started trailing down her throat, nipping and kissing along her pulse, she was rendered helpless. He had removed her hands from him and left them to hang at her side. She fisted them as he dipped lower, tickling her chest with the bit of scruff on his jaw then smoothing over the spots with licks and bites.

Her breasts ached. She longed to reach up and cup their weight. Half a dozen times she started to, but he must have been paying close attention because he easily pushed her hands back to her sides, yet avoided the spots needing his kisses the most.

"Dammit, Seth," she finally gasped as he seared a trail with his tongue that ran the valley of her breasts. He continued on to her navel, dipping in and then suckling until her muscles there spasmed in reaction. Even the pant of his breath was erotic. She felt everything, could damn near feel his heartbeat and hers rhythmically echoing in the room.

He chuckled and dropped to his knees, tracing his hands down the sides and back of her legs as he blew hot air on her pussy. How she remained standing was a mystery. God, he tormented her, and she loved every second of it.

With one finger he reached up and slid into her folds. More of her cream escaped, dampening her thighs. Her eyes were locked on his as he pulled his finger out and slid it into his mouth.

She practically came from the way his eyes darkened then closed as he licked her from his hand. "I will taste you again," he promised.

She nodded. At this point, she wasn't going to let him stop without doing just that.

He kissed her thighs and licked the moisture there. His fingers cupped her ass, kneading the flesh there, pulling her ass cheeks apart and causing her back entrance to react to the pressure there.

When he slid a damp finger from her pussy, up the crevice of her ass and back down, she nearly fell from the delirious sensation he left behind. She'd heard tales of anal sex but never could understand the appeal. But right now she couldn't help but wonder what new feelings he could awaken by plunging in her rear opening. She moaned thinking about the prospect of his thick cock pressed deep into her ass.

He'd make it good. Oh Lord, the concept alone had her shuddering. She widened her stance to keep from toppling over. She was light-headed and had nothing to grip but Seth's shoulders.

That hold was barely enough when he leaned forward and placed his mouth over her cunt and lapped at her folds. The wet, hot tongue was lethal against her clit, vibrating the nub until she cried out and dug in her nails. She wanted him to stop, yet she didn't. The edge was so close, yet she wasn't nearly fulfilled enough to fall over.

When he pressed something cool and smooth against her, she didn't question, just arched into it, needing to be filled. Her body jerked as he twisted it slowly just inside her pussy. Her muscles clamped down on it. She closed her eyes and moaned.

Too slow! He'd pulled her vibrator out and slid it back in—fucking her with it—his tongue mercilessly lapping at her clit as he very slowly slid the fake cock upward. The turning killed her. The gentle friction against the most sensitive spot inside her made her hiss through her teeth and fist her hand in Seth's hair.

How she wanted it to be *his* cock inside her, yet there was something so . . . arousing about him fucking her with her own vibrator.

"I can't decide whether to simply feast on you and make you come this way or turn you around and enjoy your sweet ass."

She whimpered, her body crying out with release with every movement he made. Anything. Something. *Everything.* She wanted him.

"Seth, please," she whimpered.

"I should be begging you, honey. Begging for all of you."

Her mind was too foggy to understand. She just wanted to come. And she wanted him to—with her. Whatever it took.

"Mmmmm." She pressed her lips together as he slid the vibrator half out of her and then pushed it back in. He hadn't even turned it on yet. Lord, she'd be done in an instant if he did.

"Like that?"

"Yeah." It was all she could do to breathe.

His lips closed over her clit and he suckled as he pushed the cock in and out of her. She moaned. There wasn't much in life better than this.

Then again.

With his mouth on her clit, vibrating with the quick movements of his tongue, he rocked the familiar cool plastic of the vibrator in and out of her wetness. She arched and twisted, sacrificing the depth of his thrusts to feel his hot mouth against her. But when he slid his other hand around her and pressed against her anus once more, she melted.

She barely remembered him lowering her to the ground. His mouth never left her body. Neither did the pressure of his hands, yet she felt how gently he stretched her out on the blankets as she tried to think around the mind-numbing sensations.

He feasted on her. She gripped the blankets and cried out, over and over as tiny peaks of pleasure coursed through her body.

Seth finally slid the vibrator from her body and lowered his mouth, using his tongue to continue the spiraling pleasure that throbbed harder with every heartbeat. She wanted him—needed him inside her.

"Dammit, Kenna . . ." He climbed over her and pressed his hot, throbbing cock against her swollen entrance.

"Seth!" she cried as she arched up. The pressure of him there, teasing the sensitive flesh of her pussy lips yet not breaching them, had her even more crazed with need than before.

His breath was hot against her cheek, the brush of it over her ear made her shiver. "I wanted your ass, Kenna. I wanted the vibrator inside your cunt and my cock up your ass."

With that, he groaned and pressed inside her.

Her toy had stretched her, but not the way he did. What a difference between the cool plastic and his hot length. She clenched the muscles of her pussy, reveling in the feeling of him filling her. With her eyes clenched tight, she memorized the way her body hummed under his hands.

He moved then, rocking slowly in and out of her. Opening her eyes, she watched his face. A sheen of sweat coated his forehead and upper lip. Lines creased his forehead. She felt his concentration, and while she ached for him to simply pound out his own orgasm inside her, his words stuck in her memory. She wanted more—she wanted everything he was willing to give her.

She gritted her teeth and held back as well, watching his features, noting the way his muscles rippled under the tight skin of his shoulders as he held himself over her, inhaled the scent of his flesh, the tang of sex mixed with the hint of sweaty bodies.

This was enough. She had come here on a whim, barely believing she'd find anything, much less this sort of bliss. It was enough to carry with her forever, to keep her soul alive. For him to remain part of her for as long as she lived.

Almost as if hearing her thoughts, he slid from her. No, wait. It wasn't enough. Not nearly enough! She gasped at the loss of sensation and searched out his eyes. Passion flared there, burning into her and chasing away the instant of cold dread that dared find its way between them.

"You with me?" he whispered and touched his lips to hers. The scent of her sex lingered there, the sweet taste infusing as he plunged his tongue between her teeth and entangled with hers.

He nipped her mouth and then repeated the question. Kenna wasn't sure what he was asking, but she wasn't daring to tell him no. He might stop this delicious torture and leave her unfulfilled. She nodded and sucked in her lip.

When she moved to sit up beside him, he shook his head and traced one finger from her collarbone to her navel. "Roll over."

She nearly laughed. Would have if his eyes hadn't darkened from the playful glint she'd just seen. He'd fisted his cock and slowly pulled down on the shaft, tightening the skin over the darkly colored head. What she wouldn't give to slip it between her lips and suck until it exploded in her mouth.

"Over," he growled again, then released himself to position her on her hands and knees.

Kenna pushed back toward him, aching to rub against his hard, damp flesh until he filled her again. She was so empty, lost without him inside her.

Instead he rubbed her ass, squeezing the skin until she nearly cried out from the pressure. His cock slid along the furrow between her cheeks. It teased her flesh, the tip of it nearly slipping inside her before he skimmed along her sensitive skin.

Her body shuddered as he inserted two fingers inside her. But he removed them all too quickly, doing little more than adding to her need, rather than satisfying her lust. Then she understood.

He used the cream to cover her rear entrance and then probed there with the tip of one finger.

She tensed, waiting for the pain. Yet her pussy throbbed with each heartbeat. She wanted this. Wanted Seth. Needed him.

"Relax," he whispered to her. He stretched her entrance slowly.

The sensations he created there were unlike anything she'd ever experienced. She never had the notion to use her vibrator there. Hadn't even touched herself there. Hadn't realized how much more sensitive it made her entire body.

"Take this. I want you to use it on yourself."

He passed the vibrator to her.

For a moment she paused. It was one thing for him to use it, but her? But then he dipped his cock into her folds once more, burying himself to the hilt and then withdrawing. She knew she had to fill that emptiness.

"Relax. Don't tighten up." Once again, he teased her tight rear opening.

As if she could relax! Her body shook with the sparks of pleasure that shot out from the place where Seth pressed his cock. She knew it was tight, felt the pressure. Even the slight twinge of pain as he entered was just an extension of her pleasure. She pushed back against him, caught in between wanting the slow possession to last and needing to feel him completely inside her.

He grunted and squeezed the flesh of her ass. The feel of her warm skin brought the edge so much closer. She could feel his cock against the walls of her pussy. It felt so empty, yet the satisfaction of him—she could feel his pulse thundering against her— was so great.

"Fuck yourself. Turn it on. I want to feel it."

She twisted the base until her vibrator shook with a steady hum. She gasped and jerked when she pressed it to her clit, amazed her body could react with even stronger sensations.

His growl indicated he too was near the edge.

"Inside."

She closed her eyes and pressed the head of the pliable plastic head into her pussy. The walls were so tight, the area so full with Seth's throbbing cock. The vibration was almost numbing—but only for a moment.

It was then it seemed her body had just come alive.

She ceased to exist. The entire core of her being rotated around the spiraling heat between her legs. Seth's fingers cut into her hips as he began to slide in and out of her ass, slow at first but gaining momentum as she pressed back against him. She wanted it. Needed it. His groans mixed with her gasps as she struggled to hold herself up with one hand while slipping the vibrating toy in and out of her cunt.

The darkness spiraled around them, pulling her so deep within it that it was light again—gloriously brilliant light that filled her with warmth. But how could she see it if her eyes were tightly closed?

But she did see it. It infused her, completing the act that for her had never been simply about physical satisfaction. Every nerve became more sensitive. Her body tensed around the double invasion. The dreamlike vision before her emphasized her body—made every touch, every moan Seth uttered so incredibly erotic. She would die from this. It felt so damn good.

Her pussy clenched around the vibrator. She felt him twitch and press deeper, if it were even possible. It was so amazing.

His hands roamed her ass, pinching, squeezing as his grunts became louder, his thrusts a little harder. She felt it as well, impending, soaring, filling her. Her ears began to ring, and in front of her, she watched Seth reach for her hand.

She felt it. Inside her soul, she felt it.

Her body erupted. She arched and gasped, unable to breathe, let alone scream his name. Fingers, soaked with her cream, released the vibrator, which fell to the blankets beneath her.

"Kenna," he hissed as his entire body tensed. The spasms that rocked her body continued as he came inside her. The heat spread, prolonging her pleasure. She shook as he muttered her name over and over.

Six

Seth pulled away, breaking the strongest connection he'd ever felt with a partner. At some point in that incredible bout of lovemaking, he'd closed his eyes. And felt a rush in his soul—a warmth he'd never known. It'd been her, touching him, reaching for him even while he was with Kenna.

But was it fair to Kenna? He pushed his hair off his sweaty forehead and blew out a deep breath. She wouldn't know he'd felt connected with someone else while making love to her—she couldn't. But that didn't keep him from feeling a tinge of guilt when she sat up and grinned at him.

If he wasn't careful, she'd fall in love with him. He could see it in her eyes, the glowing warmth, the innocent way her entire being was opened to him.

"Drink?" he asked, handing her a bowl of melted snow. As hot as it had gotten in the room, he was surprised the water hadn't come to a boil. He wished the power would come back on. A shower would be nice. The pulse in his groin jumped at the thought of soaping up her body and rinsing it clean.

He took a drink of the cold water after she'd had her fill. But he couldn't keep his eyes off her. Hell, he should be more worried about himself falling in love with *her*.

She'd relaxed. He realized she hadn't truly done that before. Her shoulders were no longer held tight. The smile that curved her lips was sensuous and casual. She probably had no idea how satisfied she looked. And how damn sexy it made her.

But...

Seth turned to the fire and fought the tug in his chest. Sex had never tugged at his emotions before. While certainly not into one-night stands, he'd never actually bedded a woman with the thought of a future together. At least beyond more casual dates.

It scared him he was thinking otherwise now.

But it wasn't because of her. The dream-like image still lingered in his mind. But he couldn't tell Kenna that and definitely didn't want to ruin her time left in Tahoe.

"I'll be right back." He took one of the bowls with him and went into the bathroom. The frigid air would do him some good. So would the icy water. He cleaned himself then splashed some water on his face for good measure.

Not that it helped. Inside him, emotions still swirled around, unsettled. Dammit, why should he waste his life—make himself feel guilty about times like this—all because of some funky feeling, some stupid connection that was probably more of a figment of his imagination anyway?

Because it was real and for once in his life, he realized he didn't want it to be. He wanted to be normal. To choose his own woman, not roam the world, wondering when he'd finally run into the person he shared the deepest part of his soul with.

"Seth?" she asked when he returned to the hearth. Her voice

slipped past the anger he'd surrounded his heart with and melted the flimsy wall easily. "You okay?"

He forced a smile—one that became genuine when he saw no apology in her eyes. "I couldn't be better." He made himself a vow as he sat down. For tonight—or for as long as Kenna was in town—he was going to ignore that tug in his head. He would push away the woman in his dreams and simply enjoy the treasure he'd been given.

When she was gone, then he could go back to his fruitless quest for his soul mate.

Kenna's teeth closed over her lip and she nodded. "Should we maybe try to get some sleep then?"

He nodded despite the fact sleep was the last thing he wanted. That was when his mind—and heart—were vulnerable. And he didn't want to dream about someone else while he had Kenna warm and willing in his arms.

Damn, she was beautiful. Her skin glowed in the firelight, a soft golden color that begged for him to touch. He almost reached out for her. But as soon as he lifted his hand, his vision clouded and it was the silhouette of another woman who stood before him.

Stop!

He shook his head and pushed his hand through his hair. Kenna gasped and watched him with narrowed eyes. Lord, she must think him crazy. "Grab the end of those blankets, let's get these straightened out," he said, cursing his stupidity. How could he think after all these years he could just exorcise her out of his life? There was no switch he could throw and then forget about her.

He shifted his mind to computing how much firewood they'd

brought in and what he figured they'd need before daylight. But that led him to mentally pointing out he and Kenna would have each other's bodies for warmth.

Sleep. Right. If only it were so easy.

It was easier than he thought. She curled against him and laid her head on his shoulder and pulled the blanket up to her chin. The heat of her body melded with his, chasing away any thoughts of the blizzard ravaging the landscape outside.

"Would you have still come to Tahoe if you'd known this is how you'd spend your first night?"

"Mmm," she hummed and snuggled closer. "I might have come last week."

He chuckled and dropped a kiss to her forehead. It was so right to have her here like this. Still, the rational side of him argued if she'd come last week, there wouldn't have been a storm and he hadn't been in town anyway, so it might have been someone else who ended up camping in front of the fireplace with her. He didn't form the words but just thinking them built a ball of fire in his chest.

As if he had any right to be jealous.

"When are you leaving?" He traced his fingers down her arm, just grazing the swell of her breast.

She sighed then looked up at him. "Trying to get rid of me so soon?" Her sweet tongue darted out and wet her lips. "Saturday. I was intending to leave early Saturday and drive all day and night. I'll do Christmas with my folks on Monday then. It's back to work for me on Tuesday."

He shook his head. "You're going to spend Christmas Day driving home?"

"Does it matter? Or are you suggesting I leave earlier? It doesn't bother me to spend Christmas alone."

He was silent for a moment. How could anyone spend Christmas alone? But what did he have to offer? "Friday night then—come with me to my mom's Christmas party."

His suggestion was met with silence. There was no way to decipher her hesitation.

"Why?" she whispered. He struggled to hear her and had no way of detecting if the huskiness in her voice was anything but sleepiness.

"I'd like—". He shifted his thought before he said too much. Her eyes were already closed so he couldn't tell if she were still listening or not. "Because I'd like you to be there with me." Why was that so hard to put into words? Why did she even question his motives? Wasn't he allowed to invite her home? As far as he could tell, she knew no one here. It was the holidays. It was a party. It was something they did every year. He usually found them tediously boring and looked for excuses not to go. Why indeed?

He looked down at Kenna's peaceful face and listened to her even breaths. Asleep she was so angelically beautiful it hurt to look at her. If he wasn't so afraid of disturbing her, he'd trace his fingers over her flushed cheeks. As it was his nerve endings tingled at the touch of her breath against his neck. Because he wanted to be with her. He asked her because he needed reassurance he'd see her after this.

Wrapping his arms around her the best he could without jostling her, he willed himself to relax and finally fell asleep.

He was gone. Kenna jerked up, squinting at the morning light coming through the unshaded windows. "Seth?" she called out, squinting in her attempt to find his silhouette lounging at the doorway to the kitchen or sitting on the couch.

She bit her lip and dropped back to her knees in front of the hearth. The room was still cool but not biting cold. Absently she acknowledged the electricity must have been restored. The storm was over. Seth wasn't stranded with her—by weather or by his gallant refusal to leave her to face the elements alone. A quick look around confirmed her thought. His jeans no longer occupied the back of the chair next to hers. Only her shoes sat beside the back door.

And for the life of her, she couldn't find an ounce of ability inside her to reach out through that once magical connection and find any trace of him.

"Oh good, you're awake," Seth said as he pushed the door open.

She sat down and gaped at him. Relief and joy flooded through her. He hadn't left. He hadn't abandoned her! At least in the sense he was still in her cabin. It hadn't all been a dream. But the sense of awareness—the sizzle of electricity between them—was gone. Completely gone. This was a handsome stranger with which she'd shared her bed. Nothing more, nothing less.

"You okay?" he bent down and brushed a hair off her cheek. She leaned into the touch, wanting to feel the crackle in the air between them.

Nothing. Not that she was unmoved by the gentle graze of his fingers across her face. But instead of her chest constricting with the fullness of emotion, it was simply a physical response to the man who had been her lover. "I got scared," she whispered, knowing she could look him in the eye and tell the truth. "I thought you'd left."

He cupped her face then and sat beside her. "I know you don't know me very well." He paused to kiss her nose. His thumb stroked her chin hypnotically. His cheeks were ruddy from the cold wind, but his eyes were clear—making her think of clear, tropical waters. "Last night wasn't a . . ." His voice trailed off and he looked around the room. "It wasn't a one-night stand. I've never done anything like that before."

Her voice caught at his next words. "There's just something . . . something about you that—oh hell." Seth leaned over her and pressed his lips to hers. His face was cold, but his lips quickly heated her body, spreading a wildfire that left the doubt in ashes. While maybe she couldn't reach out mentally, she couldn't deny the way she reacted to him. No other man could make her feel so—so everything—with just a simple kiss.

"You don't regret it, do you?" Seth made her smile. He leaned his forehead against hers so that he was too close for her eyes to even focus on his.

"Not on your life."

"Good." He stood back up and held his hand out to her. She pulled the blanket with her and wrapped it tightly around her like a giant robe. "Go get dressed. I want you to see outside."

His face glowed like a child, that is, until he let his eyes trail up and down her blanket-covered body. A spark of hope filled her when she felt him touch her with his look, the way he mentally pushed the blanket out of the way and appraised her bare body.

"I'll, um, just get some clothes," she said, giggling as she bolted toward the bedroom that held her suitcase. There she couldn't get dressed fast enough, half worried Seth would come in and see her, half wishing he would.

She doubled up on socks and cursed herself for not packing warmer clothes. Who would have known? She had driven south, not north. It wasn't supposed to be colder here than at home!

"You putting on everything in there?" his voice trailed from the doorway with a teasing lilt.

"Almost."

"Gonna make it tough on me to get back down to skin, aren't you?"

That caught her off guard. Her face must have mirrored her thoughts.

"Unless you don't want me to," he quickly added.

Kenna, you fool. It doesn't matter that you can't reach him mentally, he's right here. Don't screw this up.

She said what came to mind. "Oh, I'm definitely getting back out of these clothes. We have power, right?"

He nodded.

"Then I have a nice hot bath coming to me."

He leaned against the doorway, folded his hands across the wide expanse of his chest and grinned.

That did it. Her breasts tightened at the thought of sinking into the hot water beside him. She could only imagine how it'd feel for his wet skin to slide against hers.

"I seriously think you're thinking what I'm thinking."

She looked at him and moaned. His eyes had gone to a deep green—the gleam there had passed playful a long time ago. She swallowed and tugged her bottom lip between her teeth, a gesture that immediately had her blushing.

He groaned.

She turned away, closing her eyes and allowing a deep breath. Magical or not, the vision of Seth and her in the tub was too real. Her heart thundered in her chest, and her hands shook as she smoothed the clothes she hadn't put on back into her suitcase.

All the while wondering why she hadn't rented a cabin with a Jacuzzi.

"Kenna?"

She practically heard his teeth grinding together. She understood it far too well. "You wanted to show me something?" It took everything she had not to say or do anything to tempt either of them anymore.

"Yeah, outside." His voice was gruff, low and it rumbled over her skin, eliciting goose bumps and sending a chill up her back. And she wasn't even outside yet, dammit!

Kenna put out her hand, hoping the simple gesture would calm their raging desire—at least long enough to see what he wanted to show her and then . . .

"You'd better stop smiling like that before you miss it."

"Miss what?"

"Shhh, and come on."

His warning sent her blood pressure sky high. Maybe she couldn't reach him mentally because she was already connecting with him on a far more real plane. Maybe the pull between them had been fate's way of leading them together. Now it was up to them.

Maybe it didn't matter because he still wanted her, she still wanted him, and there was nothing here to keep them from realizing those desires.

"Close your eyes," Seth whispered as he led her through the front door. She did as he asked, knowing she was giving in to her heart and falling head over heels for him. How could she not? He made her mouth water and her heart sing. The soft touch, the almost childlike playfulness in the way he held her hand and guided her through nearly knee-deep snow. She shuffled slowly, placing more and more trust in him with each step.

"Open."

She gasped. They were on top of the world. Below them, a winter landscape was laid out as an artist would have painted it. Trees were blanketed in snow, their branches bending with the weight of it. The air was so still. The extreme contrast to last night's storm made it even more amazing. Even the breath she drew in seemed cleaner, fresher. Sure, she'd woken up on snow-covered mornings back home, but never had dawn loomed with such pristine pureness. There wasn't another house in sight, even another cabin, though she knew they dotted the mountainside. A few lazy spirals of smoke along the edge of the glassy lake beneath them was the only proof there was civilization nearby.

"What do you think?"

"I think this is heaven."

"Heaven wouldn't be so cold," he countered, but then pulled her back and wrapped his arms over her shoulders. They stood there for several long minutes. It felt right. The peace inside her mirrored the appearance of the calm around her. Oh she loved him all right. She'd be a fool not to love a man who could appreciate a sight like this.

"We've got each other to get warm if it gets too cold."

"I think you're on to something there." He hugged her tight

then released her. "I'm up for some coffee, and you'd said something about a bath?"

Without looking back, she sprinted toward the door.

"By morning we'll be able to get out of here."

Kenna looked up at Seth, who was stretched out in front of
the fire beside her. The light of the Christmas tree and the fire
were the only lights they had, despite the return of full power. It
was so cozy this way.

They'd spent the day laughing as if they'd been a couple for
months instead of hours. An earlier snowball fight had turned into
another session of lovemaking. She still wasn't sure how they'd
ended up in the bathroom, but she'd never look at a sink the same
way again. Now he was talking about leaving. Inevitable, sure,
but it seemed to dull an otherwise stellar afternoon.

"Good," she tried to laugh. "A trip to the supermarket is rather
on the top of my list of necessities."

"What? You didn't like my idea for dinner?"

They'd eaten slightly stale crackers with peanut butter for
lunch. Kenna wasn't buying into the idea of vegetable soup made
by dumping everything from the lazy Susan into the pot and
heating it up.

"Oh yeah. Sure."

He laughed and rolled over to straddle her. "C'mon, I even offered to cook it. How dare you insult my secret family recipe?"

She tried to retort, but Seth brought his mouth down and
sealed hers in a heated kiss. Her fingers slid up over his bare chest.
Who needed food anyway?

—◦◦—

Seth stood outside the cabin. It was barely dawn. He'd been up for hours, catching snippets of rest between the crazy nightmares that seemed to reach in and jar him awake with their intensity.

The last one had done him in. His dreams were always weird anyway, so the meat of the dream made little sense. He just remembered—way too clearly—the end where he was outside a building and *she*—his soul mate, his life—was inside. Locked inside. At one point, he heard her pounding on the glass to get out, pleading to him by name to set her free. He'd tried, moving in typical dream slow motion, he'd kicked and slammed and pried at the door, then moved to the window. All the while, knowing if he didn't do something quickly, something bad would happen. While he didn't believe she would die, it was more the threat of never being able to reach her again.

He shivered and pushed his hands farther down in his pockets. The dread had already set in. The dream wasn't like others with her in them. He'd imagined her as just a person he knew. There was nothing mysterious or magical about her and there'd been none of that psychic connection.

Which mirrored real life in a way that made him wonder if he'd made a grave mistake.

Hadn't he pushed her away? Hadn't he chosen Kenna over her, just for the time he had with her, based solely on the fact he wanted a warm female in his arms? No way he could downplay the chemistry he had with her, but that was physical. The woman who had the key to his soul was much more important to him. Now it looked like she was gone.

Glancing back at the door, he sighed. He'd never felt this torn.

Hell, he'd never let himself feel torn. There'd always been *her* and Samantha. The latter never did more than rile his temper or fray his nerves. The other he never talked about, never did more than accept—but she was . . . everything.

It was time to go. He had no future with Kenna. He hadn't had to stay another night but did because he wanted to and felt she wanted him to. Now he couldn't help but wonder if the price he paid was worth it.

Around him the world seemed perfect. Anyone else would say it was heaven-like, so peaceful and pristinely white. Nature untouched. For his heart, it simply felt like hell had frozen over.

⁂

"I heard you got stuck in a cabin with a gi-i-i-rl!" Gina taunted him as she launched herself into his hug.

She filled his world with sunshine anytime he'd been down, and this time was no different. "That I did, little sis. But you're not supposed to know that kind of stuff." He twirled her around and put her down, then ruffled her hair.

"Hey, I'm nine now, you need to stop doing that."

He chortled and took a step back. "I do, do I? Who says?"

"Me."

"I'm the big brother. I can do it whenever I want to." He reached out to do it again but stopped when he sensed his mother entering the room. Normally he didn't pick up any vibes from his mother. He wondered if she knew what had happened. "Hold on a minute, Geen. Mom?"

"I was just going to call you. I hadn't heard from you and was worried you were really good and stranded."

"I left early this morning. Stopped home to shower and get fresh clothes." And then stood on his balcony for nearly an hour, staring at the side of the mountain where Kenna's cabin was nestled and wondered if she'd found his note yet.

"Who is she?"

Alarms went off almost immediately. Mom never worried about his dating life, rarely asked about his personal life. He'd mentioned to his mom over the phone only he'd helped to guide a lost tourist to her cabin and had gotten stuck there because of the storm. No mention was made of her age or even that she was alone. Which meant Mom knew something.

"Just a tourist. Her name's Kenna. I invited her to your Christmas party. I doubt she'll come." Certainly not after she read the note.

"Why's that?"

He found himself biting his lower lip, which made the image of Kenna doing it pop into his head. An unfamiliar tightness lodged itself in his chest. What had he done? "She, um . . ." He turned to get away from his mother's knowing eyes. She had a way of making him feel ten again. "She's not here to socialize. I think she's running from something, but she got defensive when I asked."

He hated it when his mother gave a slow, knowing nod. "And that's it?"

Shrugging, he nodded. "Pretty much."

"So why do you look so blue?"

Shit. Why did his mother have to be psychic? She wasn't going to buy the joke-like answer that had popped into his head.

Instead, he pulled his gaze from hers and ended his part of the conversation. "I was going to see if you or Rich wanted to pop up and check on her. You know, make sure she didn't get her car stuck or anything. I had a message on my machine. They need me down in Phoenix for some promo pictures. After the blizzard, I could do with some warm weather."

When his mom opened her mouth, he interjected. "I'll be back on Thursday. I wouldn't miss the party for the world."

Kenna fell back onto the couch and blinked through the rush of tears. Angrily, she swiped them away and reread the letter. The handwriting was messy, almost as if leaving it had been a hasty afterthought.

"Bastard, lying, conniving motherfucker!" she hissed as she reread the part that had taken a jagged blade to her chest and extracted her heart. . . . *someone I have a special connection to, a woman I love and I can't risk everything for a weeklong fling* . . .

"Fling. He called the most incredible, amazing sex of my life a goddamn *fling!*" With every bit of hate she could muster, she balled up the letter and tossed it in the fire. Then stabbed it thoroughly with the red-hot poker, imagining she was torturing him with it.

"I hope you feel that, Seth Parker, you asshole."

The paper blackened and fell to ash amid the logs. She'd need more wood. What he'd brought in was quickly dwindling. She clenched her teeth and got up, then took a deep, healing breath.

The pain was inevitable, she hadn't kidded herself about that.

But she'd expected a different ache, not this ripping, wrenching, heart-splitting feeling his words had managed.

Mumbling every insult she could think of, then making up a few more, she tugged on her warmest clothes and set about finding the woodpile.

Seven

Two days later

*Y*ou must be Kenna, the girl Seth helped out."

Kenna stepped back from the woman who stood between her and the fresh baked pastries and blinked.

When she didn't even attempt a response, the woman spoke again. "I'm his mother, Margaret. Nice to meet you."

She took the elder woman's hand and shook it slowly while studying her face. She could see Seth's resemblance, especially around the eyes. "How did you know who I was?"

She wasn't buying into the idea Seth would have described her appearance, at least enough she'd be recognizable at the local supermarket.

"You're the only stranger in here, dear. I saw a car with Michigan plates in the parking lot, so that helped too."

Kenna smiled but refused to join in the woman's laughter. There's no way Seth had told his mother what had happened between them, yet the pain from it felt so very fresh. Suddenly the apple turnover—or the rest of the food in her cart—seemed much less appealing.

"He, um," Kenna paused and sucked in her lip. Then released

it and swallowed. "He left without letting me thank him. He's very noble. I was lost—and then the power went out. He helped with the fire and brought in wood and stuff." Oh God, her face was hot. Meant she was blushing. Babbling and blushing and acting defensive. Please let this woman just nod, smile and walk away.

Yeah, right.

"He's always been like that. His dad was like that too, but he didn't get to know him well—he died when Seth was seven."

"He's a good man. You should be proud." Kenna bit her tongue after saying the words and turned her cart to go.

"He mentioned inviting you to the party?"

Kenna straightened her shoulders. "He did, thank you, but I'm afraid it was just part of conversation. I didn't come here to socialize." In the grocery store *or* any part of Lake Tahoe, period.

"I know why you came."

Kenna watched as Margaret reached down and brushed the key ring Kenna had laid across the top of her purse. At first she bristled—how *dare* this woman touch something of hers. But then the hair on the back of her neck stood up and goose bumps dotted her arms. One of her key rings held an old Celtic knot charm. She couldn't even remember where she got it.

No wonder Seth's necklace had seemed familiar. The design was exactly the same.

"The knot of destiny," Seth's mother whispered. "I knew it was you. You came by the house one night, didn't you?"

Kenna swallowed, unable to lift her eyes from the curved and twisted brass charm. "How?"

"Mom, can I have—oh! Hi!" A slender dynamo propelled itself against Margaret's midsection and snapped Kenna out of her haze.

"Gina, your manners."

The little girl held out her hand. "I'm Gina."

Kenna found her smile and energy infectious. "Kenna McGurly. Pleased to meet you."

"Are you the girl Seth got trapped with?"

Kenna's mouth popped open.

Margaret gasped. "Gina!"

"Sorry."

Trapped with? Out of the mouth of babes, wasn't that the line? Kenna pasted on a smile and nodded at Margaret. "I need to get going. Very nice to meet you. You too, Gina," she added.

She couldn't get out of the store fast enough.

So that's what he'd told his family, huh? That he'd been *trapped* with her?

It'd been two days since he'd left without a goodbye. She hadn't seen or heard anything from him. The snow was melting, turning the beautiful winter elegance into a dripping, muddied mess. Funny how nature had a way of mirroring her feelings.

She fumed all the way back. At one point, she thought about reaching out to him but then decided better of it. He didn't want her.

It wasn't until she was back in the cabin that she thought about what Margaret had said. *I know why you're here.* Kenna dug her keys out of her purse and fisted the ensemble of decorative rings she'd collected since she started driving. It hadn't been a figment of her imagination. She carried the same token Seth had worn around his neck. Coincidence?

No. A blanket of melancholy settled about her shoulders. She'd been right with her initial observation. It had been Seth who'd been able to touch her soul. But he already had someone else. Trying to sort it out, she imagined he'd been satisfied with simply having her as a mystical person, a dream figure. He probably never imagined a woman with nothing more than a dream would drive all the way here and threaten his perfect life.

No wonder he'd shut her out. It wasn't that he hadn't known, it was more he didn't want to have to deal with it. Pissed her off even more he'd so easily made love to her. What had he been thinking?

For the first time since she arrived, she'd regretted the trip.

Cabin fever made her crazy. It wasn't that she wanted company—solitude suited her just fine. But everywhere she went in the small house she thought of him. The blanket on the bed had been the one he'd draped over her shoulders. That pillow had been the one he'd slept on. She'd made the mistake of using it for a nap the day before and had been overwhelmed with the way his scent had clung to the cotton.

The mere act of curling up in front of the fireplace with one of her books had the same effect. She couldn't concentrate on the story. She kept thinking about what they'd done there and then visualizing Seth with some gorgeous debutante.

Heaving a sigh, she went to the front window and looked out. "Son of a—" Why was she surprised to see Margaret and Gina getting out of the white sedan parked behind her car?

She opened the door and crossed her arms over her chest. "Something wrong?" she questioned as soon as she knew they were within earshot. She didn't want to be mean or inhospitable, but there had to be some ulterior motive and frankly, she didn't want to deal with it. If she hadn't prepaid for this cabin for the rest of the week, she'd be halfway home by now.

"Kenna, I tried to catch you before you left the store. Gina and I were talking about the party. We could really use some help with getting the house set up."

She couldn't believe it. "I'm sorry?" Kenna asked, knitting her forehead and frowning. Was this woman really suggesting what she thought she was?

"I'm not going to beat around the bush. I know more about you than you think I do. Come on down to the house—you can help us decorate and we can talk. It's got to be a better option than going stir-crazy in here."

Margaret glanced behind her at the house and smiled.

It was the most preposterous thing Kenna'd heard yet—that is, until she realized she was actually considering it.

Gina piped up then. "It'll be fun, just us girls. I hate it when Dad and Seth help with the decorations. They always want to do the same old things."

"And you like to do what? Be creative?" Kenna was drawn to children, even the very observant eyes of Seth's little sister.

"I picked you. Mom said I could have someone come help and I said I wanted you."

"She did," Margaret said, nodding. "Of course, you were my first thought and I probably would have invited you anyway, but Gina has always been around older people—except at school of course. She's very mature for her age, but I'm afraid I'm old. You're just right to her."

Kenna would bet money they'd concocted this in the car on

the windy drive up. Still, she wavered. Gina, bless her heart, already knew how to use those huge, expressive eyes to get her way.

"Excuse me if I'm slow, but we just met. Isn't it strange for you to have followed me home and are now begging me to come help you decorate your house for the holidays?"

"You're Seth's friend. He's talk—"

"We just met, but we're hardly strangers. I know my son was rather . . . affected by you."

Affected. Sounded too much like infected. "I see," she said, but didn't, really. Why would Seth have talked about her if he had someone special in his life? She was sure he'd simply explained to his family and to his dear love Kenna was nothing more than a mere lost tourist. And why wasn't Margaret standing on her future daughter-in-law's porch, pleading with her?

"So you'll come?"

Kenna glanced behind her. The fireplace was cold. The book she'd left turned over on the fireplace mantel had no pull to her.

"Seth won't be there," teased Gina. "He's in Arizona."

That caught her attention. "Arizona?" she repeated.

"Promo photo shoot with their new uniforms. He should be back tomorrow night or Friday morning."

Seth was gone and she hadn't even realized he'd left town. The connection was gone. Dead. Her heart was empty. "Promo shoot? Uniforms?" she asked, forcing a smile. It was normal to be curious, right?

Gina's eyes got huge. "He's a famous baseball play—"

"He plays minor league baseball. You didn't know?" Margaret cut in, staring at her intently.

"No." Kenna shook her head, wondering what else she didn't know. She bit her lip then saw Gina's smile fade. Ouch. "Holiday deco—"

"You'll come?" Gina said, grabbing her arm. "Please?"

"All right. Just because I'm a sucker for Christmas lights." She glanced up at Margaret just in time to see Seth's mom's face quickly morph from a studious frown to a pasted smile.

"Excellent. Follow us."

⟡

The house was everything she'd imagined. In her dreams, she'd imagined a four-floor great room with a solid wall of windows facing the water. Actually seeing it made her hands shake with excitement. The decorations were a bit different, but the way a balcony jutted from each floor and half-floor sublevels—landings that were large enough to boast room for a settee or decorative tea table—was an architectural genius. Yet the way the house was literally built into the cliff made it possible and pleasing to the eye.

"If you want lights around the window, you've got the wrong girl for the job," she teased, pointing to the highest point, four stories up.

"You mean you can't fly?" Gina laughed and pretended to pout. "Here I thought you were some snow fairy come to grant me wishes."

Margaret snorted. "Excuse her, I don't know where she comes up with some of this stuff. She's nine for goodness sake. I don't know how I'm going to survive those teenage years."

Kenna smiled at her then looked down at Gina. "Snow fairy? Is that a good thing? It sounds like a good thing."

Gina nodded, her dark eyes twinkling with mischief.

"Okay, if I *were* a snow fairy, what would you wish for?"

Without a beat, she said, "I'd wish you'd marry Seth so you can be my sister."

Kenna straightened awkwardly and felt her face heating up. She looked helplessly at Margaret. How to answer *that?*

"You're going to scare her away, talking like that," her mother finally hissed.

Kenna closed her eyes. It was almost funny the way she spoke, as if Kenna couldn't hear. Gina didn't apologize or even admit it was a joke.

Time to put a stop to this now. "Gina, I hope you didn't lure me here on some false hope. I don't think Seth likes me like that. Besides, we just met. People don't get married so quickly. What about his girlfriend, anyway? Don't you like her?"

Margaret coughed lightly. Kenna stayed focused on Gina, believing the girl's reaction would tell her more than Margaret would.

"Samantha?" she snorted. "She just thinks she's Seth's girlfriend. I don't like her much. She talks baby talk to me."

Kenna didn't feel so bad disliking this Samantha sight unseen now. Baby talk? How did Seth put up with such treatment? Another reminder he technically was a stranger to her. It was time to move forward. "About those decorations?"

"Don't worry about Samantha," Margaret whispered as she led Kenna toward the deep closet holding the holiday decorations.

She let the woman's words slide as she realized the closet was as big as her bedroom back home. If anything, it was continued proof she and Seth did not belong together. Their worlds were way too different.

Mother and daughter exchanged a few looks while the three of them dressed the giant tree and hung garland from each of the banisters. The occasional comment like, "Seth made this ornament in grade school," popped up, but Kenna wouldn't encourage conversation about him.

When they were done, Margaret sent Gina in to make hot cocoa then led Kenna to the cozy fireplace alcove on the third floor. She had a feeling this was the true family room. Books lined two of the walls, floor to ceiling. The third wall was all stone with the generous hearth centered beneath a thick mantel beam. Photographs dotted the mantel—not purchased works of art, but real family portraits and favorite snapshots.

"What happened to make him leave without saying good-bye?"

Kenna turned to Seth's mother, once again getting a glimpse of deeper lines around her eyes and a worry that made her eyes more opaque. "Seth? I-I don't think I know myself."

"Then nothing happened between you?"

Kenna turned back toward the fire, unable to have this conversation.

"Seth has a psychic gift. As do I. As do you."

Kenna swallowed and turned to deny it but couldn't. Margaret was in her head already, whispering something to her with a rhythmic cadence. It soothed and relaxed her. She sighed and closed her eyes.

"Seth used to love it when I sang to him as a little boy. He'd wake up in the night and I could lull him to sleep without even leaving my room."

She felt it, the special mother-child bond. It filled her with such warmth—an overwhelming sense of peace and richness. Something she'd never known. But just as quickly, it faded.

"I find it incredibly brave—and hardly coincidental—the way you ended up on our doorstep the night of the storm. Fate has its way. Fighting it won't help anything."

Oh, how she wanted to tell this woman everything. Tears threatened her eyes. For the first time in her life she felt someone knew what she was dealing with, someone understood the connection that was more powerful than touch, more communicative than simple speech. What would Margaret say if she told her it wasn't *her* fighting—it was her son who had pulled back and put a lock on his soul?

Where the heck was Gina with the cocoa, anyway? "Fate doesn't consider the reality of the world."

"Then why'd you come?"

That question was fair enough and had been something Kenna'd been asking herself over the last two days. Truth was, she hadn't expected to do more than learn who Seth was, and perhaps a bit about him. She'd no intentions of starting a relationship. Ironic—*fate has its way*. "The opportunity came up. I told myself those doors only stand open for a short time, and if I didn't go now, I probably never would." She waved her hand and stared toward the fire. "I just ended a relationship at home. Everyone thinks I came here running from what happened."

"Did you?"

Kenna shook her head. The emotions were all laid out. The questions were more than spoken words. She couldn't stop now even if she wanted to. "The breakup was a good excuse, but in truth, while it stung my pride, I'm glad that chapter is over. This was my way of checking out all my options before starting the next chapter." The words came out of her mouth before she realized what she was saying. She had, on some subliminal level, hoped for something. Well, she had, there'd be no other reason to travel all the way here. She hadn't expected it, but hope had been there. "Plus, I figured I'd give myself a vacation as a Christmas present." She forced a laugh.

Margaret just smiled and twisted her rings.

"Did you forget? We have to make cookies tonight!" Gina walked in the room, as if on cue, holding two mugs of steaming chocolate.

"I didn't forget, hon. We'll make them. We've got tomorrow morning too, you know."

Kenna watched the interaction between mother and daughter. All afternoon the two of them exchanged banter that at times seemed anything but parent and child, but always was full of love. Her childhood had been fine, if a bit sterile in comparison. She hadn't realized just what was missing.

"I should get out of your way then, since you have all these preparations."

"No, stay. Pleeease?"

Kenna sipped her cocoa. The longer she stayed, the more attached she became. Which meant the harder it was going to hurt to turn around and leave.

"Gina, no begging. Kenna, hon, you're welcome to stay and help. Unless, of course, you had something else planned for this evening."

They were good. Both of them, smiling up at her. Maybe fate had its way after all. She was enjoying this. Perhaps Seth was only part of the pull. While Margaret hadn't touched her mind since her initial comment, she knew the woman commanded a great skill over her abilities. At this point, she wouldn't doubt if somehow Seth's mother had played mental matchmaker with the two of them.

Over the chaotic fun of making three batches of cookies at once, Margaret quizzed her further, asking simple questions about her life, her job, and then offered up equal amounts of information about Seth's father and her current husband and life in Tahoe. Gina piped up with details of school and her friends—and the icky boys who pulled her hair and tried to knock her books out of her arms. What Kenna wouldn't give to go back to those days. Life was so simple at nine years old.

"Look, Kenna," Gina said proudly, displaying a sugar cookie decorated with a happy face. "It's you!"

"Me? Oh no, that's too pretty to be me."

"Is not." The deep, gravelly voice made Kenna's legs weak. Her stomach clenched. She knew her face was immediately beet red.

Eight

"Seth!" Gina threw herself in her brother's arms, giving Kenna an opportunity to catch her breath and put the cookie sheet on the counter. She glanced over at Margaret, who was smiling. She had known. Seth wouldn't have shut out his own mother. She'd known he was on his way home and had done her best to keep Kenna there. Successfully. At least the annoyance of getting caught in this matchmaking ploy helped her gain her balance emotionally.

"Isn't it cool how Kenna's helping us make cookies?"

Kenna couldn't help but sigh as Seth ruffled his sister's hair and smiled at her. Lord, the man was beautiful when he smiled, his mouth outlined by the deepest dimples possible, the corners of his eyes creasing. It left her breathless. And it wasn't even aimed at her.

"It's cool if you want it to be. They sure smell good." He grabbed a chocolate chip off the counter and nodded at Kenna and his mom. Then he was gone again, leaving three females staring at the doorway that swallowed him up.

Thank God Margaret had set the oven timer because Kenna

had totally lost track of what she had been doing. She was too busy mourning over the hole in her chest left from yet another affirmation. Whatever she had once felt with Seth, it was now gone.

While the minutes stretched and her nerves stretched with them, the pile of cookies grew. She jumped at every noise, expecting it to be him.

His mother said nothing. That perplexed Kenna even more. Gina rattled on about how she was going to get to visit Seth during spring training camp. When the last cookie was out of the oven, Kenna glanced at the clock.

"I need to go."

"Thanks for everything." Margaret's words carried a deeper meaning, but one Kenna didn't grasp. She wasn't sure she wanted to.

Gina hugged her tight and made her promise to come to the Christmas party. The little girl wasn't going to let her go without her crossing her heart. Kenna complied but knew she'd feel like a heel when she bypassed the party to get an early start on the long drive home. She had a feeling she was going to need all of those long and lonely hours behind the wheel to sort out what had happened in the previous week.

Kenna cursed her timing. Seth hadn't left—he was leaning against the driver's-side window of a new Mercedes talking to a gorgeous blonde. She didn't need any psychic ability to know that was Samantha.

Averting her gaze, Kenna walked straight to her car and got in. Seth called her name, but she pretended she didn't hear him. Last thing she needed to do was throw a wrench in his relationship. Her life might be all screwed up, but she didn't need to create havoc on other people's lives.

The ache in her chest exploded into a thousand pinpoints of agony as she drove away. She fought the tears, God, she fought them with everything she had. She didn't even know why she was crying—it was a by-product of the pain she felt, pain that was the first contact she'd had with Seth in over forty-eight hours.

Why are you doing this to me? she cried out to him mentally, knowing he couldn't hear her. They weren't telepathic, only flashes of emotions traveled the tenuous connection. She wondered if he'd meant to share his pain with her. Scenarios played out in her head as she drove. In one, she imagined he'd come to his senses and realized he was losing her. In another, likely more realistic setting, Samantha learned of his infidelity and was breaking off his relationship.

When no bright truck lights blinded her in the rearview mirror, Kenna realized no amount of wishful thinking would make dreams come true. She should just be glad the connection didn't seem to be irreparably severed. Perhaps over time they could regain what they had.

－⊂∙⊃－

"What's wrong with you?" Samantha's shrill voice was not what he was interested in hearing.

Kenna's taillights disappeared around the corner. He should follow. He had to follow. But then what? Admit he'd lied to her. Goddammit, why had he done that?

"Go home, Sam. It's been a long day and I'm not interested in going out."

His luck couldn't have gotten worse. Sam had passed him as he'd driven home from the airport. He'd come to his mother's instead of his condo so he'd have a reason not to invite her inside. But then he'd seen Kenna's car and wondered what he'd done to deserve this game of emotional dodge ball.

"But—"

"I'm not interested. Go home." He couldn't help but sneak another glance toward the now dark road.

"Who was she?"

"Huh?" He almost blurted out things he hadn't yet admitted to himself. Like *she* was the woman he couldn't stop thinking about every minute he'd been gone. "Her? She's none of your business."

He turned and walked into the house.

"Where's Kenna?" his mother asked him when he passed the doorway to the kitchen.

"Gone." He wasn't going to hash this over with *her* now too. Christ. Couldn't anyone leave him alone? What had she been doing here?

"Seth?"

"Not tonight." He felt his mother's hurt immediately. It was lessened only by the realization she wanted him to feel it, wanted him to remind him that he'd struck out at her when it wasn't her fault. "I'm sorry!" he yelled from the doorway to his bedroom. Make that the guest room. Hell, he slept here as much as he did at home.

───∽∾───

"What are you going to do?" Mom's soft voice filtered through the closed door about an hour later. He'd been awake, lying on top of the neatly made bed, hands folded under his head.

"About Kenna? Nothing. She's just a tourist on vacation. She'll be gone in a few days and life can get back to normal." Except that the past few days had been hell on his heart. His dreams had been empty. He could pull up recent memories of the woman that had connected to him, but ever since he'd pushed her aside to spend time with Kenna, he'd been unable to feel her. To feel anything but lonely.

"You really believe that?"

What the hell did she want him to believe? "Yes. I do."

Silence. While he wanted his mom to let the subject go, he knew she stood there, debating on her next question. He was, after all, grown and she tried to never interfere. "Whose idea was it to bring her here?" he preempted.

"Gina's. And mine. We saw her at the grocery story. She's a nice girl."

Oh hell yeah, she's hot as hell, sexy as sin and totally turned his world upside down. There was just someone else in the way. "Yep. I'll see you in the morning."

He heard her footsteps. The subject would come up again.

Seth woke up to the sound of a woman crying. He leapt from the bed and stubbed his toe on the corner of the dresser. Cursing, he hopped on one foot toward the door and opened it.

By then he realized the sound wasn't real.

Cold chills covered his flesh. After closing and locking the door, he backed up to the bed and sat, numb. Why? Why was she crying? The dream was gone. There would be no more answers. While he should be ecstatic she hadn't left him, the connection had been so—different. He felt nothing.

Nothing.

Just an emptiness that hurt nearly as much as if real pain existed. But that was his own. He should have felt the ache that drove her to such intense sobs. God, that broke his heart all by itself. So far away. So unreachable.

Shit, he just wanted to drive his fist through the door. If he could jump in his truck and find her, he'd go without hesitation, gather her in his arms and make her stop. Or make her share with him once again.

He dressed and made his way down the dark back steps and through the long hallway on the main floor. It was late, or early morning. Everyone was asleep. It had snowed, a light blanket that temporarily hid the invasion of men. He stepped outside, leaving one lonely pair of footsteps behind him.

Damn, he hated this loneliness. Helpless, that's what it was. "Where are you?" he whispered. "Show me where you are!"

Still he felt nothing. Complete emptiness.

He stood at the edge of the water and looked across the dark lake. On the far side and down, houses were white dots, their Christmas lights reflected in the black liquid. There was no horizon. Water met land met sky. And she was out there, somewhere.

"Seth?" He turned to see his mother standing on the landing of the top floor. It'd been years since she'd reached in and spoken to him mentally. He'd nearly forgotten she could.

Making his way inside, it dawned on him. Maybe the reason he couldn't feel was because the connection wasn't true. His mother had channeled it. He picked up his pace, determined to find out just what she was trying to do to him.

"Why?" he asked her.

"You did this," she said. He cringed at the defeat in her voice. "You shut her out, didn't you?"

"Would it really change things? I'm done with all your hocus pocus crap, Mom. It was fun while it lasted but lately all I'm feeling is heartache these days. Destiny be damned. I can't sit around waiting for fate to happen."

She laughed then, low enough to now wake anyone else but rich enough to know how genuinely funny she found his words. "Fate won't come to you, boy. You have to go get it."

His mother left him standing there, puzzled.

"Damn it," he muttered under his breath. The one thing that had been eating at him was the way he'd walked away from Kenna. He pushed his hand through his hair and glanced behind him. She was up there, somewhere, alone. His body responded as he thought about curling up next to her sleeping figure and sharing her warmth.

While he couldn't fool himself into believing there was any future with her, this whole psychic shit had forced him to push away the one woman he'd met who made him even question what he wanted.

No more.

He took the steps two at a time, grabbed his wallet and car keys and left without looking back.

The nose of his truck led him up the mountain. He slowed to consider his decision only when he pulled into the driveway behind Kenna's car. What if she didn't want to talk to him? He'd been stupid, leaving without explanation. And on what pretense would he say he came back?

She'd listen, he'd stay until she understood.

A light went on in one of the rooms soon after he knocked. Barely a moment later, her sleepy voice filtered through the oak door. "Who is it?"

His body responded. His own voice croaked when he responded. "Seth."

"Oh my God, is something wrong?" Kenna opened the door and grabbed his wrist, pulling him inside. Her fingers dug into his arm as she studied his face.

"No, no. At least not like you mean." Lord, what was he doing here? He'd never really considered that his experience with women usually ended before he faced dealing with this kind of thing. "I was, uh . . . thinking of you."

Her eyebrows lifted and she took a step back.

He closed the gap and took her hands. "Look, Kenna, I'm sorry."

"Seth, you shouldn't be here."

At least she didn't tell him to get out. Yet. "No, this is exactly where I should be. I've thought about you all week."

"No." She tugged her hands free and turned around. He held his breath. His heart paused as well, waiting for her next move.

With her back to him, her voice low, he almost didn't hear her ask, "What about . . . her?"

"I lied."

When she turned around again, her eyes flashed with anger. "You're lying now. I saw you with her. Just . . . *hours* ago. Don't play me."

"Kenna, please."

"Did you come here for a quick lay? Sorry, Seth, you might

not believe this, but I didn't drive all this way for a no-strings love affair with some spoiled rich boy."

"Then we'll add strings, dammit. I'm not leaving."

She stopped then. He swore he could see the pulse beating at her neck and the way her eyes roamed over him but wouldn't meet his.

"Nobody makes me feel the way you do," he said, hoping it was something she wanted to hear. It was the damn truth, but it sounded so corny being said out loud.

"And I'm supposed to just melt in your arms like some trusting romance novel heroine?"

"Can't blame a guy for hoping." Ow, was that strike one, or two?

"Why are you here—I mean, it's nearly two in the morning, Seth."

"I had a nightmare and realized—"

"Realized your guilt was drilling holes in your stomach and so you came to make yourself feel better by apologizing. Sex would be a cool side effect."

He hadn't expected this to be easy, but she was putting up a real effort. All the while, he noticed how she trembled and tried to wrap her arms around her chest. She was warding him off. Instead of aiming for her heart, which she was clearly protecting, he went for her smile instead. "Damn, caught me. Can you help?"

"Bastard," she whispered, but he saw the twitch at the corner of her mouth.

"What?" he asked, stepping closer. He saw slight confusion in her sleepy eyes. He didn't touch her but simply breathed in her scent. A fresh scent, like a mixture of fabric softener and fruity shampoo. Amazing how something so simple could send his blood pressure soaring. "What did you call me?" Leaning forward, he whispered in her ear.

A light shudder coursed through her. Her lips parted and her eyes finally locked with his.

Then the white light wiped out the beautiful vision before him.

He blinked then lifted his hand to his burning cheek. "You hit me? You hit me, dammit."

"Damn straight, Seth. This isn't a game and I'm not one of your silly conquests. Don't play games with me."

She hit him! He walked past her and sat down on the couch.

"What are you doing? You—"

"Bastard?" he provided, lifting an eyebrow, then wincing. Ow, she had a good arm on her.

"That's not even enough."

"Okay, in all seriousness, Kenna, I came here because I'd finally pulled my head out of my ass and realized you were more than just—okay, we're being pretty damn honest here, so I'll say it—you weren't just a flyby fuck."

"Nice," she spat out, pacing the length of the living room. "Forgive me for not being more hospitable, but did I tell you what time it is already? I'm tired, I'm not thinking straight and having you in my living room again is playing havoc on my ability to rationalize." She stopped and stomped, hands clenched into tight fists at her sides. "Damn you, Seth."

He was up and had her in his arms before she moved again. The kiss wasn't gentle, but he was past trying to be gentle. This woman had gotten into his bloodstream and every minute they postponed the inevitable ate through his patience. She moaned as he nudged her lips open and thrust his tongue inside.

She was a drug. The more he had, the more he needed. And he was going on a binge right now, one he had no interest in stopping. He traced the curves of her waist and hip then closed his hand over the cotton-covered flesh of her ass. He nearly overdosed on desire when she pushed her body against his.

"Kenna," he whimpered.

"Shut up," she answered. "Before I come to my senses."

He reached down and picked her up, drawing out yet another deep, devastating kiss before asking her, "Which bedroom?"

"Behind you, you jerk. But our conversation isn't over."

"Of course not," he agreed, murmuring against the silky skin of her cheek. He crushed her against him as he carried her, but that's what he wanted—needed—this sensation of being closer than skin. It was two in the morning and his body was on fire with need for her, yet his heart was awake enough to know it didn't end there.

He'd deal with it all in the morning. Right now he needed to show her just how much he missed her.

He lowered her next to the bed. It was dark, too damn dark, but he refused to break contact with her and search out the light switch. Seeing her would probably be too much for him right now anyway. In the dark he could focus on the feel of her skin, the scent of her, and listen to those whimpers and moans that drove him straight to the brink.

"No, you can't sit down yet." She was exhausted. He'd seen it on her face, yet she held on to him with the same sense of need that coursed through him. "Let's get this off." He tugged up on her oversize T-shirt and peeled it off, letting it fall where it may. Her skin was on fire. She felt so small and delicate beneath his hands as he memorized her contours. His fingertips grazed her waist then traced her ribs before taking her breasts in his hands.

He moaned as she did. She pushed into his touch, her nipples hard buds against his palms. There was no such thing as enough of her. The more he experienced, the more greedy he felt. He wanted to taste each inch he touched, licking and nipping at her until she cried from the pleasure of his attention.

"Seth," she gasped when he pinched the tips of her breasts before lowering his head to taste.

Her flavor, a tangy sweetness that was unique to her, exploded against his tongue as he outlined her nipple. Her fingers fisted in his hair as he pressed the flat of his tongue against that sensitive peak then blazed a trail through the valley until he reached the other distended bud.

Her breaths came harder. She leaned against him, drunk from the passion. It intoxicated him, yet he couldn't stop this worship of her body. He straightened, nipping her soft skin all the way back up to the nape of her neck. The way she moaned against him was maddening. He wanted her. All of her, not just to be inside her physically, but to be one with her.

God, that had to be the late hour and the intense chemistry between them that filled his head with such thoughts. Yet he couldn't deny it was true. She did things to his insides that he'd never known to protect himself against.

"Get your sweats off," he commanded, stepping back to remove his own clothing. It gave him a second to catch his breath and remind himself that she was leaving all too soon. An emotional attachment would do neither of them any good.

But when her body melted against him . . . her fully naked and pliant body pressed against his length, he realized he was in no position to worry about the difference between love and lust. Lust was manageable. He could deal with it. And right now he was going to give it his best shot to make this a very memorable night for Kenna. Because he had a real good feeling that it was too late to save her heart.

"Touch me," he said, guiding her hand to his throbbing hard-on. Air hissed through clenched teeth when her hand tightened around him and immediately stroked his full length. One touch and he was out of control.

"C'mon," he said, pulling her fingers from his body and lifting her up onto the bed. "I think we should finish that in here. Sex in a bed would be good, huh?"

She giggled, a soft, sleepy sound that tightened something in his chest. His cock ached, the feeling of a warm, soft female body half-beneath him tearing his thoughts from the sound of her laughter to the heat of her skin and the need he had to feel it around him.

Forcing himself to slow his pace, he stroked her body. His fingers danced over her skin. He listened to her gasps and sighs and felt the flesh shiver and tremble beneath him. God, she was beautiful.

Finally, he pressed between her legs and stroked her pussy, his fingers coming away soaked in her arousal. The scent drove his need even higher. She cried out, lifting her hips from the bed with each pass of his fingers over her hidden bud. The gasp on her lips turned into a low moan when he pressed inside her.

Kenna didn't need to say a word. Her body was completely in tune with his.

Nudging her knees apart, he rose above her, wishing like hell he'd turned on the light so he could watch the rapture cross her face when he slid into her depths. He loved the way her eyes darkened then those lashes fluttered closed. The way her lips pursed then opened as she gasped in pleasure.

It was all he could do not to drive madly into her, over and over.

Maybe it was good the light was off. He had to close his own eyes as he slid into her tight, wet pussy. Watching her might have been his undoing.

She wrapped her legs around his lower back, pulling him deeper. He held still, desperately searching for a thread of control.

"Seth," she whispered. "Please."

She moved, lifting her hips and rotating them, her tight cunt squeezing him mercilessly.

"Kenna," he growled. He drew back and loved her with full, slow strokes, gritting his teeth, squeezing his eyes, holding his breath until he felt her body begin to shudder beneath him. This woman was the death of him—and the life. How the two were mixed he didn't know and found he didn't care. She cried out, her body tightened and shaking beneath him with the force of her orgasm. He let go, pumping into her as his own peak shattered any rational thought.

─────

Kenna woke up in the morning, her body sore but sated. "Mmmm," she murmured as she snuggled into the pillow and moved closer to the middle of the bed. Wait. Surely he wouldn't do this to her again. But the sheets were cool against her bare skin.

"Asshole," she hissed as she sat up in bed and looked around. Sleepy satisfaction quickly turned to anger. At herself. She'd let this happen, hoping maybe it was different, maybe he'd come to his senses and understood their destiny.

Ha. She needed "fool" tattooed on her forehead for this one.

Had he even left a note this time? She pulled on her T-shirt and discarded sweatpants and pushed her hair back out of her eyes. Dammit. It was bright. What time was it anyway?

There was no reason not to wake her. What happened to honesty?

Stupid questions. Stupid move. Way to go, Kenna. Way to freaking go.

"Hey there, sleepyhead."

She stopped short and gasped.

Oh God. She backed up against the door frame, both in shock and because he completely stole her ability to speak, even to breathe. He'd left his shirt off. He'd pulled up his jeans but had left them unbuttoned and only zipped a little more than halfway. She damn near drooled at the way the cords in his arms tightened under the flesh as he draped them along the back of the couch. She didn't care about the knowing smile flitting at his lips. Let him watch her drink him in. She was past caring.

"You're doing it again," he warned, his eyes narrowing but twinkling.

"Doing what?" she managed to gasp. This wasn't the first time she'd seen his physique, but it was the first time she'd taken a moment to really appreciate it. That and the fact this man, with this body, had come back to her. Mousy little Kenna. Damn.

"You're chewing on your lip. You know what that does to me, don't you?"

"Makes you hungry?" She sniffed the coffee appreciatively. "Sure makes me hungry."

He growled, letting her mind imagine he was telling her he was hungry for her. If only this could be real life instead of some fantasy. In just a little more than twenty-four hours she'd be leaving Tahoe and this would be a sweet memory.

Damn, it was tempting to walk up to him and run her hands down his muscular chest just to feel his skin trembling beneath her fingers. Her eyes kept straying to the dark line of hair that started at his navel and disappeared in the shadow of his jeans. She hated his zipper at that moment.

"I'm going to see about breakfast. Care to join me?" She walked into the kitchen, asking herself what in the hell she was doing. Playing a game? A dangerous game. Well, what did she have to lose, really? Her heart was history, had been that very first night. Seems like even with the sex connection, he had no intention of allowing her to find him in her dreams ever again. So really, what *did* she have to lose?

Kenna smiled up at him when he walked up behind her and rubbed his hands up her arms. It was such an intimate touch, something she easily equated with longtime lovers or even comfortable married couples.

"What'd you have in mind for breakfast?"

Lord, could she really do this? "Eggs, I need to get them cooked up or throw them out." She reached for the carton and moved out of the circle of his arms. The little dip in his eyebrows gave her the boost she needed to continue.

Emotional suicide. "Your mom and sister are great." She steered the conversation toward a neutral subject as she pulled out the fry pan and pointed to the toaster. "How do you want this?"

"Got cheese?"

She nodded. "And ham. So omelet or scrambled?"

"Oh, let's be daring. Go scrambled."

Whatever that meant. "I love your house."

She whipped eggs while he diced.

"Mom's house. I've got my own place."

She poured the concoction in the skillet and glanced up at him. "It's great though. Certainly one of a kind, right?"

"Far as I know."

She nodded. The food was a great distraction. "I had a dream once about a house like that. Was weird to walk through it. Kinda like déjà vu."

"Really? Scramble, already," he said, pointing.

His face told her nothing. Should she drop it or try again?

"It was weird. While walking through it with your mom, all the details of the dream came flooding back. Ever have that?"

"Not about a house," he chuckled.

She looked him up and down then snorted. "Nah, I can't see you dreaming about a house. More like sports and girls."

"Hey," he said, pointing the forks at her. "That's . . . .sexist."

"Oh, tell me I'm wrong."

"You're not." He finished setting the table.

She grinned. Score one for her. She served their food and sat down. Time to shift the conversation in another direction. "Last night," she said, pausing to chew a bite of toast. "You said something about adding strings. Were you just saying that to lure me in the sack?"

God, she wished she had a camera to see the shock on his face. "Kenna, what are you doing?"

She took another bite, chewed and swallowed then took a sip of her coffee. "I'm eating, Seth. Why? Is there something wrong with your food?"

He growled. Kenna hid her half smile behind her coffee cup. All fair, and all that.

"So," she said when he dug into his breakfast again. "What were you planning to do today?"

"No plans."

"Ah. Well, I told your mom I'd help her cook for tomorrow. Gina wanted to make some more cookies and candy. I had a lot of fun with them yesterday."

He grunted. Oh, gee, did he want to spend time with her? Well, then he should have asked.

"I'm sure you can help out," Kenna invited, trying to maintain an innocent look. As if he'd accept her offer.

"I've got things to do."

She let up and finished her breakfast. It was one thing to distance herself and let him know what it felt like to be nothing more than the flavor of the week—no strings indeed—but quite another to be a complete bitch to him. "Well, you know where I'll be." Standing, she picked up her plate and cup and smiled sweetly. "I'm going to get in the shower." After rinsing the plate, she walked toward the short hallway leading toward the bathroom. "Oh, Seth? You might want to pick up some more condoms before coming back tonight."

Once out of the room, she let the sassy smile slide from her face. Truth was, she'd made all of it up about his mom's invitation but figured he wouldn't call her bluff. If they couldn't use the help, she'd take a driving tour of Tahoe. Anything to keep from looking like she was sitting around, waiting for Seth to come to his senses.

Seth lowered his coffee cup and stared at the doorway. Who was the woman who'd just walked through there? Get more condoms? And what was this sudden interest in his family? Did she have some kind of ulterior motive . . . or did his mother? It'd certainly be easier to comprehend if Kenna wasn't leaving town in two days. Two days.

He stared at his reflection in his coffee cup. In one week this stranger from another state had walked into his life and wreaked irreversible havoc on, hell, *everything*. He didn't want to think of doing anything with Samantha. That shallow woman would never satisfy him ever again. Gina would probably babble about Kenna for months, longer if she managed to convince her to stay in touch. Did he want to stay in touch? What benefit would there be?

Grrr. He got up and dumped the rest of his uneaten food in the garbage and washed their plates. The sound of the shower lured him in that direction. But then what? Climb in with her? Closing his eyes, he visualized her lithe body turning under falling water, rivulets streaking down her bare hips and legs. Damn. Well, there was no reason to deny they agreed on one thing—their physical attraction.

"Seth? You out there?"

He had to reach down to adjust his swelling cock. Swearing under his breath, he stepped up to the door. "Right here."

"I didn't grab a towel. Can you bring me one?"

Mercy. Nothing like having her rip any sense of control right out of his hands. "Sure." Even his voice betrayed him and shook with his effort to sound nonchalant about her request. It wasn't like he hadn't seen her naked before.

Christ.

He was totally unprepared to see her like that. Standing there, as if inviting him to come up from behind and press his cock into her glistening pink slit. She had one leg up on the edge of the tub and was leaned over, applying some kind of lotion to her ankle and foot. Her ass was lined up just right.

"Here," he croaked, handing her the towel. He was hot and cold, way too consciously aware she was intentionally baiting him but too male not to react—and react hard and fast.

Shit.

"Where are you going?" She had the nerve to taunt him when he purposely turned and walked out of the much too small and steamy room. He couldn't decide whether to count himself the luckiest man alive or be completely angry the way she acted so flippant.

"Out to wait for you to finish up."

"Oh," she tossed her hair up and looked at him. The sideways, shy smile, those white teeth tugging on her bottom lip . . . the devastating curves of her trim body. For all his size and muscle, he was helpless to fight it.

"You're doing this on purpose," he said, striding back into the room and yanking the towel from her hands. He pulled her upright, wrapped it around her middle and then turned her so she faced him—a safe arm's length away. "Don't play with me, Kenna."

"What?" she asked, her eyes widening.

He wasn't buying it. "This . . . hell, I don't know what you're doing."

"I don't understand. You came back—you admitted you came back because we're so great in bed together. I didn't think there was any reason to be shy about it."

Why didn't he let her get dressed before starting this debate? Hell, how was he supposed to answer that? What business did he have suggesting she was acting like a tart when he drove her up here just minutes after meeting her and announced he was staying the night? And she was damn right, he never denied he'd hoped to rekindle their attraction, but what was he supposed to do, lie to a tousled, sleeping, delicious-smelling woman?

"Shy. Right. Of course not." How about speechless? Unable to wrap a coherent thought around his tongue because he was too busy remembering how good she'd tasted—and wondered just how she'd taste now, all fresh, still damp from the shower?

"Is that how things are going to end with us then, with a thanks, it's been fun, the sex was great, can I call you if I'm back in town?"

"I doubt I'll ever be back in town, Seth. But do you have an alternate ending, seriously?"

He didn't, but her voice had dropped a bit and her smile wobbled. Relief coursed through him. So she did feel . . . *something*. He wasn't sure if it was his heart or his ego more pleased to learn that bit of information. Shaking his head and releasing her, he said, "No, I don't. You've probably got the right attitude about this."

"Good," she said then turned away. But he'd gotten a glimpse of something on her face before she turned away. As if she wished he'd come up with a different answer. Oh hell, it's not like he was unaffected either.

"You'll be at the party then, right?" He knew this would be their last chance to be alone. Yet he couldn't bring himself to pull her in his arms and admit what his heart was trying to tell him.

"Yeah, I have a feeling your mom would come get me if I didn't show up."

"I'll see you there."

He reached up and touched her shoulder, turning her face to his. As he expected, the light had gone out in those beautiful eyes. She tried to grin, a lopsided attempt that made her look even sadder. "I'll miss you," he whispered. With a light brush of his lips across hers, he left.

Nine

Kenna stared at the doorway, wondering where she messed up. Wasn't it *her* that was supposed to leave Seth all baffled and questioning? But it wasn't the first time in her life a man had pulled one over on her. One of these days she'd learn to stop gambling with her heart.

But she wouldn't let tears come. No way was she going to let him make her cry. This was as much of her doing—if not more—as it was his, and she knew no matter what, she'd be leaving at the end of her week's vacation.

"Get a freakin' grip, Kenna. You knew this was going to happen within minutes of meeting him. Consider it one helluva week and be done with it."

Oh, as if she were ever any good at self-pep talks. She dropped her towel and dressed, all sense of fun having faded with Seth's abrupt departure.

The thought of going to Margaret's and helping Gina with the rest of the Christmas preparations had less allure than it had earlier. What if Seth came by? Then she chuckled. What, now she was avoiding him? God, her mind was a mess. She didn't know what she wanted—or what she *should* want.

❦

"Kennaaaaa!" Gina's wail echoed through the great room. She was enveloped by a pair of thin arms.

"Lord, Gina, let the girl get through the door." Margaret tsked her daughter. "I swear, no one would believe you just turned nine."

"It's okay," Kenna laughed but pried the girl's arms from around her waist. "It's nice to be welcomed. I thought I'd come by to see if you needed more help. Last night you said you weren't finished baking."

Margaret nodded, but her eyes clouded for an instant. "Lots to do today, girls, shall we get at it?"

The afternoon went quickly. When the pastries were cooling, they ducked out and built mini snowmen along the sidewalk. Gina's melodic laughter was therapeutic to her heart. It wasn't until Richard, Margaret's husband, walked in that Kenna realized she hadn't thought about Seth in hours.

"You ladies did a fantastic job. House looks great. Smells good too."

Gina blushed and shrugged. "Mom said I was a giant help."

"That you were, midget," Margaret agreed, then smiled at Kenna. "And I'd still be working if it weren't for you. I'm going to shower and get ready for the guests."

"I should be going. I need to get packed up."

"Coming back, aren't you?" Richard asked.

Gina's fingers latched onto her arm with a death grip. "Kenna, no. You have to come to the party!"

"I'll come. Just for a little bit. Then I've got to get going back home. It's a long drive."

"I wish you lived here."

"Gina!"

"It's okay." Kenna knelt down beside Gina so she actually had to look up to the girl. "I think we can still be friends when I go home, right? I'll get your phone number and address and give you mine."

"I have e-mail!"

Kenna chuckled. "Well, that's even better then, isn't it? We'll stay in touch that way."

As she drove back she realized the heaviness in her chest wasn't from simply leaving Seth behind and losing the connection she'd felt she'd carry with her forever. No, she was going to miss Margaret and Gina as well. They'd welcomed her into their home as if she was family.

Seth's truck sat in her driveway.

Kenna sat in her car and stared at it for the longest time, not sure what could be left to discuss. He opened his door as she walked up toward the truck.

Her breath caught and her heart thudded in her chest. Lord, he looked . . . devastating. Dress clothes were certainly a weakness, but Seth in a suit that was only a notch less dressy than a tux was dangerous to her health. The appealing, citrusy scent of his cologne wafted toward her, making her knees actually start shaking. How was she supposed to survive this?

"I wasn't expecting to see you until tonight."

"Hell, I thought you left town already." He sounded mad. The tension lines in his forehead slowly smoothed as his eyes roamed her.

Sorry you walked out the way you did? She couldn't say it. Seth's eyes had darkened. She just blinked up at him.

"You need to get dressed to go."

"Yeah." She bit her lip, tugging at the sensitive skin with her teeth.

When he groaned, she tore her eyes from his and walked up to the door of the cabin. "Coming in, or do you want me to move my car so I can meet you there?"

He didn't say a word, just followed her.

"I had fun with Gina today."

"Thank you. You have no idea what your friendship means to her."

"Seth, I barely know her but I had lots of fun. I felt her age again."

"I think she's finally able to be her age again. She had a not-so-savory life before she got placed with us. She's a foster, you know."

So many things she didn't know. Her heart went out to the little girl with the beautiful smile. "Your parents are angels for taking her in."

"Kenna, dammit, I didn't mean to get you down. I was just thanking you for spending time with her. And wanted to make sure you didn't disappoint her tonight because you might be angry with me."

"Wouldn't dare." She squared her shoulders and smiled at him. So he hadn't come back because of her—it was all about Gina. Which she didn't mind, in fact, it endeared her to know he was so protective of his foster sister. Her fault, really, for setting herself up like that. To what end? Why couldn't her heart realize hope meant nothing in this situation? "I'm going to go get dressed now."

"Fine."

She let her eyes linger as he pulled off the long overcoat and folded it over the back of the recliner then sat down on the couch.

Oh Godddd. She sprinted to the bedroom to escape the emotion that threatened to tidal wave her. Too late. She shook, wanted to scream, cry, laugh—all at once. Her fingers all turned into thumbs and she couldn't stand still. Her bags had been neatly packed, but she tore them apart looking for the slender black dress she'd brought—just in case. Then came the heels. Hose? In this weather, they'd probably be good, but she was damn near sweating just trying to get her body to obey.

She should not be smoothing her hands up over her breasts as she lifted her shirt up, imagining Seth's fingers doing the same. She should not shift her hips, imagining his hard body would be there to press against. She shouldn't even care if he liked her dress.

Kenna glanced at the door at least a half dozen times, expecting and then anticipating his silhouette to darken the doorway. Nothing. She cursed her nervousness as she applied a light coat of mascara and then smoothed a soft gloss to her lips. Her hair was staying down. She had no patience or vision for some elegant style. A few brushstrokes had it gleaming. Good enough.

The woman staring back at her looked the way she felt. Scared. Out of her league and certainly not ready for a holiday party. *Act. Pretend the man out there is here for every reason you want him to be. Pretend, dammit, or you'll just make a fool out of yourself.*

"Nearly ready?"

She whirled at the voice in the doorway, having given up on

him caring one bit about what she was doing. "Um, yeah. I think. Have I forgotten anything?"

Her heart skidded to a halt when he tilted his head sideways, smiled just enough for the dimple-like creases on either side of his mouth to deepen and said, "Your smile."

She licked her lips and smiled, the false upturn of her lips turning genuine as she watched him look her over. There was no mistaking his appreciation. At least she had that. If nothing else, she had that.

"Ready," Kenna said, slapped the cover down on her suitcase and followed Seth out.

"Ride with me?" he asked.

Unfortunately her heart heard, "Be my date?" She shook her head. "You're host, or co-host at least. You can't leave the party to bring me home, and honestly, I don't intend to stay long. I'm leaving right after I get packed."

"Tonight?"

She should have sassed back with some answer about having gotten all he was going to get from her, but there was no reason to cheapen the moment. Truth was, she saw something in his eyes that made her wonder if he fought the same emotional demons she did. Ah, probably just wishful thinking.

"Yeah, tonight. It's a long drive and I want to be able to relax and unpack, you know, wash clothes and stuff before I go back to work." She ignored the fact it meant she'd be spending Christmas day alone in her car. There was no Christmas this year for her anyway, unless she counted this.

He nodded. "Guess I'll follow you."

Seth did follow her, at least part of the way. He turned off at an intersection she didn't know. No matter. She knew her way, and it wasn't like she was at this party just for him. In fact, she reminded herself sternly, he had made sure she was coming so she could see Gina.

"You look fabulous. Where's Seth?" Ah, so Margaret knew her son had been with her.

Kenna shrugged then removed her coat and gave it to Richard. "He turned off."

His mother raised an eyebrow but could respond no further because a couple had just entered the door behind Kenna. They'd talk later, Kenna was sure. In fact, as her husband took the couple's coats, Margaret met her eye and nodded toward the kitchen.

She'd decorated and cooked but somehow hadn't fathomed the magnitude of people milling around the expansive home. Margaret hadn't given her details really, other than most of her guests would be locals, but that some of her old friends and those spending some holiday time in the area would likely stop in. The party was an annual thing.

Heck, back home this would qualify for front-page billing on the newspaper. Considering this was Lake Tahoe, she could only imagine what kind of celebrities would appear.

But it wasn't a famous face she scanned the crowd for. It was Seth. She couldn't help it. The third-floor balcony offered the best and most private view of the entire area.

Gina hadn't popped out of some corner and dragged her off to whatever it was nine-year-olds did during such an adult-oriented social gathering. Margaret was still stuck at the door, ushering in her friends and neighbors with elegance and grace.

Kenna avoided small talk and prowled the sublevels when her

balcony got too crowded. It wasn't that she was antisocial, but she didn't even register on the prestige level filling the room. The woman beside her at the buffet wore at least twenty carats in diamonds on her neck, hands and wrists. Kenna immediately had balled her hands into fists to hide her chipped and unpainted nails.

"There you are!" Gina called. "Come on up!"

She was on the top floor and dressed like an angel. Kenna hastily climbed the steps to join her ally. "Okay, do you know what's so great about these parties?"

"Mom says they just exchange gossip. The women try to out-do one another's dress or jewelry and the men talk business or golf. And of course, they eat and drink."

Sounded like exactly what was going on. For a nine-year-old, Gina was pretty perceptive. "So I suppose everyone's talking about me, wondering who the geeky girl in a department store dress is, right?"

Gina's laughter had to carry down several levels, but Kenna didn't care. The bubbly sound was contagious and soon they both were giggling at the abundance of oversprayed hair and gaudy baubles.

"I wasn't supposed to monopo—monpolol—something—I wasn't supposed to take up your time."

Who wouldn't choose to sit and talk to this beautifully dressed, immaculately mannered little girl over the heavily perfumed rich women and their busybody attitudes? "I don't know anyone else here other than your mom. She's busy at the door. So I'd rather be with you. At least I don't have to worry about embarrassing myself because the correct way to eat a brownie is with a fork or something."

Gina brought a white-gloved hand to her mouth with mock horror. "I've already been warned. No finger food. See?" She wiggled her fingers.

"How about I go snag us some cookies and we can eat them with our fingers if we want to."

"Just don't get any on your dress," her mother warned, sneaking up from behind and winking at Kenna. "I'll walk down with you."

"Thanks for inviting me, but I don't think I'll be sticking around long. I really don't have the . . . practice at things like this. Look at me, I was hiding out in the loft with a little girl."

"She loves it, and you're not doing anything wrong."

"Yeah, but I bet there are tongues wagging already."

Margaret's cheeks deepened to a dark rose and she lowered her head. "Oh, they can't figure you out. But don't be alarmed, they mean no harm."

Kenna just rolled her eyes. Oh, wait until Seth arrived. They'll probably catch her staring, breathless at him and . . .

"Here." Margaret pressed a folded slip of paper in her hand. "Don't open this until you've gone."

She looked down at it. It was warm, almost as if there was a life to the paper. But she knew better. That damn hope inside her just wouldn't give up, would it? "Now . . . cookies, you said?"

Kenna returned upstairs to Gina, a large bounty of cookies in one hand and the mysterious paper in the other. She was tempted, sorely tempted to peek. Instead, she waited until Gina was distracted and tucked it in her bra.

"I think you made this cookie," Kenna pointed to a smiley face with chocolate freckles.

Gina laughed. "Mom did."

"Oh, yeah right."

A burst of laughter filled the space from below. Young men. Seth. Kenna lowered her cookie to her plate and brushed the crumbs from her lips.

"Yep, I think that means Seth's here."

Great, even the little one could read her every thought. It was better for her to stay well hidden and save Seth the bother of having questions raised about their relationship. "I . . ." she stood up and swallowed. "I'll go see."

The top-floor loft extended farther over the room than the lower levels, making it impossible to see everything that was going on. But she didn't need to see everything. Seth was on the ground floor by the entrance leading out to the porch. Apparently he'd entered that way, as he still had his jacket on. Seth, about six guys who looked about the same age, possibly younger, and several beautiful women. One of them clung possessively to Seth's arm.

Kenna wanted to throw up. How—how *could* he? She clenched her fists so hard she knew she left marks. But the sharp pain in her palms was nothing in comparison to the ripping of her chest. Damn near brought tears to her eyes.

She wanted to leave. Now.

"Gina, honey, I—" The young girl's downturned mouth tore at Kenna. It wasn't fair. Not to Gina, and Gina was really the innocent here. Kenna knew there was another woman—they hadn't talked about it recently, but Seth had told her about *her*. "I think Seth's busy with his friends. So let's enjoy our picnic."

A half hour later, Margaret came and tugged Kenna away, insisting she wanted to introduce her to some of her friends.

A backdoor exit would have been much more appealing. She vowed to take advantage of any exit she could as soon as possible.

She felt the instant his eyes landed on her. Someone threw a switch and her senses came alive. She had thought the connection severed—that she'd never know such a feeling again. Warmth washed over her, a fullness that surprised her—even though it'd been merely days since she'd felt it.

Margaret sighed. Kenna guessed she felt it or at least knew about it. But there was no way she could put things into words at that moment. The introductions were a blur. She could pinpoint Seth by the power of his gaze, even as she smiled into the eyes of Margaret's neighbors and said the proper greetings.

Someone thrust a drink in her hand. Margaret lifted it out and promised to return with water. Kenna was lost and found all at once. She was on the third floor, in the family's nook with some of Margaret's and Richard's closer friends. Seth was on the half floor below her. He'd shrugged off the blonde, but she still stood as close as possible and pouted up at him. Disgusting. She couldn't imagine Seth with someone like her. But then again, she didn't know him all that well.

"Here."

Kenna took the water from Margaret and gulped it down. "I need to get out of here."

Margaret followed Kenna's gaze and hissed through her teeth. "Already?"

"I've seen enough."

Once again, Margaret shocked her. "I'm so glad to have met

you, honey. Just remember your special gift. And come back any-time, you're always welcome here."

And with that, Margaret led Kenna through the master bed-room, retrieved her coat and then took her to an elevator that connected the room to the garage. "You parked up by the road, I take it?"

Kenna nodded.

"Take care." With a quick, motherly peck on the cheek, Margaret gave Kenna a push into the elevator and hit the button.

⟿⟾

"What are you doing?" Seth demanded of his mother when he finally found her in the kitchen, fussing over several plates of food that were poised to be taken out.

"Here," she said, thrusting a bowl of whipped dessert in his hand. "And bring the punch bowl back with you. I was dreading having to carry that heavy thing up the stairs."

He sighed and glared at his mother.

"Well?" she asked, tapping her foot.

Didn't matter how old he got, he wasn't going to win a battle of wills with her. But he had questions, lots of questions. The wave of emptiness was like a jug of icy water poured over him. He'd pulled away from his teammates and raced outside. The feeling was so much stronger there, but he couldn't pinpoint anything. His breath had felt like icy shards as the wind swirled around him.

The darkness gave him no answers, however. So he stomped back in to find out what his mother knew. Which was a lot, based on the sly smile she couldn't hide behind all this fussing over the food.

"Here, now tell me what you know about this . . . magic crap."

"Son, you said you don't believe in destiny, so why should you care?"

Seth watched her deftly fill the punch bowl as if this were nothing at all. "Destiny, fate, whatever this is—it's disrupting my life. Destiny is about as real as Santa is to me right now. Want to fill me in on what's going on here?"

"You hate it when I interfere. So I haven't."

"Liar."

He saw it then, the extra light in her eye. "You are lying. You know."

"Listen," she said, turning away from him and picking up a set of keys. "I've got a ton to do here. Kenna just left but she won't get far without these."

"She left?"

"Said she'd come to see Gina, who's now in bed. And she mentioned something about getting on the road right away."

Kenna left? He hadn't even had a chance to talk to her, much less introduce her to his friends. She'd been with Gina and he hadn't wanted to interrupt them. "Fine," he said to his mother, grabbing the keys.

He circumvented the party and cut out through a service door. Best to get this over with so he could quiz his mother further. But when he hit the cold air again, the feeling hit him. Full in the chest, he felt a sense of helpless desperation. And longing. That more than anything made him stop in his tracks and look around. Why now? Was she here? He hadn't sensed anything since he'd pushed her away to enjoy his time with Kenna and now it was back—with an intensity he hadn't anticipated.

Twice he paused to go back. Kenna would go back in to look for her keys eventually.

In the meantime, he could search out—

She stood beside her car. The light up here was poor, but he could see her silhouette. The thick winter coat, the line of her dress that hit mid-calf. God, she had to be freezing. But she was digging through her bag, her back to him.

"Kenna?" he said, jogging the rest of the way to her. "Here. Mom found these."

"Oh thank God." She pushed her hair off her forehead and took the keys. "I wasn't looking forward to going back in there."

"Why?"

He was close enough now to see her features. Her eyes flickered over his face then fell. She fiddled with her key ring. "I don't fit in there. But it was fun—with Gina. We snuck cookies up to the upper level."

"So I heard."

She nodded, still not looking up at him. Her voice strained, she said, "I'm leaving, Seth. Not sure what to say, other than goodbye."

"Yeah, nice knowing you just doesn't work here, does it?"

Christ. He wanted to kiss her. Such a sucker for the way she tugged her bottom lip into her mouth and looked so— "Let me see your keys." Now his chest hurt—pounded as if it were going to explode out of his chest. Yet there, in her fingers, was something he hadn't expected to see.

Coincidence. That familiar brass knot hanging amid her key rings was simply a coincidence.

Her features were blank but she still wouldn't look him in the eye. More proof it meant nothing.

"I need to get moving. I wanted to get back, changed and on the road here soon."

"You shouldn't have this many key rings on here, Kenna. Weighs down the ignition."

Kenna blinked up at him, her mouth falling open. She snatched them back. "Thanks. I'll be sure to lighten the load when I get home."

Shit. Not a way to end things, not when he had so many questions. "Kenna, wait. I—" Christ, how was he going to say this? "Why did you come to Lake Tahoe?"

"I—" Seems she was out of words as well, but the tight set to her lips said it had more to do with frustration. "I was chasing a dream. Now goodbye, Seth."

Just like that, she turned from him and unlocked her car door. He let her get in but stopped her from closing the door. "What dream? Tell me, Kenna. What were you hoping to find here?"

Tears glistened in her eyes as she looked at him then aimed her eyes forward. "You wouldn't understand. Fate has this way of torturing me. Give this back to your mom. Tell her she's mistaken. Now, if I can please go?"

He took the piece of paper, glanced at the words, *He's the one*, which was written in his mother's formal handwriting. If it were possible for his heart to skip a beat, his did, but how could he believe such a thing if Kenna was walking away?

Seth reached in and placed his hand over hers and squeezed.

He wasn't expecting the jolt of electricity that soared through his body or the way lightning seemed to hit his very soul at the contact. Her sad smile said everything he felt in his heart.

He stepped backward, staring at her. He couldn't even speak

to stop her as she started the car and then pulled her door closed. The glare on the window prevented him from seeing her as she backed up, paused then sped into the night. After watching those twin taillights disappear into the night, he looked down at his hands.

Something in the snow caught his attention. Had she dropped something? His ragged breath left his body as if he'd been hit in the chest. A charm, the charm. Somehow coincidence wasn't going to explain this one away.

He fisted the metal token, finding its cold weight heavy in his hand as he ran inside to find his mother.

"You knew."

"You didn't believe in destiny. Nor do you want me to interfere, remember?"

He growled and slammed the charm on the counter.

"You let her leave?"

"What the hell was I supposed to do? She clearly didn't want to stay."

"Do you blame her?"

Seth looked at his mother incredulously. "What, are you on her side now?"

"No. I'm just saying. She took an incredible risk coming here, following nothing more than a feeling in her heart. You found each other almost immediately, and I know you had to feel something—a pull, a tug, some sort of familiarity."

Seth laughed then. What a damn fool he was. All this time he'd been looking for someone who had been right here. The bitch of it was he'd pushed Kenna away—oh God, what a mess.

"I screwed up, didn't I?"

"You just going to let it go?"

Seth glanced up at the clock then picked up the charm from the kitchen counter. "Let it go? You got to be kidding me. No way am I wasting another minute thinking about it. I'll follow her to the end of the earth if I have to just to convince her how I feel." He rubbed his hand over his face and looked up at his mom.

Her gentle smile said it all.

"I've got to be back in Arizona on Thursday. If I make it, I'll try to stop back here on my way through. But I'll call you."

"We'll be here. Go."

He dropped a kiss on her cheek and raced out the door.

Kenna stood on the porch of her cabin and looked out over the darkened landscape. It was clear now, the stars dotting the heavens with amazing clarity, the moon reflecting on the still water below. It was picture perfect. But then her eyes strayed to the house at the bottom of the hill. She couldn't see it specifically, with the cliff side and foliage, but she could see the glow coming from it.

She pushed him away. Not that a hug and kiss goodbye would have made her feel any better. It was protection, the way she brushed off his questions. Her heart ached.

"Seth," she whispered into the night, the tears finally tracing down her cheeks. "Oh, Seth."

She couldn't find a happy ending to this story. It wasn't possible. He had a life that kept him busy and a warm, loving family here. She had a job and ties in Michigan. Long-distance relationships didn't work, but rational answers did little to soothe the ragged chasm that'd been slashed through her heart.

Oh, it ached. She pressed her fist to her chest to make sure the gaping hole wasn't real. She sobbed. For all the lost dreams, for the broken fantasies and unrealized hopes. For the shattered innocence of one girl, one boy and the fairy tale of happily ever after.

She'd hoped, God, she'd hoped so strongly that the magic of Christmas would make the impossible happen. What a fool. The only thing the holiday would be good for this year would be to remind her how alone she felt. If she let it. But then again, her initial purpose for coming was to discover the truth—and she had. The answer to the question she'd posed to herself for more than half her life was now answered. *Merry Christmas, Kenna.*

Sniffling, she went inside and chided herself on breaking down.

It would be the last time that happened. She washed her face then pulled on jeans and a sweatshirt. As she circled the house, the events of those first few nights replayed in her mind. She'd felt him so intensely then. They'd connected on a level she hadn't thought possible.

Even now, however, she could feel a trace of him. She felt his anger, his confusion. Perhaps his girlfriend had seen them together. Perhaps he was regretting what he'd done with her.

"Goodbye, Seth," she whispered as she pulled her suitcase out the door and closed it behind her. That chapter of her life had ended. Fate wasn't writing this story, she was. Her mission was done. It was time to move on.

Ten

Seth stopped as if a brick wall had formed in the road in front of him.

Goodbye, Seth, echoed through his head.

"No." He pushed his truck harder, cursing the slow vehicle in front of him. In his hand he held the charm. He had to get to her—had to reach her.

Then what?

He hadn't planned that far. But he'd do something—anything to get her to stay. He'd pay for the cabin, hell, he'd buy the cabin. She didn't have to go home.

But as he thought those things, he realized Kenna wasn't going to allow it to happen at all. What his mother said boggled his mind. Kenna was one helluva woman. What kind of strength and will did it take to drive a half continent away to find the person who spoke to your heart? He'd never been courageous enough to even consider it.

"Thank you!" he called to the driver who finally made a painstakingly slow turn at the next crossroads. Yet he knew he was going to miss her. This destiny crap spoiled the future sometimes.

He knew she was gone—he could feel her getting farther and farther away.

Yet he continued to the cabin. Maybe it would hold some answers.

Empty. Dark and cold. The door was locked. Hell, he was disappointed not to find a "Dear John" letter taped to the door.

"Kenna!" he shouted over the lake. Sweet God, it hurt. What was he going to do now? Follow?

He had to. How could he not know?

Walking back to the truck, he felt her, reaching. He closed his eyes and held out his hand. The cold air sliced through his lungs, but even that sensation faded as he tuned into her.

She turned to him and he could finally see her face. But the smile was gone, replaced by heartbreak so deep and painful he stepped back at the staggering weight of it.

"Remember me," she whispered, and reached out. Her fingers failed to reach him, however, and he was left standing there, aching for her touch—for the sense of heat to revitalize him, to give him hope.

But that's what he'd done to her, wasn't it? Turned her away because he'd wanted some shallow, physical-only relationship. He didn't know! He turned and kicked the tire to his truck. Dammit, how could he have known?

Wait.

She was close, he knew she had to be. Keys. Surely she had to drop them off somewhere.

He jumped in the truck and backed out of the driveway with more speed than was safe. Nothing mattered now, nothing except finding her, facing her—knowing she was the one who had been with him his entire life—and would continue to be, whether they were hundreds of miles apart or not.

He owed her an apology and so much more.

His advantage was knowing the narrow roads and shortcuts. He nearly spun the truck around as he blew the stop sign and negotiated the sharp right turn. There were two or three main offices downtown. If she were renting from a private owner, he was shit out of luck.

"Where are you?" he asked aloud. Yet he couldn't pinpoint her. How had she found him, anyway? So damn accurately?

Hell, she probably paid more attention to her ability, honed it. He picked up the phone, knowing there was one woman who had more power than anyone he knew.

"Find her," he barked when his mother answered the phone. "I don't have time to explain. Tell me who she rented the cabin from or where she's at on this godforsaken mountain before I kill myself trying to find her."

"Schmidt's," his mother said and hung up.

"Schmidt's," he repeated. A well-known real estate company that had an office on the main road. He gunned the engine and pushed as hard as he dared in his effort to find her there.

"Dammit, Kenna, don't go!" he shouted, knowing he lacked the ability to touch her the way she did him. "Please wait! Wait."

He got behind her, waving to the car he cut off in his effort to get right behind her. He flashed his lights and was ready to start honking the horn if she didn't pay attention.

She pulled forward then signaled left. Maybe? His hands shook as he watched her, waiting for some signal she was pulling over.

He nearly laughed when she finally did. He hadn't believed she would, but he was prepared to follow her all the way to Michigan if he had to. He pulled to the side of her car in the very same fast-food restaurant where they'd first met.

Just like before, she got out of the car and ducked in through the glass doors before he could catch up.

"Kenna, wait," he called, giving chase.

"Get me a coffee, Seth," she said. Her voice was steady, sure, but her face denied any calm demeanor. He'd expected to see she'd been crying—mirroring the ripping emotions he'd felt radiating from her.

"You won't run? 'Cause dammit, I will chase you down. I'll follow you all the way if I have to."

Her eyes met his with a connection that spanned the distance between them and erased everything around them. He nearly drowned in the emotion mirrored there. Shit, he felt like crying from the pureness he saw. "I believe that," she said, her voice low and shaky. "But I want coffee."

"Coffee, right." But he couldn't tear himself away from her face. This . . . *this* is what he expected to feel the moment he met her. This overwhelming fullness in his chest. The rightness threatened to burst out of his soul. The need to wrap his arms around her and never ever let her go. He couldn't move for the perfection of her. Afraid if he touched her, she might dissolve or, worse yet, flinch at his touch.

Could it hurt to love so much?

"I'll, um." Words were not easy. "I'll get your coffee. Sit down."

He ordered, paid and returned to her, all as if in a blur. His mind was racing with possible solutions. He could relocate. Didn't matter where his home base was. Heck, he could play for a team up there. Or convince her to move. Eventually. He couldn't swamp her with that just yet. Shit. He couldn't—wouldn't let her go.

"I'm sorry," he said as he sat the steaming cup in front of her. "You have no idea how." He paused to pull in a hard-earned breath. How could such emotional unease manifest itself so physically? "How sorry I am we wasted this week."

"It wasn't wasted." It was all she said. She kept her eyes averted, toying with the plastic snap top on her coffee.

"It needed to be more. God, what we could have learned, done together."

"I'm not sorry I came," she challenged with fire in her eyes.

"But I shut you out. I thought—" Shit, this was hard to say, but he couldn't let it hang between them. "When I left you that letter about someone else, well, that someone else was you—I didn't know. How could I know?"

"But I saw you at the party with—whatshername... Samantha. Gina said she was your girlfriend."

"She was just a girl I dated on occasion but not my girlfriend. I wouldn't lie about it. But I don't love her, never have, never will and she won't accept that. Even when I was with her, I thought about you, about those mysterious ways you'd touch me in my sleep. I could hear you whispering to me. All I wanted—my whole life, all I wanted was to meet *you*."

One side of her mouth curled up. "That's how I felt in here, five days ago."

"Really?"

She nodded and stirred her cup.

"Here." He pushed the charm between them. "You dropped this."

She looked up at him then covered the token with her hand. "I did?" Then she slid it toward him. "Keep it. It can be your Christmas present. It's the symbol of destiny."

"We have a destiny."

"And it was to meet here. It was for this to happen. I'll never forget you, Seth. You'll live right here, forever. But fate wasn't kind. We're way too different. Our lives won't mesh."

"The hell they won't," he nearly yelled, unable to accept how easily she was going to throw what they had together away. "I'll do anything. Anything to have you. I'll go with you right now."

"You can't desert your family. I have a life back home, one not so easy to walk away from."

Seth clenched his fists and stared at her. "I won't give up."

"I didn't expect you to." She bit her lip then and a tear flowed down her cheek. "I stayed up last night, trying to think of a way we can do this. I can't ask you to come to me, I can't imagine moving here."

"Then let's meet halfway. I hear Iowa's nice."

She laughed then, the slow, easy chuckle a healing balm on his bleeding heart. "I do love you."

Tears filled his eyes, but he wouldn't blink or turn away. He stared at her, wondering how he'd survived so many years without this woman. "Kenna, I love you too." It was amazing how easily those words came out. As he said them, the weight lifted from him. He pulled in a deep breath, swiped at his eyes and leaned forward. He picked up her fist, dropped the charm into it and closed it inside his hands. "No matter what we have to do, we're going to be together."

She swallowed then tugged at her bottom lip as she nodded. She was the most beautiful woman in the world at that moment. He'd die for her. Move mountains if he had to. Destiny had brought her to him, and he wasn't going to let anything tear them apart.

"Listen," he said, "come home with me. I need to pack. We can leave first thing in the morning. We'll figure out the next step when we get to it."

"Are you always going to take charge like this?"

"Honey, if I was taking charge, I'd just take you back to my condo and make it your home. It's much closer."

She laughed then. It was finally okay. He smiled back at her. They were going to be okay.

"So is this where I'm supposed to tell you that I really don't mind leaving Michigan?" Kenna said, tilting her head.

It was all he could do to keep from pulling her across the table and into his arms. "You're just saying that."

"Not really. If it meant so much, I wouldn't have jumped in my car and driven all this way, searching for something."

"You're amazing," he muttered, still awed that she'd actually come blindly to search for him.

"So where's that condo of yours?"

His pants got incredibly tight at the way her mouth curved around the cup as she took a drink. She was his. *His.* He didn't care if they lived in a cardboard box under the freeway if it meant he could possess her forever.

"Shouting distance from Mom's house, actually. Let's get you settled in, and we can negotiate this all tomorrow."

"Or we could just let destiny take its own path."

"Um, no," he said, watching her fist the symbol that had been so much more than just a charm. "Destiny takes too long and it doesn't communicate too well. After all, we lost the best half of the week already. Let's do it our way from now on."

"That sounds like a dream come true."

"It's not a dream anymore," he whispered. "I want to see you every waking moment. Not just when I close my eyes."

"Me too. Merry Christmas, Seth."

Seth growled and reached for Kenna's hand. His fingers threaded with hers, the coolness of his charm between their palms. This was one dream from which he never wanted to wake.